# SHOSHONE VALLEY

*Brad Dennison*

Author of
*THE LONG TRAIL and WANDERING MAN*

Published by Pine Bookshelf
Buford, Georgia

*Shoshone Valley* is a work of fiction. Names, characters, places, and incidents are either the product of the author's imagination or are used fictitiously. Any resemblance to actual persons, living or dead, events or locales is entirely coincidental.

Copyright 2016 by Bradley A. Dennison
All Rights Reserved

Excerpt from Thunder, Copyright 2016 by Bradley A. Dennison
All Rights Reserved

Cover Design: Donna Dennison

Editors: Donna Dennison
    Martha Gulick

Copy Editor: Loretta Yike

### *THE McCABES*

The Long Trail
One Man's Shadow
Return of the Gunhawk
Boom Town
Trail Drive
Johnny McCabe
Shoshone Valley
Thunder
Wandering Man

### *JUBILEE*

Preacher With A Gun
Gunhawk Blood (Coming Soon)

### *THE TEXAS RANGER*

Tremain
Wardtown
Jericho (Coming Soon)

To my wonderful wife and partner in life, Donna
You make everything complete.

# PART ONE

## *California*

### 1

Montana
April, 1882

BREE WAS in a range shirt, a split skirt and boots. She was standing near the corral with a cup of coffee, looking off at the meadow behind the house, and watching the horses. Some were grazing and others were frolicking in the morning air. Running and chasing each other.

Johnny walked up to stand beside her.

She said, "I feel bad dragging you and Jessica and Cora all the way in from the canyon. But I'm glad you're here."

"We were thinking it might be a good idea anyway. Jessica's due in about a month, and it would be difficult for Granny Tate to get all the way out to the canyon. Besides, Jessica would have it no other way. Aunt Ginny's planning a wedding, and even though I doubt she really needs any help, Jessica won't even think of staying away. For a woman, there's something magical about a wedding."

Bree nodded. "I can't believe it. In just twelve days, I'll be Mrs. Charles Cole."

Johnny nodded. "You'll always be my little punkin'. I hope you know that."

She grinned. "I wouldn't have it any other way."

She noticed her father had a coiled up lariat in his hand.

"So, what-cha doing?" she said.

"I was thinking on going out there and fetching Midnight for you."

"Why? You want to go riding?"

He nodded with a smile. "We used to do that a lot. We haven't been able to as much, now that I've moved out to the canyon. It'll be my last chance to ride with my little girl before she becomes a married woman."

She gave him a look that said, *get serious.* She said, "Pa, I'll always be your little girl."

Johnny was riding Thunder, and Bree was on Midnight, and they were moving along the valley floor at a shambling trot. All about them was grass standing tall and green. Another half mile on their right would be the Harding farm.

She said, "Is Thunder the best horse you've ever had?"

He nodded. "One of the two. The other one being Bravo."

"I still miss Bravo. He died a hero. Saving me."

Johnny nodded. "He was an incredible horse. When I rode cross country with your uncles, I did every foot of the journey on Bravo."

"What was the valley like, that first winter you and Uncle Joe stayed with the Shoshone?"

"Come on. I'll show you."

He turned Thunder off to the left, and Bree followed him to a ridge that was covered with tall pines.

Thunder was a mountain horse and handled the slope with ease. Even though Midnight had been born and raised at the ranch, she was the daughter of Thunder, and showed it as she matched him step-for-step.

They came out on a rocky cliff near the top of the ridge.

Johnny swung out of the saddle and Bree did the same. They left the reins trailing, and she followed him out onto the ledge.

The wind was stronger out here. It made the brim of Johnny's hat shake, and Bree reached up to place a hand on the crown of her own hat to keep the wind from lifting it from her head.

"Look off to the valley," he said.

She did. A good chunk of the valley floor was visible. Mostly grass, with a few trees scattered. She could see a ribbon of blue winding its way along—the small river that ran from one end of the valley to the other.

Johnny said, "You can't see any of the farms from here. Or the trail that leads to town. This view is about the closest you can get to how things looked then."

"You told me about how you met Ma. Christmas night, when you and Aunt Ginny and I sat up talking. And I know you brought us here after Ma was killed."

He nodded.

She said, "You've never talked much about the in-between things, though. Like, Zack was with you and Uncle Joe when you first came here, right?"

Johnny nodded again.

"How did he tie into everything? And why wasn't Uncle Matt with you?"

"Well, to tell the story proper, we have to go back to when I was still courting your mother. If you remember the story, your Uncle Matt was going to marry Verna."

Her turn to nod. She said, "That horrible woman who almost got you and Dusty and Uncle Matt killed a couple of summers ago. When you rode out to California to visit Ma's grave."

"Your Uncle Joe and I always had a bad feeling about her. So did your mother. But we didn't know just how bad. It's a long story, though."

She shrugged. "I have all day. Aunt Ginny and Jessica are going to town to make final arrangements at the church. They won't need me until tomorrow."

Johnny glanced off at the sun. By where it was hanging in the sky, he estimated it was maybe nine in the morning.

"Well, all right. If you remember right, your uncles and I were working for the McCarty Ranch out in California. We were using assumed names, but then we found out our cousin Thad confessed to the murder of that constable in Missouri, and we were cleared."

She nodded. "That's when you rode into town to see Ma."

"That was the summer of fifty-eight. An awful lot seemed to happen in that summer."

"When you rode into town, how did you know how to find her? I've always heard her parents didn't want you seeing her."

He nodded. "That's right. But I had found out from some of the men at the ranch that she worked as a school marm, at a one-room school at the edge of town."

Bree was giving a big, beaming smile of surprise. "Ma was a school marm? How come I never heard this before?"

He shrugged. "I suppose it just never came up in conversation. She wasn't a school marm for very long, though. Only a few months."

"Was that because of you?"

He nodded. "Because of me and her parents."

"Did they really call my grandfather Doc Buzzard?"

Johnny chuckled. "That they did."

"We've never met them. Are they still alive?"

"Far as I know. I didn't bother with a visit when I was out there last. They wouldn't want to see me, and I sure didn't want to see them."

"So, when you rode into town to see Ma, you found her at the school?"

Johnny nodded. "I left Quint in charge, and I saddled Bravo, and I rode on into town..."

# 2

## California
## September, 1858

MATT HEADED off to the corral. They had mustangs to break, and he and Corry were the two bronc-busters.

Joe said, "I'm gonna go watch the action. You coming?"

Johnny shook his head. "I'm heading to town. I'm giving myself the day off. Tell Quint he's in charge."

Joe said, "You're going to town?"

Johnny said, "There's a girl in town. The daughter of Doc Buzzard. And I'm riding in to see her."

Joe smiled. "About time."

Johnny slapped Joe on the shoulder and said, "I'm gonna marry that girl."

Joe watched his brother run to the stable, and he laughed.

Johnny had been thinking he was going to saddle up Bravo and ride directly into town, but then he realized he was dressed for work and was a few days removed from his most recent bath. So he turned away from the stable and bee-lined it to the bunkhouse.

Johnny felt like his steps were lighter than usual. He found himself smiling and almost laughing. He felt free.

The reward for him and his brothers was a burden that he knew had been weighing him down. He hadn't realized how much.

First order of business, a hot bath. There was a tub at the back of the bunkhouse, and he intended to use it. The stove was still hot from morning coffee, so he threw two more chunks of wood in and then set a pot of water on top for boiling.

Once he was bathed and his face shaved, he put on the Mexican vaquero pants he had bought in Texas and a white shirt and string tie. Then he shouldered into his gray vaquero jacket.

His gunbelt was draped over a chair. He grabbed it and buckled it on. The gunbelt had been specially made for him when he was with the Rangers—he hadn't spent all of his money on tequila and women. Most men of the time wore their gun on their belt. Either high on the hip at one side or toward the front and turned for a cross-draw. Johnny's holsters were extended down a few inches from the belt. This allowed him a little easier access to his guns. The leather connecting the holsters to the belt was double-layered and stiff, so the guns wouldn't flop about as he rode.

He headed to the stable, and once Bravo was saddled, he started for town.

As he rode up to the school house, two kids were running from it. A couple of others were walking. It was early afternoon, and school had apparently let out for the day.

One boy looked to be about ten, with hair cut squarely above his eyebrows.

Johnny said, "Excuse me, is the school marm still in the building?"

The boy looked up at him. "Miss Marker. Yes, sir. She's still there."

"Much obliged."

Johnny swung out of the saddle. He gave Bravo's rein a half turn around the railing of a small set of stairs that led up to the front door.

The prettiest girl he had ever seen was behind the desk, focusing on some papers in front of her. Her hair was the color of corn silk, and it seemed to grow in natural ringlets. It was done up in a way that let some of the ringlets fall behind her head.

Johnny took off his hat, and she looked up at the sound of his spurs jingling as he walked up to the desk.

"May I help you?" she said.

But then she recognized him from the dance, and Johnny saw a little smile forming.

"Mister McCabe," she said.

"No *mister*," he said. "For you, it's always Johnny."

"So tell me, are you always this forward?" The smile was still there.

He found he was smiling, too. "Only when I need to be."

"So, what brings a dashing desperado to the town school?"

"Well, the thing is, I heard a rumor."

She raised her brows. "What kind of a rumor did you hear?"

"That the school marm had no one to walk her home. I thought, now that's a crying shame. So I saddled up my horse and rode on into town. A gentleman can't let a lady walk home by herself."

She was smiling, and she glanced downward for a moment. A hint of shyness. Then she looked back up at him. "I surely appreciate the effort, but I've been walking home every day since summer school began."

"That's about to change."

She raised a brow. "Oh, is it now?"

"I'm good at predicting things like that."

She let out a giggle. "I do have to finish correcting these papers."

"I could help you with that."

She was giving him a look that was somewhere between skepticism and a silent laugh. "Could you?"

He shrugged. "Well, I can read and write. I might not be the best at spelling."

"So, you did get some schooling, while traipsing around the country and being a desperado."

He nodded. "Oh, yes. Every now and then, we desperados have to take a break. That's when I'd get my schooling in."

She laughed.

He said, "Tell you what. I'll sit down and wait all patient-like. And then when the papers are corrected, maybe you could join me for a cup of coffee down at the café. Then I'll walk you home."

"Well," she leaned her head a little to one side. "The problem is, I don't really drink coffee. I drink tea."

He rubbed his chin and squinted one eye, as though he was in deep thought. She giggled again.

He said, "Maybe I can have a cup of coffee and you can have a cup of tea."

"Are you always this good at figuring out solutions?"

He nodded. "Only when I have proper motivation."

He sat in the first row of desks while she worked. She looked up at one point and he was looking at her. She smiled and he returned the smile. Then she went back to work, but peeked up over a sheet of paper at him and they both laughed.

She finally decided she wasn't getting any work done. "I'll grade these papers at home tonight."

She packed them into a valise. Johnny then took the handle, and said, "Allow me, ma'am."

As they were walking toward the café, the boy Johnny had seen earlier called out, "Good night, Miss Marker."

She said, "Good night, Timmy."

Then she said to Johnny, "I know they call me Miss Buzzard behind my back."

"That's cruel."

She shrugged. "I understand why. I know how the town sees him."

"But they can't know him like you do. There must be a lot of redeeming qualities about him."

She shrugged again. "Not really. He's my father, but he is what he is."

They found a table in the café by the window. Johnny kept his hat with him—there was a hat rack by the door, but a cowhand didn't let go of his hat. It was too valuable a tool. So he balanced it on his knee.

Lura ordered a cup of Earl Grey tea and Johnny ordered a coffee. Both arrived in a cup and saucer. Johnny was again glad he had let his mother teach him how to balance a cup in a saucer.

The coffee was weak and thin. Not the trail coffee he preferred. But at the moment he didn't care. All that mattered was he was at a table with Lura, looking into her eyes and talking. Sharing a moment with her.

Lura took a sip of tea and talked about her father. Apparently her opinion of him was no higher than anyone else's in town.

"He can't really be that bad," Johnny said.

"Really?" She cocked a brow at him.

"A guy who was really a buzzard wouldn't be able to have such an incredible daughter."

She hadn't been expecting him to say that. Her cheeks grew a little red and she had to look down a moment.

*She doesn't know she's beautiful,* Johnny thought to himself. One of the things he liked the most in a woman was when she didn't know she was beautiful.

"I am very different from my father," she finally said, looking back at him. "From my mother too, really."

"How is that? I don't mean to sound like my brother Matt—if you want an earful of philosophy, just let him get wound up and he can talk for hours. But it seems to me we're largely influenced by our role models when we're growing up."

She took another sip of tea. "I have an aunt in San Francisco. Virginia Brackston. I spent every summer with her. I was going to go there this summer. In fact I was considering moving there to live with her. But then I was offered the position of teaching summer school here. In a lot of ways, she's more like a mother to me than my own mother."

"Your aunt must be quite a lady, then, because she did a great job raising her niece."

Lura blushed again. But this time she didn't look away.

"Why Johnny," she said, "are you throwing compliments at me just to embarrass me?"

He shook his head with a smile. "I could throw

compliments at you all day, and it still wouldn't cover how I feel about you."

"But we just met a few weeks ago at the dance."

"And yet, I feel like I've known you forever."

She was smiling, and leaned her head a bit to one side the way a woman will when she's smiling at the man she loves. "I feel the same. I've heard of this, and read about it, but never actually experienced it."

"I want to see you again."

"When?"

"Tomorrow night, for dinner. Then the next day. Saturday. How would you like to go for a picnic?"

"That would be so lovely. But I must confess, I've never been on a horse. I'm no cowgirl."

"There's a buggy at the ranch. I'll ask Mister McCarty if I can borrow it."

"That's right," she said, realizing something she had forgotten. "You're the ramrod of the Bar M, aren't you? How are you going to run the ranch if you're always running off with me?"

"I'll find a way. When something's worth doing, you find a way."

When the tea and coffee were done, he walked her home.

The Marker house was a small building with white clapboards and a peaked roof, on a side street. There was a small picket fence lining the property, and a few flowers grew alongside the walkway.

"How do you make flowers grow? It's so dry, out here in California."

"It's my mother's doing. She could make plants grow on solid rock, if she tried."

They were at the door, so he handed her back her valise.

He said, "Tomorrow night for dinner, then?"

She nodded with a smile. "Absolutely."

"I'll pick you up at, say, five o'clock?"

Another nod and a smile.

He stood looking at her. Her eyes were green,

gentle and yet somehow magical at the same time.

He reached up and touched her cheekbone, and she closed her eyes the way a woman does when she likes a man's touch. Her skin was smooth and soft. Again, Johnny found the word *magical* came to mind.

Then came the kiss. Light and ethereal. Like a breeze on a spring day.

"Should I pick you up here or at the school?" he said.

"Probably the school would be best."

Something about the way she said it made Johnny think there was more behind the statement than might be apparent at first. He was about to ask, but then thought better of it.

He touched the brim of his hat with a grin. She gave a chuckle. He said, "Then, I'll see you tomorrow, Miss Marker."

"I'm looking forward to it, Mister McCabe. Or is it, Reynolds?"

He gave a full smile. "It's McCabe. No more Reynolds."

"A man of mystery," she said.

"You never know."

He waited until she was in the door, then he turned and started back to the school house.

And yet she had him wondering about what she had said. That he should meet her at the school. Not the words, but somehow the way she had said it. Something almost cryptic, and like she was trying hard to make it seem not so cryptic.

Maybe he was making something out of nothing. But his gut told him no. Pa had always been big on trusting your gut.

# 3

LURA SHUT the door. Her father was standing in the center of the room, staring at her. His long, hooked nose. Thin, graying hair. His narrow jaw.

He *did* look like a buzzard, she had to admit.

He said, "You were with that cowhand. The one from the dance."

She said, "He's not a cowhand, Papa. He's the ramrod of the McCarty ranch."

"Same difference."

"What does it matter? He's a good man."

"What matters is I'm your father, and I'm telling you that you are not to see him."

"I'm nineteen. I can see whomever I wish."

"Not if you are to live under my roof."

"That can be remedied."

She went to step around him, but he grabbed her by the shoulder and spun her around. The valise fell out of her hand and landed on the floor by her feet.

He said, "Don't you turn your back on me. We're not finished discussing this."

But she wasn't afraid. She felt fury rising up. "Don't you ever dare touch me like that again."

He stared at her. She stared at him.

Then she grabbed the valise and said, "I have some papers to correct. I'll be at the school."

She headed for the door, pounding her heels into the floor.

Her mother was standing in the doorway that led from the parlor to the kitchen. She had hair that had one time been the color of Lura's, but was now streaked with white. Lines were carved into skin that had once been porcelain.

"Lura," she called out. "Please don't go."

The doctor said, "You leave, you don't come back. Do you understand?"

Lura pulled open the door, then she turned back

to them. "If that's the way you want it."

And Lura was out the door.

"Lura!" her mother cried out and ran to the door. But Lura pulled the door shut.

Her mother turned to the doctor. "Jonathan. Do something."

He shook his head. "Sabrina, let her go. If she wants to go, then she can go."

He turned and headed to the kitchen. A cup of coffee was waiting for him. A cup he had abandoned when his daughter had arrived at the front door with that cowhand. Swaggering around in his Mexican pants and his two guns riding low on his hips, like some sort of outlaw. What if the neighbors saw?

Sabrina followed him into the kitchen. "Jonathan. We can't just let her move out. Where would she go?"

He pulled a chair out from the table and sat. He lifted the cup and took a sip. It was getting cold. He muttered a curse. He had let his coffee grow cold over an ungrateful girl who had no respect for her parents or her family name.

"Jonathan. We can't just let her leave."

He set the coffee down. A man couldn't just drink his coffee in peace around here.

He said, "Maybe it's better this way. We've had her here for nineteen years. Maybe it's time for it to be just us here."

"Just us?" Sabrina took a step back. "You want her to leave, don't you?"

He drew a weary breath. "I did what you asked. I raised her like my own and I never told her the truth. And I've had to look at her every day. And every time I look at her, I don't see anything of myself. I see you in her, but there's nothing of me."

Sabrina said, "She's your daughter too, Jonathan. It's about the man who raised her."

He pounded his fist onto the table so hard the cup and saucer bounced a little. "She's not mine. Every time I see her, I'm reminded of it. I've had to look at her every single day for the past nineteen years."

Sabrina took another step back, and her mouth hung open a moment. Then she said, "I never knew you felt that way."

He nodded impatiently. "Well, all right, now you do. It's too late to do anything about it. But she's made her bed, and now she can lie in it. If she wants to leave, let her. But if she stays here, she doesn't see any cowhand. The next thing you know, she'll be seeing the swamper down at the saloon. Or the boy who shovels stalls at the livery."

"Jonathan," she said. "I asked you to never tell her the truth about her father. But that's all I've ever asked of you, over all the years. But now I'm asking you this—don't make her leave. Please. For me."

There was a quick knock at the front door. He looked at Sabrina, but she wasn't moving.

He got to his feet and said, "I'll get it myself."

He went to the door. It was Marshal Brannigan.

"Doc," he said. "I hate to bother you, but we need you down at the saloon. There's been trouble. A man got himself stabbed."

"No bother at all," the doctor said. He welcomed the interruption. His coffee had gone cold, anyway. "I'll get my bag."

He went into the kitchen. He had dropped his bag on the table when he got home from the office.

Sabrina looked at him, pleadingly. Her eyes were filled with tears.

He gave another weary sigh.

"All right," he said. "Fine. But you take care of her. And keep that lowlife cowboy out of this house. I never want to have to look at them or see the two of them together."

"Thank you, Jonathan."

He made a huffing, hissing sound through his teeth. Then he grabbed his bag and followed the marshal to the saloon.

Sabrina grabbed her shawl and scurried off to the

school building.

She found Lura behind the desk, a quill pen in hand.

Lura looked up. "Mama."

Sabrina smiled, and hurried to her daughter. Lura stood and Sabrina gave her a hug.

"My baby," Sabrina said. "You've always been the center of my world. You're all I have."

Lura nodded. She was wiping away a tear. "I'll be all right, Mama. I'm getting paid enough with this job to pay for a room at the rooming house. Mrs. Swafford's."

"Nonsense. Your home is with us."

"He doesn't want me there, Mama. I don't think he ever has. He's always acted like I was just in the way. Even when I was little. The only place I ever felt wanted was at Aunt Ginny's in San Francisco."

"I've always wanted you. And so has he. He just has a hard time showing his feelings. You know that."

"Well, I'm tired of it."

"Please don't leave. Give him one more chance."

Lura gave a reluctant nod of her head. "Maybe. All right. For you, Mama."

"Thank you."

"But I have to ask you, are you still going to be seeing that young man?"

"Yes, Mama. That's not going to stop."

"Why? Just to spite your father?"

Lura lowered herself back to her chair. "No. Nothing I do is because of him. It's because..."

She looked off into space, trying to find the words. "It's hard to explain. At the dance a few weeks ago, when he walked across the room and our eyes met, it was like I had known him forever. When we danced, I don't think we shared one word. We didn't need to. I was where I was meant to be, and so was he."

Her mother said, "I understand. But your father never will. Can you see the young man, but away from the house? Can you make that compromise?"

Lura was about to say *not a chance*. She was

going to ask if her mother would have made that compromise. But something about what her mother had said a few moments ago. Lura was all she had. Her mother had said that more than once when Lura was growing up, but it was like she was hearing it differently this time. Maybe it was that now, she was hearing it with the ears of an adult.

Lura said, "All right, Mama. For you."

Her mother clasped her hands in front of her. "Thank you."

Lura stood by a window and watched her mother scurry home to cook dinner. She noted her mother seldom walked when she was going from one place to another by herself. She scurried, almost like she was somehow afraid. In fact, it seemed there was a little edge of fear in her mother most of the time.

Lura knew her mother had never really been happy. She didn't think her parents had ever been in love. There was a bond of sorts between them, but nothing more.

She wanted to spend the rest of her life with Johnny. She had known that ever since the dance. But even if she hadn't met him, she knew one thing—she would rather be alone for the rest of her life than have what her parents had.

The man at the saloon had taken a knife to the ribs. He was sitting on the floor and the side of his shirt was soaking in blood.

Doc Marker pressed a handkerchief into the wound, and told the man to push down on it with his elbow.

"Hold that tight," Marker said. "You're going to need stitches, but I can't do it here."

Marker looked at Brannigan. "Can you get him to my office?"

Brannigan nodded.

The man with the wound tried to get to his feet, but was a little shaken. He had not only lost a lot of blood, but before the knife had even been drawn, he had taken a punch to the face. Brannigan and a deputy helped steady the man and walked with him out the door.

Marker went ahead of them, and he fished keys out of his jacket pocket and unlocked the door. He was the first into his office. It had gotten dark, so he struck a match and got a lamp burning.

The man with the wound was about thirty. His hair was a few months removed from a barber shop, and he needed a shave. His clothes were trail worn, and even though the marshal had taken the man's gun, Marker could tell this man was a ruffian. Probably a two-bit outlaw. He wore his holster at his left side and turned for a crossdraw—no cowhand would bother with that—and he had a knife sheath in his boot.

Brannigan said, "Doc, if you have this under control, the other one in the fight got away."

The man said, "He started it, Marshal. Honest."

"That's for the prosecutor to decide. But," Brannigan looked at the deputy, "we've got to find him."

Marker said, "I'm all right, Marshal. Go do what you have to do."

Brannigan slapped the deputy on the shoulder and said, "Come on."

When the door shut and Marker was alone with the man, Marker said, "You're lucky. The blade almost slipped between your ribs. If it had done that, it could have gone into a lung."

"You mean I'm gonna live?"

Marker gave him a long look. "Yes. That's what it means."

Marker got some alcohol and a cloth to wash the wound out. "This is going to sting a little."

It did. The man flinched as Marker applied the alcohol.

Then it was time to go to work with the needle and thread.

"Just between you and me," Marker said, "do you

have a price on your head?"

The man shook his head. A little too quickly, Marker thought.

"No, sir," he said. "I'm an honest man."

"Too honest for a job?"

"What kind of job?"

"The kind that might be frowned on by the marshal, but one I'm prepared to pay handsomely for."

This had the man's attention. "What do you want done?"

Marker was silent a moment, giving the man a long look and deciding if he really wanted to say what he was about to.

He said, "How much would you charge to kill a man?"

# 4

MONDAY MORNING, Johnny had coffee with Frank McCarty.

Johnny said, "The corral is done. I'm thinking on heading out to the mountains again in a couple of weeks for some more mustangs. Matt and Corry are already pretty much done with the last ones."

"Good. I might have a buyer for some of them."

This had Johnny's attention.

McCarty said, "I know a rancher down closer to Stockton. Tom and his young wife Victoria. It's a small ranch, but I think it's going to grow. He's not much older than you are, but there's something about him. I think he's going to do well. I sent him a letter explaining that we're expanding into horses, and he wants to ride up and check out our stock."

Johnny nodded. "Excellent. We'll have some good stock waiting for him."

McCarty took a sip of his coffee. "I understand you've started seeing Doc Buzzard's daughter."

Johnny grinned. The name still struck him funny. "Yes. We had dinner a few times last week, and a picnic. We're going on another picnic next Sunday, after church."

"I always wondered about that family, just between you and me." He set the coffee cup down on the saucer. "The girl is about as pretty as can be, but it's hard to believe an old vulture like Doc Marker could produce a girl with looks like that."

Johnny laughed. "A lot of us have wondered about that. I haven't talked to him. She meets me outside their house or outside the schoolhouse. That family seems to have problems."

McCarty was silent a moment, then said, "It's not really my business, of course, but I consider you to be practically part of our family now. I have to say this, because I would if you were my son. Keep in mind, the apple doesn't fall far from the tree."

Johnny thought about that for a moment. He realized—he didn't really know what Mr. McCarty was talking about.

The look on his face must have said it.

McCarty said, "You have said what you want is to eventually build a ranch of your own. You want a good woman to raise children with and a warm hearth to rest beside after a hard day's work."

Johnny nodded. McCarty had gotten him talking about what he wanted one evening after one glass of tequila too many.

McCarty said, "I've known Doc Marker for a long time. They don't call him Doc Buzzard for nothing. He's a mean-spirited man with as dark a soul as any I've ever seen.

"One time, I got myself gored pretty bad by a steer. Deep cut on my arm. I still have the scar. But I wouldn't let Doc Buzzard touch me. We had a trail cook who had been an Army doctor at one point. I had him stitch me up.

"What I'm saying is, I don't think that man knows the first thing about family values. He's no one I would turn my back on. If that's the way his daughter was raised, could she really be the woman to stand alongside of you?"

Johnny knew Mr. McCarty wasn't criticizing for the sake of criticizing. He hadn't thought about, but now that Mr. McCarty raised the point, it was worth thinking about.

"I suppose," Johnny said, "I don't know."

"I don't mean to talk bad about the girl. I just want you to think long and hard about it. And if you decide she's the one for you, then you have my full blessing."

Johnny headed back to the bunkhouse. He was going to plan the next expedition into the mountains to go mustanging. He knew Matt and Corry would want to go. Johnny had told them both to stay behind the last time, and they balked at the idea. Johnny liked that in his men. They were part of this ranch and wanted to share in the work. But Johnny felt that if the Bar M was going to be serious about branching out into horse ranching, he wanted his two bronc-busters to remain free of injuries.

The bunkhouse was in sight and Johnny saw smoke coming from the stove pipe and hoped there was coffee brewing. That was when he heard the sound of shod hooves on the ground behind him. A horse wearing iron shoes makes a different sound than one that's not shod.

Johnny turned. He didn't feel like he was on edge, but he supposed he always was. His right hand moved partway to his right-hand gun without him even intending it to, almost as a reflex.

And in the saddle sat a man he hadn't seen in two years.

He had a floppy hat, a jaw that was covered with whiskers. His shirt was a faded brown and his pants a faded black that looked almost gray. His vest had belonged to a three-piece suit at one time, and was now frayed and torn. He wore two guns, like most Rangers did in Texas.

Johnny broke into a smile and said, "Zack Johnson."

Zack grinned. "I heard a rumor that you were the ramrod of this spread. Thought I'd ride out and see if you're hirin'."

"Our payroll is full. Why you asking?"

He shrugged. "I'm looking for a job. I'm a little tired of chasing renegades and desperadoes. Thought I'd like to chase stray cows for a while."

"You're hired."

"Thought you said the payroll was full."

Johnny said, "For you, there's always a job open."

Zack swung out of the saddle, and he and Johnny took each other into a long hug.

Zack followed Johnny to the bunkhouse, and Johnny introduced him to Matt and Joe.

Matt said, "Zack Johnson. The man who took the arrow to the leg, that time Johnny shot down five Comanches with five shots."

Zack was smiling. His smile was big and wide. "You've heard the story."

Joe said, "I think half the country has heard the story."

Johnny got out a bottle of tequila. It was a Monday morning, but no work was going to be done today, now that Zack was here. Johnny waived the no-drinking policy and pulled the cork on the bottle.

He put Quint in charge for the day, which didn't help matters much because Quint wound up sitting in the bunkhouse with the McCabe brothers and Zack Johnson as they told the stories of their days with the Texas Rangers.

Hardy joined them. Along with Corry and Chip. Valdez and Moses Timmons soon came by.

Word spread around the ranch that Zack Johnson was here, and it wasn't long before McCarty himself was standing in the bunkhouse doorway listening.

The men of the Bar M had heard the name Johnny McCabe before they had ever met Johnny and his brothers. And the name Zack Johnson was sometimes spoken along with Johnny.

Zack said to Johnny, "You ever tell these men about the time you used a bullet like a billiard ball?"

Johnny was sitting on the edge of the table. He shook his head, but Joe said, "Yeah, he told me about that once, when we were riding back home."

Matt said, "I never heard about it."

Zack was in an upright chair in front of the stove. He was leaning the chair onto its back legs, and held a tin coffee cup full of tequila. He had pushed his hat back.

Zack said, "Johnny was using a Colt rifle."

He looked at Johnny and said, "You still have that

rifle?"

Johnny shook his head. "Traded it in for a Hawken, back in Texas."

"A Hawken? You have it here?"

Johnny looked over at Chip, who had pulled up a chair by Johnny's bunk. "Hey, Chip. Hand that rifle over, will you?"

The Hawken was held up by a couple of pegs on the wall. Chip got the rifle and handed it to Zack.

"Well, look at that," Zack said.

Zack handed the rifle back to Chip and got on with the story, telling about how banditos were hiding behind rocks, but with other taller rocks behind them.

"So, Johnny just sights in on the rocks behind them, and just like you would with a billiard ball, he ricochets a bullet off the rock, and it hits one of the men."

Chip's mouth was hanging open. Hardy said, "Are you funnin' with us?"

Zack shook his head and raised one hand. "I swear to the Almighty. One of the finest pieces of shootin' I ever saw."

Corry said, "Did he really shoot down five Comanches with five bullets?"

Zack nodded. "I was there for that one, too. Did that with his pistols."

Johnny said, "Zack, everyone here has better things to do than listen to my old adventures."

"No we don't," Corry said.

Valdez was grinning. "Please. We want to hear all about his adventures."

And so Zack told about the five shots Johnny made while ten Comanches were riding down on them. Plucked them out of the saddle and then executed a border shift and was ready for five more shots, but the remaining five reined up and thought better of it.

Zack told of raids into Mexico, chasing Mexican border raiders.

Zack said, "Remember that time your rifle

wouldn't fire, and two banditos were riding up beside you? One on one side and one on the other? One of 'em had a pistol out and your rifle wouldn't fire, but then you turned the rifle around and rammed the rifle stock right into his face. And then the gun went off and took the other one clean out of the saddle?"

Joe said, "That really happen?"

Johnny nodded. "Turned out the trigger had gotten damaged. But when I hit the bandito in the face, it jarred the gun enough so it went off. Turned out his partner was at the other side of me, and right in the line of fire. I was lucky I didn't shoot myself by accident."

It was late into the afternoon when the men dispersed. The cook was getting supper ready, and the tequila was gone. Matt went back to the main house with Mr. McCarty.

Johnny had lost count of the glasses of tequila he had downed, and when he went to the stove to put some coffee on, he found he had to concentrate a little to walk a straight line.

Joe was still at the table, and had lit up his Indian pipe.

Zack said to Joe, "Your brother was known for putting away some tequila. Let me tell you. One time after chasing border outlaws, we celebrated for an entire weekend in a little town near the border. At one time he was standing on the saloon roof, shooting at plates as people threw them into the air. Filled with tequila and howling like a wolf."

Johnny looked at him. "I was not howling like a wolf."

"Yes you were, old son. You were just too drunk to remember."

Joe was grinning.

Zack said, "What I could never figure is how you could be that drunk and still hit those plates that were being tossed up. You never missed one."

"I remember the restaurant owner wasn't too

pleased about his plates being broken that way."

"But he wasn't going to say much, not when the town was filled with drunken Rangers shooting off their guns."

Johnny arranged the wood in the stove and struck a match to some kindling. Then he put a kettle filled with water and coffee on the stove. They went outside to wait for the coffee water to boil, because it was going to get mighty warm inside.

Johnny said, "What're you doing all the way out here? Did you quit the Rangers?"

Zack nodded. "There comes a time when you just have to move on. They were talking about making me a captain, and that job involves more politics than anything else."

"So you quit and rode west?"

Zack nodded.

Johnny waited. He knew Zack well enough to know when something was wrong. Zack had always been quick with a laugh, but now he seemed a little solemn.

Zack said, "We were in a bad one, Johnny. A bad fight, about a year ago. Just south of the border. A bunch of banditos came north and raided. Hit a couple of small ranches. We followed 'em about thirty miles into Mexico, to a small town."

Zack looked at Joe and said, "We were never shy about crossing the border. I'm sure the diplomats and heads of state wouldn't like it, but they weren't there doing the fighting."

Joe was sitting on a bench by the door. He nodded and took a puff of smoke. "That's often the way."

"Well, it turned out there were a bunch of 'em waiting for us. We rode into a trap. They caught us in a crossfire and killed seven of us. Remember Roy Jenkins?"

Johnny said, "They didn't get Roy?"

Zack nodded. "Bullet to the head. Sam Tucker, too."

"Not Sam."

Zack nodded again. "Caught one in my arm, too. But I was able to turn my horse and get out of there. Only four of us made it out alive. Hesky Jones was one of 'em, but he died of his wounds a few days later. Took three shots to the chest."

Johnny shook his head. "They were good men, all of them."

Zack said, "When Hesky was dying, he said if I ever see you again, to let you know how much what you done meant to him."

Johnny said to Joe, "Hesky was an escaped slave. A little older than Nate, but not much. I drew him up some false freedom papers, and he showed 'em to the captain. On our recommendation, he was let into the Rangers."

Joe said, "They let colored men ride with white? You don't normally see that."

Zack shook his head with a chuckle. "You don't there, either, but the captain made an unofficial exception for Hesky. He was a natural horseman and a good shot with a rifle, and an all-around good man."

"That was a good thing you done," Joe said. "Never did take to slavery. You see it among the Indians, too. They take captives in battle, they often keep 'em as slaves. That was one part of their culture I didn't like."

"Seeing those men go down," Zack said. "It did something to me. My arm healed fine, partly because the captain gave it a treatment with his corn squeezin's."

Zack shook his head. "That's not something you soon forget. The bullet caught me just below the elbow and now the grip in my left hand isn't what it used to be. The doctor said it probably never would be. The bullet took some muscle. But all of those good men being killed. Some of them were close friends of ours. I suppose it did something to me. I just couldn't do the job, anymore.

"The captain said a man can handle only so many

battles before he has to walk away. He told me maybe it was my time to walk away. And like I said, they wanted to make me a captain, but I wanted none of that. So I rode.

"I've just been drifting for months. Working a little here and there. Then I heard in a saloon over in Camanche that you were running the Bar M, so I rode on over."

"Glad you did," Johnny said. He looked at Joe and said, "This man and I have saved each other's lives more times than I can count. He's like a brother to me."

Joe nodded. "Any brother of yours is a brother to me."

# 5

IT WAS Wednesday afternoon and Doc Marker was thinking of closing up shop for the day. He had sat in his office and read the paper for a while, then he had taken an inventory of supplies—an inventory he didn't have to take, but he was growing bored. No children to deliver. No one needing a bone set. He found himself wishing for a gunfight at the saloon, so he could have some wounds to patch or even just a death certificate to fill out.

He didn't feel morbid wishing for business. The cowhands and saddle bums who shot at each other in the saloon were men he had no compassion for. As far as he was concerned, they could kill each other off.

He decided to reach into the bottom drawer of his desk. A place he went to every so often to lighten the burden a little. A steel flask was waiting for him, and he pulled the cork and took a swig.

Whiskey. It tasted a little metallic because he had poured it into the flask days ago. But he didn't drink it for the taste.

The desk was old and battered. About the best you could find here on the frontier. He felt it was appropriate for this small, shabby office.

He belonged in Boston, he thought. Or Philadelphia. He had been destined to be a surgeon at a fine hospital. He had come from money and success, and such things were expected of him.

In his early days of practicing medicine in Boston, his hair was longish and he wore a thick mustache. Anything to distract from his long, hooked nose and his jagged frame.

Of course, his name hadn't been *Marker* then. But he couldn't use his real name anymore, because he had killed a man.

Not that the man didn't have it coming. The man had been tall and handsome. Rugged, but not overly so.

Just enough to catch a woman's eye. A smile that could have been designed by an artist. Charismatic in that way of some men who simply walk into a room and all eyes are on them.

The man had made Marker feel small in front of the woman he had been engaged to marry. She was a Boston socialite and came from a family with more money than they would ever know what to do with. She and Marker had been at a ball, and when the man arrived and the socialite saw him, her eyes sparkled. And when the man asked her to dance, she said yes and walked away from Marker like he wasn't even there.

The man played polo, and it was just a few days later that he was carried into the hospital where Marker was working. The horse and rider had gone tumbling with two other riders on the polo field. Horse hooves had torn into the man's leg. Looked like the femur was broken.

It was all too easy for Marker to end the problem. One of his medical professors had said if the femoral artery is nicked, a man can bleed out in seconds. Marker decided to test the theory, but with more than a nick. A full-fledged swipe.

He hadn't counted on a nurse seeing it. As the man bled out and went unconscious for the last time, Marker looked quickly at the doorway, to make sure it was deserted, to find a nurse standing there. She had seen the entire thing.

Marker considered taking care of her too, but he didn't quite know how to do it on a moment's notice. She didn't give him time to think about it. She turned and ran.

Marker found himself in jail. The man's family was well connected and the district attorney was going for a charge of first degree murder. The society girl gave him back his engagement ring. His family informed him that should he somehow avoid the gallows, he could consider himself disinherited.

Marker was in his jail cell one night, with a week's

worth of whiskers on his face, and still in the same clothes he had been arrested in. He was sitting on the bunk, his face buried in his hands.

He hadn't heard the turnkey coming down the row of cells. But he looked up at the sound of the key in the lock.

The man was about fifty, with gray hair and a round stomach. He wore a navy blue smock with a badge pinned to it, and a military-type kepi was on his head.

He swung the door open and said, "All right, Doc. Come with me."

"Why?" the doctor said.

"You got a visitor."

"At this hour? It must be after ten."

The turnkey beckoned with his fingers. "Come on with you."

Marker got to his feet. He left his jacket and tie in the cell.

The front office was empty except for the turnkey himself, and a man Marker hadn't seen since medical school.

"Troy," he said.

Troy smiled. He was cleanly shaven, and in a tie and jacket. "Jonathan."

They shook hands, which led to an embrace. Old friends from medical school. Fraternity brothers. They had chased girls together, emptied bottles of whiskey together, and laughed at each other for their hangovers the next day.

Troy said, "I wish I were seeing you under better circumstances."

Jonathan nodded. He was about to say that he hadn't done the crime, but Troy knew him better than anyone ever had. He found himself saying nothing.

Troy said, "I'm not going to let them hang you."

Jonathan shrugged. "I don't really know what to do. My family has disinherited me. I have only the money in my pockets."

"Come with me."

Marker looked at the turnkey, who said, "I don't see anything."

Troy said, "I paid him well. Now, come with me."

Troy had a buggy outside, which they got in. Then a ride to an apartment Troy kept in town. Jonathan enjoyed a bath, and then at Troy's insistence, he shaved the mustache. And then Troy cut Jonathan's hair until it was short cropped. It was then parted in the middle and slicked down with hair grease.

The following morning, Troy drove him to the train station and handed him a ticket to St. Louis.

Jonathan said, "I'm afraid you're going to bring on a world of troubles for yourself."

Troy said, "Not at all. My father has been one of the largest contributors to the governor's election. And to the mayor's. Money opens doors and makes things happen. I'll be all right."

"How can I ever repay you for this?"

Troy shook his head. "You were the closest person to me in my life for a number of years. You would have done the same for me."

Jonathan didn't know that he would have. Troy was taking on a lot of risk. Despite the connections Troy's father had, it was still a risk. Jonathan didn't take risks for others. But he instead said nothing, and let Troy take it as Jonathan being overcome with emotion.

Troy slapped him on the shoulder and said, "Go get on that train. You'll have to use a different name, of course."

Troy grinned. "Remember all of the poker we played in school? You can call yourself Jonathan Marker."

That got a snicker out of Jonathan. "That would be funny."

Troy handed him a carpet bag, and a billfold.

Troy said, "That's filled with cash. Five hundred dollars. Get yourself to Saint Louis and disappear.

Maybe go to San Francisco. Use your new name and build a life for yourself."

They shook hands. Troy said, "Get going. They're boarding the train."

Jonathan stepped onto the train and never looked back.

He didn't stay in St. Louis for long. He felt maybe he should go further west. Troy had mentioned San Francisco, so Jonathan decided to make it his destination.

He remained in St. Louis long enough to find a man who could forge documents. Now Jonathan Marker was a graduate of the Harvard Medical School, with the diploma to prove it.

He set up shop in San Francisco. He decided he was a young doctor from Boston who wanted a fresh start in another part of the country.

Rather than work in a hospital, he became a general practitioner. He delivered babies and set broken arms. And he met Sabrina Brackston, the daughter of a wealthy shipping magnate. Not wealthy on the level of the family of the Boston socialite he had been planning to marry, but wealth is relative. In a city like Boston, the Brackstons would have been considered well-off but hardly the upper crust. But in a sleepy little place like San Francisco before the gold rush, they were socialites.

Sabrina Brackston was no one Marker would normally look at. She was pretty enough, but she didn't strike him as gifted intellectually. Educated, but not very good at putting together ideas. However, you couldn't ignore her father's bank book. The girl was lonely and she was carrying the child of a man who had abandoned her before marrying her. Many liked to pretend children didn't come into the world before a wedding and that there was no consummation of relationships before vows were exchanged. Marker happened to know a lot more of it went on than society wanted to admit.

He stepped in and married Sabrina. Saved the

honor of her and the family. Except somehow the gruff old man who was her father didn't take to Jonathan.

Jonathan said to him once, "I know you don't like me, sir."

The old man said, "It's not that I don't like you. It's that I don't trust you."

The old man had a way of fixing a glare on you that could cause your knees to turn to jelly. Sabrina's older sister Ginny could do it, too. Jonathan spent as little time with them as possible.

He and Sabrina moved to Greenville, off in Calaveras County. A small town but with a couple of large ranches and a few farms. There were also two vineyards nearby. Jonathan gave a speech about small town people being the salt of the Earth. Really, he just wanted to be away from the old man. He didn't plan to be away forever, just long enough for the old man to live out his final days. Then Sabrina could get her half of Brackston Shipping, and she and Jonathan could move back to San Francisco.

The old man stabbed at Jonathan from the grave, though. In the will, the entire company went to Ginny. There was also a partial stake in a ranch outside of San Francisco, and a stake in a land development company. They owned a few thousand acres of undeveloped range in Calaveras County. All proverbial small potatoes, but they were part of the larger package. However, according to the will, none of it would go to Sabrina if she was still married to Jonathan at the time of the old man's death.

Ginny was nice enough to give her sister some of the money anyway, which was enough combined with Marker's income as a doctor to provide a comfortable life in the small town of Greenville, but nothing more.

After the gold rush in '49, the little land development company found itself swimming in dollars, and Ginny bought into a timber company to provide lumber for shoring up mines as well as shipbuilding. She was living the life Jonathan could have lived, had the old man not been so hard to impress.

And so here Jonathan was, in a town overrun with cowboys and farmers. Country folk with their country ways. It was better than prison, he supposed, but not much. At least it was better than the noose that would have been waiting for him back in Massachusetts.

Sabrina and her daughter visited Ginny a few times a year, but Ginny seldom came out to Greenville. Jonathan was fine with that. He didn't mind having the house to himself, and he certainly didn't want to see Ginny any more than he had to.

When Sabrina's daughter turned twelve, she started spending summers with her Aunt Ginny. Jonathan was fine with that. Three months without the little brat underfoot.

Now the girl was eighteen and seemed to have a romantic interest in one of the local cowhands. Well, that was going to end. Not that he necessarily thought a cowhand would be bad for Lura. He didn't actually waste any of his energy caring about Lura's well-being. He was concerned about how it would seem to others for him to have a cowhand for a son-in-law. Someday, if he ever found his way out of his exile in Greenville and was able to return to San Francisco, he doubted the high society folk would find it droll that his son-in-law was a cowhand.

He took another belt of whiskey. That was when the door opened.

A man Marker had never figured to see again stepped through. The one with the stab wound from a few days ago.

"What do you want?" Marker said, too weary to care about niceties. "Did your stitches come loose?"

He shook his head. "Not at all. I just wanted to tell you the county prosecutor decided I acted in self-defense. He's not filing any charges."

Jonathan gave a weary sigh. "I'm thrilled for you."

"I remember you talkin' about a job offer."

Marker stood the whiskey flask on the desk. He

walked past the man to the door, and locked it.

He said, "If I'm ever asked, we never had this conversation."

The man nodded. "Them's the kind of jobs that pay the best."

"Two hundred dollars. That's almost two years pay for a cowhand around here."

The man nodded. "All right, you've hired yourself a man."

"There's a cowhand working for the McCarty ranch. The leader, or *ramrod,* or whatever they call them."

"Yeah. I know him. Turns out he's Johnny McCabe."

"I forget what his name is. It doesn't matter."

"Oh yeah, it does. They're talkin' about him from here to Texas. They say he's killed more than twenty men in gunfights. They say he's the best shot with a pistol there ever was."

Marker didn't have patience for second-rate hero worship. "It doesn't matter what they're saying. He's just a man, like any other. And he can die just like any other man."

"Die? *He's* the one you want killed?"

Marker nodded. "He's the one."

The man stepped back. "Not for two hundred. If even half of what they're saying about him is true, I need a lot more than two hundred."

Marker sighed wearily. "All right. Two fifty."

The man shook his head. "Five hundred. In cash. And I need half of it up front."

"*Five hundred?*" Marker shouted the words, then cringed at the thought that he might be overheard. Like with most frontier towns, the walls of many of the buildings in Greenville were slapped together and didn't block sound very well. He didn't want anyone passing by outside to hear him.

He said more quietly, "Five hundred?"

The man shrugged. "If you don't have the money,

then I'll find another job somewheres else. Takin' a shot at McCabe is a risk you've gotta pay a man for. There's also his two brothers to deal with. One of them spent time with Injuns. They say he's scalped a man before."

"I'm not paying you five hundred."

The man shrugged. "Then good luck finding someone else who will do it for less."

He started for the door.

"All right," Marker said. He gave a sigh of exasperation. "Five hundred it is."

The man nodded. "Half up front."

"That'll have to wait until the bank is open tomorrow."

"Do you want him killed at a particular time?"

"The sooner the better." Marker thought for a moment. "He's taking my daughter on a picnic Sunday, after church. They'll be somewhere outside of town. That might be a good opportunity."

"Do you know where they're goin'?"

"No I don't."

"Don't matter. I can track a man, and I can do it so's he don't know he's bein' followed. The only problem is your daughter will be there. I gotta do it in a way so she don't get hurt."

Marker waved off the notion with one hand. "Don't worry about her. Just make the shot count."

"Your daughter?"

"I'm not paying you to ask questions. Just to do a job."

The man nodded. "Yes, sir."

"Come by tomorrow night, after hours. I'll have the first half of the money for you. After you do the job, come and see me. I'll be here at my office Sunday evening. After I pay you the rest of what I'll owe you, you'll need to ride hard and fast. I don't want the law finding you. And if they do, remember, I'll never admit to hiring you."

"I'll remember. But no one will find me. I won't stop riding till I hit Mexico."

Marker let him out the back door, then went back to his desk and the flask of whiskey that was waiting for him.

# 6

JOHNNY STOOD in front of a small mirror that was held in place on the bunkhouse wall with a nail. He was in a white shirt and was tying a black string tie.

Matt said, "Well, you're getting quite good at that. But then, you had a good teacher."

Joe was sitting at the table with a cup of coffee in hand. "Didn't Ma and Pa ever teach you to be humble?"

Matt grinned. "They tried."

"Cain't fault 'em for that."

Zack Johnson was leaning a hand against one bunk and had a cup of coffee in hand. "I still can't believe you're going to be setting foot in a church."

Johnny nodded. "That I am. I go every Sunday now. It gives me a chance to see Lura."

"What are times coming to?"

Quint was sitting across the table from Joe. He said, "You ain't seen the gal he's courtin'. Prettiest gal I ever saw. If a gal like that took a shine to you, you'd be goin' to church, too."

Johnny said, "We come from church-going folk. Went to church every Sunday when we were growing up."

Zack grinned. "A lot of good it did."

Matt said, "Can you imagine what he would have been like without all of that church going?"

Johnny reached for his guns, but then stood with the gunbelt in one hand. "I don't normally take my guns to church, but Lura and I are going on a picnic lunch afterward. I don't normally go far without my guns, but I don't want her to think I'm some sort of desperado. I want this day to be perfect."

"I'm sure you'll be fine," Zack said. "It'll just be you and the girl. You won't need your guns. There aren't any banditos around here."

Johnny glanced at Matt. He knew Matt understood.

Matt said, "Tell you what. Don't worry about it. And, in fact, don't worry about the food, either. I'll ride into town behind you and stop in at the restaurant. You'll have a full picnic basket waiting for you in the buggy when you get out of church."

"I can't ask you to do that."

"You didn't ask. But this way, you'll be able to go from church right to the picnic. Much more romantic."

Matt slapped Johnny on the back. "And you can always bring a rifle with you in the buggy. She won't think you're a desperado for having a rifle with you."

Johnny arrived at the Marker house in a black buggy. Leaning against the seat was his Hawken rifle.

He didn't go in, because her father had said he didn't want to see Johnny at the doorstep. So Johnny just brought the horses to a stop and waited.

Lura was out the door in less than a minute. Johnny hopped down to meet her.

Her hair was done up and she was in a dress with a lacy collar and lace at the cuffs of her sleeves.

"You look incredible this morning," he said.

She smiled. "You always say that."

"Because it's always true."

He took her hand as she climbed up into the buggy and then he climbed up behind her and took the reins, and they were off to the church.

When the church service was done, they found a picnic basket waiting for them on the buggy seat. Johnny grinned.

Lura said, "Where did that come from?"

He said, "My brother Matt is hosting our lunch. Sort of."

Johnny flipped open the basket. "A roasted chicken. Potato salad."

He grinned. "A bottle of wine. Riesling. It must go with chicken. You can trust Matt for that sort of thing."

Lura gave him a look of intrigue. "I've never tasted

wine."

That got a surprised look out of him.

She said, "I *am* a Baptist, you know."

"Well, girl, it's time for you to partake of the wild life."

She giggled.

Johnny noticed something else toward the bottom of the basket. He moved aside the potato salad, and he saw a revolver. Matt's .36 Navy.

Johnny smiled. "Matt thinks of everything."

"What is it?"

He put the wine back and flipped the basket shut. Now was not the time go into how uneasy he felt not wearing his guns. That was a long story that would take a long time to tell.

He said, "Nothing. Let's go."

He took her hand as she climbed up into the buggy.

Johnny had left the buggy near the church. A white building with a peaked roof and a steeple. As Jonathan and Sabrina Marker were stepping out the front door, Jonathan first shook hands with the reverend. A man with white hair and eyes that squinted behind a pair of spectacles.

"Great sermon, Pastor," Jonathan said.

Sabrina then shook the pastor's hand and said, "It was one of your best. I really loved how you compared Daniel and the Lion to the railroad..."

Jonathan glanced toward the buggy and saw Johnny and Lura in the seat. Johnny was turning the buggy around, and they started away, Johnny keeping the horses to a walk.

Jonathan glanced across the street. The man was standing there. Jonathan still didn't know his name, and didn't want to. The man looked like he was wearing the same clothes he had earlier in the week. Not a man you wanted to stand downwind from.

Jonathan looked at him and nodded. The man

nodded back. The man watched the buggy move away down the street, and then he strolled to a horse he had left tethered to a hitching rail. He moved casually, as though he had no particular place to go. A hurrying man can draw attention. A strolling man is often not remembered. He swung into the saddle and then began walking his horse down the street.

There was a saloon across the street from the Baptist Church. According to town statutes, saloons were to be closed on Sundays. However, the saloon across from the church slid around those laws by not actually taking cash for the drinks it served on Sunday. Tabs were unofficially recorded and paid up later. It helped that the owner was on the city council.
The saloon was less upscale than the *Cattleman's Lounge*. The bar was made of wooden planks nailed down to a frame made of two-by-fours. The floor was dirt, and the only drinks served were whiskey and beer. Nothing fancy. The beer was bottled only—no kegs—because it was easier and therefore cheaper to transport them.
Joe was standing in the doorway of the saloon. The day had become hot, and there was a light breeze outside. Joe had his floppy, tattered hat tipped back on his head. He was in a range shirt and canvas pants, and his pants were tucked into black riding boots. His long knife was in a sheath at his side, and his pistol was tucked into the front of his belt. In one hand was a bottle of beer.
Joe's gaze was on the man who had just saddled up and started off down the street. He glanced back over to the church to Doc and Mrs. Buzzard. They had finished talking to the preacher and were walking away down the street.
Joe had watched Johnny and Lura climb into the buggy and watched Johnny turn the team around and start off down the street. Mighty nice thing, Joe thought, watching Johnny and Lura. They had a love that

reminded him of what he almost had with the Cheyenne girl.

He had then noticed Doc Buzzard glancing across the street to the saddlebum who had been lounging in front of the saloon. The doc had nodded toward him, trying to be discreet. Problem was, Joe was there, and Joe missed little. Joe had watched while the man nodded back. Joe then watched as the man mounted up and rode off down the street, in the same direction Johnny and Lura had gone.

Joe stepped back inside and took a sip of his beer.

Matt was at a table, engaged in a game of chess. He was playing a Swedish man who had thinning hair and a thick beard that rivaled Joe's. The man was in a broadcloth shirt and suspenders and ran a sawmill by the Calaveras River, which was just outside of town. He spoke little English, but he knew the game of chess and knew enough English to say *check* and *checkmate*.

Joe stood the bottle on the table. He said, "Want to finish my beer?"

Matt's elbow was on the table and his chin was in his hand. He was looking at the chessboard trying to figure out what to do.

He said, "Finish your beer? Not really. Why?"

"Gotta go kill a man."

Joe turned and headed for the door.

Matt continued to look at the board. He had lost a rook and a bishop. No matter what move he made next, he was going to lose the second bishop.

Then it dawned on him what Joe had just said. He looked at the doorway, but Joe was gone. He got up and ran out to the boardwalk, but there was no sign of his brother.

He went back to the table and sat. Lars slid his queen diagonally along four squares, and said, "Checkmate."

Matt blinked and looked at the board.

Lars laughed, and picked up Joe's beer and chugged it down.

# 7

JOHNNY GLANCED back over his shoulder again.

Lura said, "That's the second time you've done that."

Johnny nodded. "There's a rider back there."

Lura looked back. The trail behind them was empty for about a thousand feet, then the trail curved and was lost from sight behind a line of trees.

She said, "I don't see anyone."

"He's holding a ways back. Every so often I see him if the trail straightens out for a bit."

"Maybe he's going the same way we are."

"Maybe. But my gut says no."

She gave a little grin. "Your gut?"

He nodded. He looked at her with a smile. She was such a stranger to his way of life.

He gave her a smile, and said, "Sometimes that's all you have to go on."

Now she gave a wide smile. "And what does this gut of yours say about me?"

"It said on that first night when we danced, I wanted to be nowhere else than with you."

She gave a nod, like she was giving it some thought. "I would say you have a wise gut."

He laughed.

He turned the horses off to the side of the road. "Let's rest the team a little."

She said, "It's only been a few miles."

"Yeah, but it's that gut feeling again."

She shrugged.

He gave the reins a little tug and the horses stopped, and he raised a foot and pushed down the brake lever.

He then got down from the buggy. He said, "Want to stretch your legs a little?"

She shrugged again. "I suppose."

He took her hand while she climbed down.

"Of course," she said, glancing to the road behind them, "this gives you quite a view of the road back there. Total coincidence?"

Johnny gave a look of mock innocence and said, "Well, of course."

She laughed and gave him a little slap on the shoulder. "This isn't the wild country of south Texas. There are neither Mexican border raiders here, nor Indian raiders."

Johnny glanced along their back trail. The road was made up of two long wagon wheel ruts with a hump of brown grass in the middle, and it stretched behind them for maybe a quarter of a mile, then was lost for a bit behind some trees, then curved back into view a full mile away.

Johnny could see the rider in the distance. Looked like he had dismounted and was loosening the cinch. Resting his horse. Odd coincidence that he decided to rest his horse at the same time Johnny did the team.

Johnny glanced at the Hawken. It was still leaning on the buggy seat. The picnic basket with Matt's gun was still at the back of the buggy. Both guns were within reach.

Johnny kept the conversation light, though. No need to let Lura know that he found himself going into full warfare mode.

It wasn't anything he thought about. He just felt the readiness for battle working its way through him. Like he somehow could feel a gunfight was coming on, and his bodying was getting ready for it.

He said, "What kind of Indians are there around here?"

"Oh," she began to stroll a bit, and he walked beside her. "Around here there were Miwok and Washoe. Or so I've heard. I've never really seen any."

Johnny glanced toward their back trail, and could see the rider was still there, standing by his horse. Johnny couldn't see him well because of the distance, but he thought the man might be smoking a cigarette.

Johnny said, "Lura, I don't want to frighten you. But there's a lot about me you don't know."

She looked at him like she didn't know what to think.

She said, "I know your heart. I could see in your eyes all I needed to see, that night on the dance floor. And the way you held me when we danced. That's all I need to know."

"I hope that's enough. You may not feel the same when you learn more about me."

He went to the picnic basket, flipped open the lid and pulled out the pistol.

Her eyes went wide. "What's that doing there?"

"The reality is I should never be far away from a gun. I have a way of attracting trouble. So far, I've stayed alive by being more dangerous than those bringing the trouble."

She didn't know what to say.

He spun the revolver slowly, checking the percussion caps to make sure they were all in place.

He said, "Can you drive a team?"

She nodded.

"We're going to drive along. There's a bend in the road up ahead."

She looked ahead toward the bend. It was maybe three hundred feet away.

He said, "I'm going to drive the buggy until it's beyond that bend, where we'll be out of that rider's sight. Then I'm going to jump out and I need you to continue driving the team along. Keep going until you hear a gunshot."

"Why is there going to be a gunshot?"

"Because that man behind us might just be riding along and mean us no trouble at all. Once I've talked with him and made sure of it, then I'll fire one shot in the air and you can bring the buggy back. But if you hear more than one shot, keep on driving. This trail will take you to the ranch. Tell Zack or Quint or whoever's there."

She said, "You're scaring me."

"Sometimes being afraid is a good thing."

Johnny tucked the revolver into the front of his belt, and then he and Lura climbed into the carriage. Johnny clicked the team forward.

They rode along at a casual pace. Once they were beyond the bend, Johnny handed the reins to Lura and then jumped out of the wagon. The horses weren't moving at much more than a walking pace, so he was able to land on his feet.

"Remember what I said," he said to her. "Come back if you hear one shot. If you hear more than one, keep riding to the ranch."

She looked at him with a combination of worry and like she thought he was out of his mind.

Johnny stepped off the road into a stand of short pines. He drew Matt's pistol, and he waited.

The rider had been about a mile back, and within what Johnny guessed to be fifteen minutes, he heard the clip-clop of iron shoes on a hard-packed dirt trail.

The rider came into view. He was keeping his horse at a pace that matched that of the wagon team.

Johnny was behind a pine. He waited while the sound of the horse stepping along passed directly in front of him.

Then he stepped out onto the trail. He kept the revolver in his hand, but held down at his side.

"Hello!" he called out.

The rider reined up and looked back over his shoulder.

Johnny said, "You looking for me?"

The rider said, "Should I be?"

"You tell me."

The rider pulled his gun. He was fast. He leaped from the horse away from Johnny as he did so. Johnny had the gun up and firing but he missed as the rider hit the ground.

The rider rolled to a sitting position and fired a shot at Johnny, but Johnny was turning and diving to one side. The rider's shot missed.

Johnny scrambled back to the pines. The rider dove for cover behind an outcropping of bedrock at the edge of the trail. The horse ran off at a full gallop.

Johnny peeked around the tree, and the rider fired. The bullet chipped away some bark near Johnny's head, and he ducked back.

Then he stepped back out into view, firing as he did so. The rider ducked back and the bullet ricocheted off the rock.

Johnny dove for cover behind another nearby tree. He then rose to his knees and dared take a look.

The rider fired and Johnny felt the breeze of the bullet as it whooshed past him.

Johnny realized he had to be judicious with his shots. He had only one gun. When he had checked the cylinder, there had been five percussion caps in place. That meant five shots. He had already used two of them. If the rider had another gun, or another cylinder to quickly reload his gun with, then he had much more ammunition than Johnny did.

Johnny decided to wait. Maybe the rider would think Johnny had been hit.

The day was warm. Johnny was in the shade of the pine, but he still felt sweat beading up in his hair and along his forehead. He reached up with his left hand to pull free his string tie and unbutton the shirt's top button. He heard grasshoppers buzzing away in a field of brown grass that opened up behind him.

The rider then fired. Once, and then again. Both bullets caught the tree trunk near Johnny's head. Still, he held tight. He could smell pine sap from where the bullets had torn up the bark.

If he was counting right, then the rider had fired four times, which meant his gun held only one more shot. No one would load all six chambers in a revolver when they were riding along on a horse. They would be risking a bullet in the leg if the gun got jarred. This meant the rider had another gun or a loaded cylinder.

"McCabe!" the rider called out.

Johnny said nothing. Let the rider think he was hurt. Zack Johnson and Hesky Jones had gotten out of a fix that way, once.

"McCabe, you ain't gettin' out of this alive! I been paid good money to make sure you're dead!"

*Paid good money?* Johnny asked himself. *Someone is paying to have me killed?*

Johnny wanted to call out and ask who hired him. But to do so would end the bluff he was trying to run. He had only three shots, and a man who believes he's good enough to make every shot count is a fool.

Then Johnny heard something he didn't want to hear. The sound of a horse's hooves on the dirt trail, from up ahead. Two horses, along with the creaking a wagon makes as it rolls along.

*No,* he thought. *It can't be Lura.*

She should have heard the shots and been partway to the ranch by now.

Then he saw the buggy coming into view from around the bend in the road. Lura was driving it. She pulled up the reins as soon as she was in view.

Johnny was about to scream to her to go back. It would be the end of his bluff, but he didn't care.

But before he could, the rider burst into a run toward the buggy.

"No!" Johnny called out.

He had three shots left, and he cut one loose at the rider.

It caught him and spun him around. Must have hit a shoulder, Johnny figured. But the man kept his footing and continued running.

Johnny fired once more, and the bullet hit the brim of the man's hat and sent the hat spinning away.

Then the man jumped up onto the buggy seat. Lura slapped at him, but he grabbed her and pulled her in front of him. He had one arm folded around her neck, and put his pistol to her head.

Johnny ran for the buggy, but the man called out, "That's far enough, McCabe!"

Johnny stopped running. He estimated the wagon to be a hundred feet away.

"Drop the gun," the man said. "Or I blow her brains out."

Johnny aimed the gun toward the man. Sighting in the way you do with a rifle. He needed to make the same shot he had done in Texas the summer before, and he had only one shot remaining.

But he couldn't find his focus. This was Lura the man was threatening. If the shot missed, she was dead. He realized the end of the gun was shaking a little.

To make matters worse, he didn't know this gun. To make a shot as precise as the one he had made the summer before, he had to really know the gun he was using. To know if the sight was even a hair off.

He lowered the gun, drew a breath, and then brought the gun back out to full extension.

"I mean it, McCabe," the man said. "Drop the gun."

Then there was a whistle off to one side. Johnny looked in that direction. So did the man. In doing so, the man's pistol was brought forward so it was aiming past Lura's face and not directly at her.

Joe was on a horse, about five hundred feet off the trail. The land about him was open. Dry brown grass and scattered scrub oaks.

Joe had his Enfield to his shoulder. He fired, and the man's head snapped back and blood spattered. Lura screamed and jumped back.

Johnny ran for the buggy. Lura was climbing down but in her haste lost her footing and fell, and Johnny caught her.

She buried her head in his shoulder and was trembling.

Johnny stroked her hair with one hand.

"It's all right," he said.

She wasn't crying, just trembling. Then she drew a breath and the trembling stopped.

She stepped back. "I'm all right."

"Why'd you come back?"

"I just had to know if you were all right. The next time, I'll follow your instructions to the letter."

Johnny said, "The next time? You still want to see me, even after this?"

She nodded. "Without a doubt."

Joe was reining up in front of the buggy. The team of horses had jumped with surprise at the gunshot, but hadn't started running.

Johnny looked at him. "I didn't know you were out there. How is it I didn't see you?"

"Ain't a man alive can see me if I don't want to be seen."

Johnny and Joe tied the body over the saddle of the man's horse.

Joe said, "I hope you don't mind me takin' that shot."

Johnny shook his head. "Not at all."

"I've seen you make tougher shots, but not when you had this much riding on it. And you didn't have your own gun."

Johnny said, "How'd you know we were in trouble?"

Joe was silent a moment. Careful of what he was going to say.

Then he said, "I saw him ridin' out after you. Figured it was probably trouble. After enough of this kind of thing, you develop an instinct for it."

Lura was sitting on a rock by the edge of the trail.

Johnny went over to her and said, "Would you like me to take you home?"

She thought for a moment. "No. I don't find that place very comforting. I'd rather be with you."

"Should I take you to the ranch?"

She shook her head, and stood. "We're out here

for a picnic. I'd like to have one."

Johnny was so impressed with the strength of this girl.

He looked at Joe, and Joe said, "I'll get the body into town."

Joe pulled his gun and said, "Here, take this'un. It's more effective in your hands than mine."

"But what'll you use?"

Joe slapped the side of his rifle. "I got ol' Bessy here. That's all I need. And my pig sticker."

He tapped the hilt of his knife.

Lura said to Johnny, "When you said there's a lot I don't know about you, you weren't kidding."

"Are you sure you're not having second thoughts about me?"

She shook her head. "Never. I know what I felt the night of the dance, and I know it's real."

"You are such a treasure, do you know that?"

She grinned. "I've always had a feeling."

He grinned back. He was looking into her eyes. The color of a summer sky with just a hint of cloud cover forming. He could look into them forever.

Joe said, "Time for me to get ridin'. Sounds like it's about to get mushy around here, and that might make me blush."

He swung into the saddle.

Johnny said to him, "I owe you, you know."

Joe shook his head. "No you don't. We're brothers. See you back at the ranch."

Joe clicked his horse forward, leading the horse with the rider's body draped across the saddle.

Joe rode easily on his way to town. At one point, he stopped to rest the horses. He dug out his Indian pipe and smoked for a while.

By the time he rode onto the main street of Greenville, it was getting dark. People were staring at the sight of a dead body across the saddle.

Three blocks ahead on the left was Brannigan's

office, but Joe rode on by. He continued on until he was at Doc Buzzard's office. It was dark enough that he could see there was a light on in the front window.

"Hey, Doc!" he called out. "Get out here!"

The door opened and the old buzzard stormed out. As if to say, *who dares bother me?* The man always looked bothered.

Joe said, "Got somethin' for you."

He backed his horse up until he was beside the rider's horse. He drew his knife and with one swipe cut the ropes holding the body to the saddle.

"What's that?" the doctor said.

Joe gave a push, and the body slid off to land in a somersault in the dirt.

"A warnin'," Joe said.

He fixed his gaze on the doc.

Marker opened his mouth like he was going to protest. Like he was going to say he didn't know what Joe was talking about. But he gave it up. For the first time, Joe saw the man not looking bothered. He looked frightened.

Joe turned his horse and started back to the ranch.

# 8

JOHNNY TURNED the buggy off the trail and onto a seemingly flat expanse of grassland. Though, flat can be a little relative. The buggy bounced and leaned a bit as the horses pulled it over clumps of sod. Lura was laughing.

Her hair had long ago come undone and was flowing down to her elbows.

When they were a few hundred feet from the trail, Johnny turned the horses toward a grove of scrub oaks.

He had brought a blanket with him, and he spread it out on the grass. Lura made herself comfortable while Johnny tended to the team. He left the harnesses in place, but unhitched them so they could move about and graze.

He was in his white shirt, but had left the jacket and the tie with the buggy. As he walked over toward Lura, he realized Joe's gun was still tucked in the front of his belt. Matt's was with the buggy.

He pulled the gun and said, "Would you like me to leave this with the other one?"

She shook her head. "Somehow, I think we'd be safer if you had it within reach."

He had to chuckle at that. "Maybe you have a point."

He sat on the blanket beside her and placed the gun in the grass, but within reach.

He said, "I know you have a lot of questions."

She touched the side of his face. "You're a man of the gun. I know that. After our dance, I asked questions. I doubt my mother would be entirely pleased with the answers, but I haven't told her anything other than you're the ramrod of the McCarty ranch. But I think she understands how I feel."

"What about your father?"

"He doesn't like anything."

Johnny laughed, and so did she.

She said, "I'll admit, there were times I wondered what kind of person I really was, as the daughter of that man. When I look at him, he seems so full of hatred. Like he's angry with the whole world. I tried for a long time to break through his shell but he won't let me, so I just gave up."

"Maybe in your case, the apple may not have fallen far from the tree, but it just kept on rolling until it was a long ways off."

She smiled. "Why, Johnny. That's almost poetic."

He shook his head. "That's my brother Matt's department."

"There are all sorts of poetry. There's poetry of words."

Johnny nodded. "Matt is sure full of words."

She chuckled. Then she looked up and he followed her gaze. The sky was a clear blue, like it almost always was here in California. A bird was flying overhead, and continued on toward the trail and beyond. Some sort of jay, Johnny thought. He didn't know birds.

Lura said, "But poetry exists in many forms. Like that bird in flight. Graceful, elegant. It's creating its own kind of poetry."

"The sound of your voice is like music, you know that? Maybe it's a kind of poetry in itself."

She looked at him long and deep, the way a woman does when a man says the right thing. Not that he was necessarily trying to say the right thing, he was just speaking from his heart.

Then she gave him a kiss, long and deep.

He said, "Maybe we should eat. You've been through a lot. And the chicken might be getting cold."

"I don't want to eat."

He nodded. "This is the first time we've been alone. I've walked you home from the school, and we've had dinner at the restaurant in town a few times, and we had that small picnic out by the church. But this is the first time we've been alone like this."

"I know." She reached up and undid the second button on his shirt.

"Aren't you concerned about what people are going to think?"

"Are you?"

"I've never cared about what folks say about me, but I'm concerned about what they might say about you. I never want anyone to say anything bad about you."

She undid the next button. "People can say what they want. They usually do."

When it was dark, they were still on the blanket. Johnny was in his jeans, and Lura was in her camisole and petticoat.

He said, "You smell like peaches."

"It's a fragrance my aunt in San Francisco gave me. Do you like it?"

He nodded. "Very much."

She said with a smile, "I heard a rumor that you brought some wine with you."

He nodded with a grin. He got up on all fours and crawled over to the picnic basket and found the wine. Matt had included a corkscrew, so Johnny screwed it into the cork and then pulled the cork out with a pop. They both laughed, the way everyone does when a cork pops.

He pulled two tin cups from the basket, and he filled each with wine and handed one to her. She sat up and took it with both hands so it wouldn't spill.

He said, "Are you sure you're all right about everything?"

She nodded. "It's not wrong when you're with the man you love. The man you're going to spend the rest of your life with."

It surprised him to hear this come from her.

"I hope I'm not being forward," she said. Then she said, "I suppose it's a little late for that now."

They both laughed.

She said, "But, I have to confess, I knew when you walked across the dance floor to me that I was going to spend the rest of my life with you."

"I had that feeling too. I didn't want to admit to it, because I was still using the name Reynolds and there was still a price on my head."

He had told her that part of his past.

She took a sip of the wine. "This is really good."

He took a sip. "I'm not really a wine person, but I have to admit, Matt outdid himself on this one. The whole meal is a gift from him."

They drank wine and ate chicken, and he told her about his background. Everything that had happened to him. The gunfights. All of the tequila.

He wanted to have no secrets from her. If they were truly going to have a life together, he had to follow the example of his own parents. As far as he knew, they had never had any secrets from each other. So he told her about the women in the border towns, and he told her about Becky Drummond. He told her about Maria Carrera, a love that might have been had things been different.

"The women in those border towns," he said, "I never should have done any of that. I was just being careless. And Becky Drummond—I did love her at the time, but it wasn't like what I feel for you. I've never felt anything like this."

They talked into the night.

At one point, she pointed up at the stars. "You see that one right there? It's really bright and twinkling?"

He nodded. "Yep."

"That's mine. I found it when I was a little girl and would look up at the night sky. It's the star I wished on."

"And what kind of wishes would you make?"

"Oh, all kinds. I wished for you, I suppose. I wished for a knight in shining armor who would whisk me away."

"I'm hardly a knight in shining armor."

She looked at him. "You're a modern-day version of it. Your brothers are too. Or at least Joe is, and I suspect Matt must be, too."

"You wouldn't have been in danger if not for me."

"That's not the point."

He touched her left hand, and ran his fingers over her ring finger. He said, "You really knew we'd be together the moment you saw me walking toward you on the dance floor?"

She nodded. "This feeling came over me like I've never had before. It was like I was being touched by destiny."

"I felt the same way. I knew I shouldn't be getting to know a girl when I had a reward on my head. I knew I might have to light out on a moment's notice. And yet I somehow found myself being drawn across the floor to you. Like it was meant to be."

He rubbed her finger again. "I would like to ask you to marry me. But I don't have a ring."

She took his hand. "We're already married in our hearts. We have been since the moment you crossed the dance floor to me."

After a time, Johnny said, "We should probably be getting back." He was sitting up and in his jeans, and reaching for his shirt. "Your father will be mad as all get out."

She shook her head. "I don't really care what he thinks. I don't mean that to sound defiant or disrespectful. I just don't care what he thinks, and I doubt he cares what I think."

She sat up and reached for her dress. "I feel sorry for my mother and the sad life she has. I really do. But I realized a long time ago the only opinion I really care about is my own, and my Aunt Ginny's. She has said more than once she doesn't care about pretenses, she cares about the heart."

"Sounds like I would like her," Johnny said with a smile.

"She has really been more of a mother to me than

my own mother."

He buttoned his shirt and said, "Knight in shining armor, hmmm?".

She nodded. "That's what I said."

"I suppose that's kind of similar to what an old friend of mine said about me once. An old scout by the name of Apache Jim."

"My, what an extraordinary name."

He nodded. "Apache Jim Layton. Spent some time among the Apache when he was younger."

She was giving a smile of wonder. "You have lived such an extraordinary life. Met such incredible people."

He nodded. "I hadn't thought of it that way, but I suppose I have. The word Apache Jim used for men like me is *gunhawk*."

"Gunhawk? Sounds like some sort of wild bird."

He laughed. "I suppose that's what I am. A wild bird. But he said men of the gun who try to do the right thing just because it's the right thing to do, are gunhawks. Even if they don't carry a gun, they're still gunhawks in spirit."

"And if I'm to be the wife of a gunhawk, if I'm going to be part of this life you live, then you're going to have to show me how to shoot."

He nodded again. "I suppose maybe I should. And yet, I feel a little guilty in a way, pulling you into this sort of life."

She laid a hand on his arm. "It's the life I want."

"The life of a gunhawk?"

"A life with you. Wherever and however that is."

He couldn't help but smile. "Where have you been all my life?"

"Right here in California, wishing on a star for the right gunhawk to come into my life."

He took her in his arms, and they just held each other. Her head was on his shoulder. He was gently rubbing her back and stroking the long hair that fell to her waist.

Johnny looked up at the sky trying to gauge the

time. The stars were as they were earlier, as they seemed to be every night in the California sky. Twinkling and without a cloud in sight.

He said, "Must be near midnight."

"I suppose we should be going, but I don't want to. I want to be with you forever."

"We'll make the wedding plans, and figure out where we're going to live."

She nodded. "It won't be soon enough."

# 9

MATT STEPPED into the bunkhouse.

Joe was standing in front of the stove with a cold cup of coffee, and Quint and Zack Johnson were at the table. Zack was smoking a cigarette and Quint had a Bible in one hand. Quint wore spectacles that wrapped tightly around his face. On the table was a kerosene lamp turned all the way up, and Quint was squinting at the letters on the page. Evan sat off a ways from the table, leaning his chair back against a wall. He was working a harmonica, filling the bunkhouse with a mournful, cowboy tune.

Corry was asleep in one of the bunks. Chip and Valdez were off with the floaters at a line camp.

Matt said to Joe, "Where'd you ride off to, today?"

"Let's talk outside."

Matt followed Joe out the door, and Zack followed them both.

Matt said, "What's going on?"

Joe told him about the man he had shot. And he told him the whole story, including the silent exchange of glances he had seen between the man and the doctor.

Joe said, "I think Doc Buzzard paid the man to kill Johnny."

Matt gave him a long look. "No. That's crazy."

Zack said, "You've gotta be real sure about something like that."

Joe pulled a wad of cash from his pocket and handed it to Matt. "Look at this."

"Where'd you get that?"

"From the dead man's pocket. I counted it. Two hundred and fifty dollars. After I left Johnny and Miss Lura, I reined up and checked the dead man's pockets for anything that might tell me who he was. I was thinkin' he might be a bounty hunter who hadn't got word that our names are cleared. But I could never quite figure just what was behind the looks that he and

Doc Buzzard gave each other."

Matt said, "Maybe they didn't look at each other. Maybe you just saw it wrong."

Joe looked at him as if to say, *are you serious?*

He said, "Buzzard looked full at him and nodded, and the man nodded back."

"So, what'd you find in his pockets? Besides this?"

"Nothin' at all. Nothin' to indicate his name. Just some cigarette fixin's, two bits in change, and them bills. The old doctor paid him to kill Johnny. Where else would a saddle tramp like him get that kind of money? That's more than a cowhand makes in a year."

"Maybe he worked some place and saved his money."

"You know cowhands. How many of them ever save any money?"

Matt nodded. "True. They blow every cent they make."

Zack said, "We've got to tell Johnny."

"You found the money after you left Johnny and Miss Lura," Matt said.

Joe nodded.

"But did you tell him about her father?"

Joe shook his head. "Not with the little gal right there with him. It's her father. And I'm thinkin' maybe we shouldn't."

Matt and Zack both looked at him.

Matt said, "He has to be told."

Joe said, "And what will he do? Will he tell Miss Lura, or will he keep it from her? Did Ma and Pa ever keep secrets from each other?"

"Not that I'm aware of."

Joe took a sip of cold coffee. "I'm thinkin' we shouldn't tell him anything about this, anything he might not want to tell Miss Lura."

Matt stroked his chin. This was a lot to think about.

He said, "All right. For now, we say nothing."

Matt and Joe looked at Zack. He said, "I'm

following your lead on this. Whatever you think is best."

Sabrina Marker heard the sound of a horse and wagon outside. She moved a curtain aside and in the moonlight she could see the wagon was a carriage. Lura was on the front seat alongside the young man she was seeing. The cowboy Jonathan so vehemently disapproved of. The one people in town were calling a gunfighter. McCabe, she believed his name was.

The young man brought the horses to a stop. Sabrina watched as Lura and the McCabe boy kissed.

He hopped down, then helped her down and walked her to the door.

Sabrina let the curtain fall into place. She had been up waiting. This was the first boy Lura had ever been seriously involved with. There had been a couple who had escorted her to dances over the past few years, but Lura had never really seemed to connect with them.

Sabrina had never quite known how to talk to her daughter. Sabrina had always been afraid of saying the wrong thing. She hated herself for her fear, but it was there. She was grateful to her sister Ginny for being the mother figure to Lura that she herself could not be.

The door opened and Lura stepped in. Sabrina heard the McCabe boy say goodnight, then the door shut.

The only light in the room was from a lantern on an end table in one corner. Lura must have thought she was alone, because she leaned back against the door for a moment and looked off into space. Her hair was hanging loose, all the way to her hips. On her face was a sort of dreamy smile.

Sabrina recognized the look.

She said, "I waited up for you."

Lura reacted with a start. "Mama. I didn't know you were there."

"You were out so late. I was starting to worry. Especially after that man was brought in dead. Apparently there was a shooting outside of town."

Lura shook her head. "I'm probably never safer than when I'm with him."

That was when Jonathan came down the stairs. He said, "It's nearly one in the morning. What are the neighbors going to think?"

Lura said, "It's not their business."

"It's that crazy aunt of yours in San Francisco. That's what it is. Encouraging that independent streak in you."

Lura gave a weary sigh. "You're just worried about what the neighbors will think of you."

He looked like he was going to say something, but then didn't. He turned and went back upstairs.

Sabrina knew the rider who had brought in the dead man was a cowhand for the McCarty Ranch. Word travels fast in small towns, and she had heard the cowhand—some said he was the McCabe boy's brother—rode to Jonathan's office and dropped the body almost at the doorway. And he said to consider it a warning.

She knew Jonathan was capable of unscrupulous things. With him, integrity was often a fleeting thing. But she had to wonder what the rider had been talking about, and if it was in any way connected to the way Jonathan had just acted.

Sabrina looked at her daughter and said, "You love this boy, don't you?"

Lura nodded.

"Does he feel the same way?"

"Oh, yes, Mama. It's like it was meant to be. We're going to build our lives together."

"You're talking marriage already?"

"I suppose it seems sudden. But when he walked across the dance floor to me, it was like I knew our futures would be entwined forever. I know it sounds crazy..."

"No it doesn't." Sabrina walked over to her daughter and took her hands. "I felt that way about a boy once, long ago."

"Papa?"

Sabrina gave an amused smile. "No."

Lura didn't look surprised. She knew what her parents had was functional, but nothing more.

Sabrina said, "I've never been close with you. I regret that, but I did the best I could."

"I know, Mama." Lura said it in a way that showed she bore no ill will toward her mother.

Sabrina said, "I'm so grateful that your Aunt Ginny is in your life."

Lura nodded.

Sabrina said, "I'm going to give you some advice. I don't do it very often, I know. I've always had a hard time reaching out to people. Even my own daughter, God help me."

Lura squeezed her mother's hands.

Sabrina said, "But I've got to say this. If you two love each other the way you seem to, then ignore your father. Hang onto this boy and never let go."

# 10

MATT AND JOE STOOD in front of the saloon. Across the street, church had let out. Johnny and Lura were walking hand-in-hand down the street.

Matt said, "It's like what Ma had with Pa. It's the same kind of love."

"I had that once," Joe said. "Or I thought I did. That Cheyenne gal I've mentioned."

Matt nodded. "What I have with Verna is, well, maybe in all honesty it's not quite what Johnny and Miss Lura seem to have. But it's good."

Joe had a bottle of beer in one hand and he took a sip. Public drinking wasn't legal, but if he saw Marshal Brannigan approaching, he would step back inside.

Joe said, "Not everyone finds what Ma and Pa had."

"No, indeed. And that brings me to something I've been thinking about."

Joe looked at him.

Matt said, "We both agree that we shouldn't tell Johnny about Doc Buzzard trying to have him killed."

Joe nodded. "Prob'ly never will be able to."

"But that's an awful lot of money. What'll we do with it?"

"I suppose it belongs to Doc Buzzard, if you're correct in what you saw."

"He don't deserve it back. But it don't seem right for us to just spend it."

"No, indeed." Matt leaned one shoulder against the doorway. "Why don't we just hang onto it for a while? Maybe a time will come when the money is needed."

Joe nodded and took another sip of beer.

A month passed, and then another. Johnny made his way to town every Wednesday evening to have dinner with Lura, and then he saw her Sunday morning for church and spent the afternoon with her.

During the week, he ran the ranch.

He went one week without seeing her at all, because he went into the mountains with some of the men to do some mustanging. Another week he and a couple of the men brought some horses to a small ranch south of Sacramento. But most weeks, he was able to see her on their regular days.

There were no more picnics like the one they had had. Too much of that would ruin her reputation. As it was, they had managed to return to town without anyone seeing them. Joe, Matt and Zack had listened for gossip and heard none.

Just like Johnny felt with Maria in Texas and Becky back in Pennsylvania, a man has to protect a woman's honor.

By the end of September, Johnny realized that autumn was just around the proverbial corner. Fall roundup would be soon. He had finished his first summer as ramrod of the Bar M.

There seemed to be no change in the weather. He said as much one Sunday afternoon over dinner with Lura.

She said, "There's very little change in the weather here. Winter will be a little chilly in the evening, but that's all. I remember we had snow, once. I think I was about ten. I woke up to an inch of it on the ground. It looked so magical. But it was gone by afternoon."

"Where I grew up," Johnny said, "we had four full seasons. Summers could be hot, and in the East, they can be humid. Makes it seem a lot hotter than it really is. But the winters would see us knee-deep in snow."

She was smiling. "It must have been marvelous."

He shrugged. "It was at first, I suppose. Every kid loves to see snow at the start of winter. But after a while, it gets to be tiresome. Winters are cold there—really cold. In the morning, you can find ice an inch thick in a water trough."

"You've seen so much of the world," she said. "I've

never been north or west of Greenville. I've never been south of San Francisco."

"Someday, I'll take you east," he said. "I want you to meet Ma."

"I would so love to meet her."

They talked long after the meal was gone. They talked of wedding plans. A small ceremony at the church in town.

"Mama wants us to wait until spring. She says there's nothing like a June bride. But I don't want to wait. I don't want to wait anymore for us to begin our lives together."

"Are you sure? The last thing I want is for you to feel rushed."

She reached across the table and took his hand. "Oh, Johnny. Rushed is one thing I don't feel. Everything is falling into place so naturally."

Johnny wasn't sure who to ask to be best man. Matt and Joe were equally close to him. And there was Zack Johnson. She planned to ask her Aunt Ginny to be her maid of honor.

It was dark by the time he got her home. As he drove the buggy along the trail back to the ranch, he saw lighting flashing toward the northeast. The stars in that direction were completely obliterated by the cloud cover. By the time he rode into the ranch yard, thunder was rumbling.

When the horses were taken care of and Johnny was walking across the ranch yard toward the bunkhouse, rain started to fall. At first in heavy drops, then by the time he was reaching for the bunkhouse door, the heavens unloaded.

He jumped in through the doorway. He was surprised to find anyone still awake. Matt was pacing about and Zack and Joe were at the table.

Johnny said, "It's comin' down hard out there. A big storm, looks like."

Johnny's hat was now wet. He tossed it toward a peg on the wall. The hat touched the peg and fell to the floor.

Johnny said to Matt, "You called me morose once. But right now I feel about as un-morose as can be."

Joe was sitting at the table, whittling aimlessly at a block of wood. Matt was across the table with a cup of coffee in front of him.

Joe said, "If I didn't know better, I'd say the boy's in love."

"Never thought I'd see it," Matt said. "The Gunman of the Rio Grande, in love."

Johnny was too happy to even take the bait.

"You know," Johnny said, lifting the kettle to see if there was any more coffee. There wasn't. "You think I'd feel like leaping in the air and screaming with joy. But strangely, I don't. I feel calm inside. Having Lura in my life feels so natural, it's like she was made to be at my side. And me at hers. It's like there was a Lura-shaped emptiness in my heart that I didn't even know was there. But now I can't imagine her not being with me."

That was when there was loud clattering of hoofbeats in the ranch yard outside. Two horses charging in fast.

Johnny went out into the rain, followed by the others. One rider was reining up and his horse slid a bit in the mud that was forming in the ranch yard. It was so dark now because of the cloud cover that Johnny could barely see him in the light from the bunkhouse window.

Then lightning came swirling down and struck the ground just beyond the ranch yard, creating a flashing blue light that made the night light up for a moment. In the light, Johnny could see it was Valdez, and the second horse had a body draped across the saddle.

"Johnny!" Valdez called out. "Quint!"

Zack caught the horse by the reins, and Valdez tried to swing out of the saddle, but fell and landed in the mud.

Another streak hit a little further out, and in the light Johnny could see Valdez's shirt was torn and his shirt and face were covered with either mud or blood.

"What happened?" Johnny had to shout over the pounding rain.

"It's Chip! He's dead!"

Quint took the body of Chip by the shoulders and Zack grabbed the feet, and they carried the body into the bunkhouse, running as fast as they could to get out of the rain. Joe grabbed both horses by the reins to pull them toward the barn. Moses Timmons came running to lend a hand and took one of the horses.

Valdez was injured and unsteady on his feet. A little disoriented. Johnny grabbed him by the shoulders and steered him toward the bunkhouse.

Once they were inside, Johnny guided him to the table, and he dropped into one of the chairs. He was soaked as though he had jumped into a lake with his clothes on, and it was indeed mud on both sides of his face and the front of his shirt.

"What happened?" Johnny said.

"The storm." He was panting for breath.

"I'll get him some water," Matt said.

There was a bucket in one corner with a dipper, and Matt fetched it. Valdez took it down so fast he got choking and had to cough some of it out.

"The storm," he said. "The herd. The storm came on so fast, they started running. And then, and then it hit. Out of the night."

"What hit?" Johnny said.

"A twister. It hit. Mud and dirt spraying everywhere. It threw a couple of trees. The cows—they were running every which way. Chip's horse went down and he was trampled. I went down too."

He took some more water. Then he said, "The herd. It's gone. I don't know how many were killed by the twister and how many just run off. But they're gone. Two thousand head. I think most of 'em might be dead."

Johnny thought about the other men, the three stationed regularly at the line camp. "What about Jay,

Rodriquez and Marley?"

"They're gone. The line shack is gone."

In the morning, Johnny and McCarty rode out to survey the damage. Joe and Matt were with them, along with Zack and Hardy. The sky overhead was blue and cloudless, and the morning was warm with just a touch of a breeze. Amazing, Johnny thought. You'd never know such a violent storm had torn through just the night before.

They came to a section where trees had been torn apart, and one scrub oak had apparently been uprooted. It was lying on the ground, with its root base still attached.

Quint said, "I've seen a twister do that kind of thing before."

They rode on and found dead bodies of steers lying in the sun. Dozens of them.

"I wonder how much of the herd was decimated," Matt said.

*Decimated*, Johnny thought. One of those ten-dollar words Matt liked to throw around. But Johnny's mood was too dark at the moment to bother teasing him about it.

"My main concern is the men," McCarty said. "We can rebuild the herd."

He said to Johnny, "You had three of them at the line shack, right?"

Johnny nodded. "The same three Cooper used to send out there. I figured the three work together well, so why change things."

"Let's head to the line shack."

The cabin that served as the line shack had been a structure slapped together with a framework of two-by-fours, and upright planks nailed in place formed the walls. The roof had been done with wooden shingles. There had been a stovepipe sticking from one wall, and two walls were lined with bunks. Enough for the three that worked out of it and any other men Johnny sent out to help.

The cabin was now gone as though it had never existed. The grass around the cabin was torn up and gone too, as though a giant hoe had been used to tear up the earth. There was a mound of dirt off to one side that Johnny remembered was where a scrub oak had stood.

There was no corral. No horses. All gone.

"I hope the men weren't in the shack when the twister hit," McCarty said.

Johnny sat silent a moment, staring at the empty spot of roughed-up earth where the cabin had once been.

He said, "According to Valdez, they were."

Matt said, "Valdez and Chip were riding night herd."

"I had sent them out because a wild cat had come out of the mountains and taken a few head."

This section of range wasn't far from the foothills to the mountains.

He said, "I figured some men riding night herd might be able to get a shot off at it. I figured the three floaters could use an extra hand, so I sent Valdez and Chip out."

They sat in silence a few moments, looking at the area. Thinking about the power of the storm and the lives of the men lost.

Then Johnny said, "We should spread out and see if we can find what's left of the herd. Try to get an idea of how many might be left alive."

He didn't mean to sound heartless, but they had to get to work. As the ramrod, it was his place to say it.

"I'm already out here," McCarty said. "I'll lend a hand."

The goal was to tally the dead steers and then determine how far those that had lived had stampeded. The men split up and rode in various directions. By midafternoon, they met up back at the site of the former cabin.

"Three hundred twenty" Johnny said. He looked to Mr. McCarty. "The count might not be accurate."

Matt had dismounted and was loosening the cinch. He said, "Some of the cows killed by the twister were pretty mangled. There's one area where it's hard to tell how many are there. Body parts are tossed all around. Possibly as many as five cows. Others are totally intact and look like they could almost be just sleeping."

McCarty nodded. "That's what I found in the section of range I covered."

He looked to Johnny and said, "How many more do you think there might be?"

"I think that could be about all. Once you get beyond a certain perimeter, there doesn't seem to be any more carcasses."

Quint said, "Lots of tracks, though."

"I'm beginning to think a lot more might have lived than Valdez might have guessed."

McCarty took off his hat and rubbed one hand through his flat, wet hair.

He said, "This is going to be a massive roundup. They could have run for miles."

Johnny said, "We're going to need to set up a cattle camp and we're going to need a cook. This could take weeks."

Quint nodded. "Moses Timmons usually does the cooking for our roundups."

"Can he cook?"

"No," Hardy said, "but that never stopped him."

Everyone had a chuckle.

"All right," Johnny said, "let's head on back to headquarters. We have a big job ahead of us, and I want to get started, but we have some things to take care of, first. Like, giving Chip a proper burial. He was a good hand and a good man. And then I'll have Moses go into town and get stocked up on supplies."

# 11

THEY HAD a table in the corner of what had become their favorite restaurant.

Johnny was in his white shirt and jacket, and a string tie was in place.

Lura was in the simple gray dress she had worn to teach school. Johnny had met her at the school and walked with her to the restaurant they both liked.

He told her about the tornado.

"We heard about it," she said. "They're talking all over town about it. Another one hit outside of town. A small one. It tore up some trees, but that's about it. The stage driver said another small one ruined a barn outside of Camanche."

"We buried Chip this morning," Johnny said. "He's buried next to True Cooper. The other three, what we call the floaters, they worked out of the line cabin that got destroyed. We never found them. That's four men dead. Four men working for me."

He shook his head. "I don't know if I'm cut out for this business of being a ramrod. Of the men killed, I assigned every one of them there."

"You couldn't have known there would be a storm like that."

He shook his head again. "I know. I'm not being rational. But I understand something my captain in the Rangers said. He said when someone dies under your command, it cuts into you. Even if it's not your fault that they're dead, they're still your men."

She reached over and took his hand. "The fact that you're so bothered by this shows that you belong in command. That you *are* cut out to be a ramrod."

"You know, you're better medicine than anything any doctor could prescribe."

The meal was served. A bottle of white wine was standing on the table and Lura's glass was partly empty, so Johnny reached over with the bottle and filled it.

Johnny was having steak and potatoes, and Lura was having a dinner of baked chicken with a white gravy over a scoop of mashed potatoes.

Johnny said, "I remember once Matt said something about not drinking white wine with steak."

Lura grinned. "I won't tell him if you don't."

"It's a deal."

They ate for a bit, then Johnny said, "I have a big job ahead of me. All of the men do. It looks like the bulk of the herd survived the twister, but they've scattered far and wide. We could be out there weeks. I hope not a month. That's why I came to see you today. I just had to see you once more before I headed out."

"Let the job take as long as it takes. I'll be here waiting for you."

It was his turn to reach over and take her hand.

He said, "Did I ever tell you I love you?"

She thought for a moment. "I don't think either of us has actually said that. At least, not in words."

"Well let me say it. Lura Marker, I love you more than I ever thought it was possible to love someone."

She blinked back a tear. "And I love you. And always will."

"When I'm back," he said, "we'll be married."

She nodded. "Go do what you need to do. Run the ranch. Round up that herd. And then we'll begin our life together."

He walked her to the front door of what everyone in town called the Buzzard's house. Johnny tried not to think of it that way out of respect for Lura. It was dark, and they stood by the front door.

She said, "I'd ask you in, but...you know."

He smiled. "That's all right. I should be getting back to the ranch. It takes a bit of work to prepare for a roundup and we're doing this one on short notice."

"Be safe out there."

He nodded. "I will. And you be well."

They kissed, and he waited while she opened the door and stepped inside.

Then he returned the hat to his head and started toward the livery stable to fetch Bravo. He was torn between not wanting to be away from Lura for possibly weeks and focusing his thoughts on the demands of the upcoming job.

Once Bravo was saddled, Johnny rode down the street, which took him past the Buzzard house. It was dark, and he looked toward the house, wondering if Lura was upstairs, getting ready for bed. He knew the upstairs window overlooking the street was hers.

The curtains parted, and in the moonlight he could see her looking down at him. He waved and she blew him a kiss.

He found himself filled with warmth. Not unlike sitting by a hearth at night, he thought, but it was a warmth from the inside out.

He thought of Pa and Ma and what they had. Their love and what their lives stood for. He thought Ma would like Lura.

He turned Bravo into the cemetery and swung out of the saddle. He walked over to the freshly filled-in grave of Chip Henry. His actual name was Hezekiah Henry and that was the name that would be on his headstone. Mr. McCarty was having the stone engraved and then it would be delivered from San Francisco in a few weeks.

He said, "I'm sorry, Chip. I wish it could have been different. You were a good man. Your shoes are gonna be hard to fill."

He thought of the other three men. They were good men, too. There were no graves to fill, but Mr. McCarty was going to have a stone engraved with the names of all three of them and it would be standing here at the cemetery.

"Well, Chip," he said. "I've got a ranch to run. I'll be seeing you."

He swung back into the saddle and turned Bravo

out of the cemetery and to the trail.

# 12

THE RANCH WAS bustling with activity.

Johnny said to Zack, "I want you to serve as the wrangler. It's not a job normally done by a top hand, but I think looking after the remuda is a real important job. I need a man I can trust."

Johnny decided there was no reason to hold off getting a new cabin built. The previous one had been slapped together but he wanted the new one to be a little more sturdy.

He sent Valdez into town to the saw mill to place an order for lumber. Once the roundup was done, they would build the new cabin.

He met McCarty in his office for a cup of coffee in mid-morning.

McCarty said, "You're four men short, now."

Johnny nodded. "I think I have enough men for the job. I'm leaving Valdez at the ranch to take care of the farrier work for the family. I don't want to take the time right now to hire new men. I'll do that when we're back."

"Do you want me to ride with you? Serve as an extra cowhand?"

"I appreciate the offer, sir, but I think we can handle it."

McCarty chuckled. "I'm kind of glad you said that. I don't know if my old bones could handle a few weeks in a cow camp anymore."

Come morning, they headed out. Moses Timmons had a wagon loaded with supplies, and a sheet of canvas was draped over the back.

Johnny rode beside the wagon, along with Joe, Hardy and Quint. Zack was riding a little behind, bringing a remuda of thirty horses. Corry and Matt were helping him.

Johnny said, "We'll use the site of the line shack

for the cow camp. We'll bring the strays back to the range in that area. Most of the grass is still good."

Quint nodded. "We'll get started while Mose sets up camp."

Johnny said to Moses, "You gonna need any help?"

He shook his head. "Nope. I've done this before, many a time."

The men split up and began a long process of searching out the steers. The men had lariats with them, and each had two canteens of water. They left their rifles at the wagon because a rifle can snag a lariat.

Johnny was wearing the leather leggings he had acquired in Texas, and his guns were in place.

He found one steer munching on grass about a mile from the new cow camp. It looked up at him as he rode up to it. Johnny turned Bravo around behind the animal and started it moving. He found another chewing on some grass under a scrub oak. This steer was not so compliant. A longhorn could run like a horse and this one went into a full gallop. Johnny spurred Bravo on and they caught up to it, and Johnny dropped a loop over the steer's horns.

By nightfall, they had rounded up thirty-two of them. Johnny assigned Hardy and Evans to take the first shift of riding night herd. Since they would all be working long days and needing sleep, Johnny planned to keep the shifts short. No longer than two hours each.

Moses had a campfire burning and a pot of beans hanging from a spit. He also had three kettles of coffee boiling.

When the coffee was ready, Johnny poured a cup.

The sky overhead was clear and filled with stars. Like it usually was in California. Like it had been during his night with Lura.

Matt said, "So, what are your plans with Miss Lura?"

"We're getting married. Probably not long after this roundup is done."

"I would say that's a little sudden, if I hadn't seen you two together. That first night at the dance. You could feel the energy in the air."

Joe poured a cup of coffee and strolled over.

Matt said, "Did you hear? Johnny and Miss Lura are getting married."

Joe nodded. "Cain't say I'm surprised."

Johnny took a sip of coffee. "The only thing that makes me feel a little bad is I don't have the money to get her a proper engagement ring. Seems to me a girl like her should have the best."

Matt said, "Maybe she realizes having the best isn't about material things."

Johnny grinned. "Yeah, she said something like that."

The following day, they were in the saddle for another day of riding about and searching. Finding a trail of longhorn tracks and following them. When a cow was found, it was driven back to the cow camp.

Johnny rode back to change horses around noon. He had been on a buckskin gelding during the morning, and Zack fetched him a bay and switched saddles for him.

Mose came over with a plate of beans.

"Eat," he said. "You boys are working hard out there. Gotta keep your strength up."

Johnny wasn't going to say no.

He was shoveling beans into his mouth when he saw a man coming in on foot. Looked like Hardy. He was hefting a saddle over one shoulder.

He walked up to Johnny and dropped the saddle to the ground. "My horse stepped in a hole and we both went down. Broke its leg right good. Never seen a horse's leg broke worse."

"You put it down?"

He nodded. "I was three miles out."

"You walked three miles?"

Hardy nodded.

Walking a great distance wasn't easy in skin-tight riding boots.

Hardy reached his right hand to his left shoulder. "Hurt my shoulder in the fall. I can hardly move my arm."

Mose Timmons had come over. He said, "Does it hurt here?" and grabbed Hardy just below the point of his shoulder.

Hardy yelped.

Mose said, "I know what's wrong. Come back with me to the wagon."

He had Hardy sit in the wagon seat with his left arm extended out behind the seat.

"Now, look over there," Moses said, pointing to Hardy's right.

Hardy did, and Moses grabbed the arm and gave a yank. Hardy yelped again, standing up in the seat.

But then he said, "I think you helped it."

Mose said, "You had a separated shoulder. It's going to be sore for a few days, but you'll be all right."

Johnny was grinning. "I never saw that done before."

Mose nodded. "I learned it from True Cooper."

By that night, eighty six head had been rounded up.

"Had a good day," Joe said.

Hardy was using a bandana as an improvised sling for his arm.

Johnny said, "How's that shoulder doing?"

Hardy shrugged, but used only his right shoulder. "It'll be all right, I'm sure."

"You've got the night off from night herd. I think tomorrow maybe you should take over wrangler duties for the day. Go easy on the shoulder. Zack can join us in the roundup."

Zack was sitting with a plate of beans. "Can't say

I'll complain about that. I don't think I'm cut out to be a wrangler."

"Me neither," Hardy said. "As soon as this shoulder is better, I want to be back in the saddle."

"No one wants to be wrangler," Matt said. "It was that way at the Broken Spur, too."

Johnny got a plate of beans and sat down. He unbuckled his gunbelt and set it on the ground next to him. Two guns were heavy to tote around all day.

He said, "*Wrangler* has to be one of the most disliked jobs on a ranch."

"That's understandable," Matt said. "It seems to be a job given to kids not quite ready to take on cowhand duties, or old men who can't do a full day in the saddle, anymore."

"It shouldn't be that way. If you think about it, a good horse is worth its weight in gold to a cowhand. When you're out there, it's just you and your horse. Where would you be without a good horse?"

Hardy nodded. "I had to walk three miles today, after my horse went down."

"It seems to me a ranch should find a good man to be the wrangler, pay him a top wage and keep him in the job."

Zack raised his brows as he tossed the idea around. "You might have a point."

"Maybe I'll do that once this roundup is over. Make our wrangler position a top job on the ranch."

The following day, the rain came in again. This was the second rain storm in a week. Johnny hadn't seen this much rain since he had come to California. But unlike the storms of a few nights ago, this was a drizzling rain that lasted most of the day.

The men found only thirteen cows.

The following day was sunny and the men got an early start. The total rounded up was now one hundred forty-two. Johnny found two that were dead—it looked like they had been injured in the stampede and then wandered for a while before they died.

That night, he stood off a bit from the fire with a cup of coffee. He was aching with fatigue and figured he'd crawl into his bedroll as soon as his coffee was finished.

But as he stood and looked off at the night sky, his thoughts weren't of his aches and pains or the work waiting for him in the morning. His thoughts were of Lura.

# 13

JONATHAN WAS sitting in his chair in the living room with a glass of brandy in one hand. Business was slow at the office so he had locked up and come home early.

It had been over a week since Lura had last seen the cowhand. Or the gunfighter. Whatever he was. Rabble, as far as Jonathan was concerned.

Sabrina was in the kitchen puttering away. Preparing dinner, he supposed. He heard the occasional clanking of a pot or pan against something.

The front door opened. Jonathan looked over to see Lura coming in. She glanced at him but said nothing. He said nothing, either. There was nothing to say.

"Lura," Sabrina said. "Is that you?"

"Mama?" Lura said.

Sabrina hurried out of the kitchen to her daughter. The daughter that cost Jonathan two hundred and fifty dollars.

Jonathan looked over at the women. Lura was setting her books down on a chair by the door. Jonathan had to admit, she looked a little worn.

"Are the little brats too much to handle?" he said with a smirk.

"Jonathan," Sabrina said.

"Mama," Lura said, "I need to talk."

Lura glanced at Jonathan. "In the kitchen."

They left the room.

Jonathan got to his feet. One practice he had made over the years was to get all of the information he could. Know as much about what was going on around him as was possible.

With the brandy in hand, he walked over toward the doorway to the kitchen. Then he stopped, wondering if he really wanted to know anything more about Lura.

In a way, he wished she would just marry the gunman and get out of his life. She had been an extra mouth to feed for eighteen years. A price he had to pay for his mistake in Boston, all those years ago. Not the mistake of killing a man, but the mistake of being caught.

He could hear their voices but not what they were saying. But he caught some words. *Pregnant. Late.*

Was he hearing this correctly? Was Lura pregnant? With the gunman's baby?

He went back to his chair and sat down. He took a sip of brandy while he tried to decide what to do.

In the morning, he sat at the table with a cup of coffee and waited until Lura left. Sabrina was preparing to wash the morning dishes, and Jonathan said, "Is she pregnant?"

Sabrina had a dish cloth in her hand. She turned and looked at him. "You know? How?"

He didn't want to admit he had been eavesdropping. He said, "I'm a doctor."

She gave a sigh of resignation. Almost saying aloud, *I should have known.*

He said, "How far along is she?"

"Just a little over two months. She didn't say anything at first, in case she was wrong."

He said, "Does it belong to that gunman?"

"Jonathan," she said, with an admonishing tone. "Of course it does. What kind of girl do you think she is?"

"I have no idea what kind of girl she is. That's the way I have wanted it, and she doesn't seem to mind too much."

"She has always wanted a father in her life. It was your choice to keep distant."

"I kept distant for very good reasons." He got to his feet and went to the stove, and refilled his cup.

He said, "Until now, what she has done with her life is of little concern to me. I don't like her seeing that gunman, but there's little I can do to stop it. But," he looked at her firmly, "I will not have her embarrassing this family by bringing that man's child into the world when they're not even married."

"Oh, Jonathan. They'll be married in a few weeks."

"People will know, Sabrina. They're not stupid. What will that do to us? I'm the town doctor. We're good, God-fearing people." He tossed the term *God-fearing* around when he needed to. People seemed to react positively to it.

He said, "Are they planning to live somewhere else? I've heard he's from Texas. Will he take her back there? Or somewhere?"

Sabrina shook her head. "He's actually from Pennsylvania, but they're going to live in this area. He's got a prominent position with the McCarty Ranch."

Jonathan looked away.

She said with a smile, "Jonathan, try to look at the good side of all this. We're going to be grandparents."

There were times Sabrina could be bullied, and there were times she needed to be gently maneuvered. This was one of the latter times.

He set the coffee on the table and took her hands.

"Sabrina, think about it. Think about what they'll be saying behind her back. The awful things."

Her smile faded.

He said, "She's a good girl. We both know that. She doesn't deserve to be talked about like that, does she?"

Sabrina shook her head.

"I know you want to be a grandmother. And you can. But the best thing for all of us would be if she went away to have her child."

"To Ginny's?"

"Yes. To Ginny's. She has gone there summers, for years. And think about how much Ginny will like having her there. I think of the poor woman, all alone in that house. Then maybe once Lura has had the child, then she can return. We can tell people that the child is her younger cousin, or something like that. Then she can marry that gunman."

"I so want to have a grandchild. And to have Lura here. I want her to be happy."

"And she *will* be happy. She'll be right here in town or nearby, and she'll raise her child. And we'll know it's really her child and you will have your grandchild. But she won't be happy if people are talking poorly about her behind her back, will she?"

Sabrina shook her head.

"You know what they'll call her? A *whore!*" He shouted the word. Sabrina blinked with surprise and her lip quivered a little.

He said, "It would break my heart if people talked that way about our Lura. You don't want that, do you?"

Sabrina shook her head. "No. That would be awful. I'll talk to her."

He stroked Sabrina's hand. "No, I'll talk to her. She and I don't talk enough."

She nodded.

He let go of her hand and picked up his cup of coffee. "And it might be best if we don't tell the cowboy that Lura is with child. That's for her to tell him. I'm sure she'll write him once she gets to Ginny's."

She nodded again. "We won't tell him."

Jonathan knew Lura stayed late after school to correct papers and whatever else it was a school marm did. He wanted to talk to her and he wanted it to be alone. No witnesses. No Sabrina with her cooing about them being grandparents.

He walked in, and she looked up from the front desk with what struck him at first as a look somewhere between fright and disappointment.

He said, "I need to talk to you."

She said, "I'm busy," and went back to the papers on the desk.

He walked up to her. "We need to talk now. Your mother told me. Well, actually, I figured it out. I *am* a doctor, you know."

She said nothing.

He said, "I'm going to make this quick and clear. No beating around the bush. You *will* not embarrass this family by bringing that gunman's whelp into our lives."

This had her attention.

She said, "There's not a lot that can be done about it now."

"More can be done about it than you think."

She gave a sigh of resignation. "All right. What is it that you're talking about?"

"Your mother's batty old sister, in San Francisco. You're going to go there."

She looked at him like he was out of his mind.

"What, have you been nipping in your brandy already? I'm not going anywhere. Johnny is here, and we are going to build our lives here."

"Yes, you are going. And here's why. If you want that child, you're going to have to have it there. You're not going to have it here."

She rose to her feet. "Where I have it is between Johnny and me."

"Sit down." He almost growled the words.

She realized she was frightened of him. She had disliked him, hated him at times. But had never been frightened. She sat down.

"You don't know what I'm capable of," he said. "Do you want to know?"

She said nothing.

"Let me tell you. I'm capable of whatever I have to do to get the job done. The job at the moment is getting you out of town. You are going."

Lura tried to sound strong. "No I'm not."

"You have two choices. One is you go to Ginny's place and have the baby there. You won't want for anything. That crazy old lady has more money than she knows what to do with. And then, maybe after a time you can come back. The other choice is we bury you in a shallow grave outside of town somewhere."

She blinked with surprise. Had she heard him correctly?

"Like I said, you don't know what I'm capable of. If that incompetent dolt I hired had done the job I paid him for, we wouldn't even be having this discussion."

Her mouth fell open. "You hired that man? You paid him to kill Johnny?"

"So you have two choices. Have your little whelp in San Francisco, or we bury you and your little offspring and never have to worry about you again."

She was silent. She didn't know what to say.

He said, "You're going to tell your mother that you like my idea of going to Ginny's, to have the baby there. You're not going to tell your mother anything about shallow graves. If you do, then you have as good as guaranteed yourself that grave. In the morning, you're going to be on the first stagecoach bound for San Francisco."

The following day, he and Sabrina saw her off. She boarded the stage, the driver clicked the team into motion, and they were off.

"I'm going to miss her so," Sabrina said. Tears were streaming down her face.

"Oh, I know," Jonathan said. He took her in an embrace. "But it's what's best."

Sabrina nodded. "I know."

He walked her home, then he went and opened the office.

He should be rejoicing, but he was concerned. Things were going a little too easily. If anything went wrong, he could be ruined.

He doubted there would be any conviction if he was caught. It would be his word against Lura's. She had no proof of anything. But if Sabrina left him, then he would have no more pipeline to the Brackston money. Sabrina's head had always been a little soft and she was easy to manipulate, but she might not be as much so if she found out about his conversation with

Lura and the death threat.

He went to his desk and pulled out the flask. He took a quick drink and put it back. Time to get to work on the second phase of his plan. To get rid of the gunman.

Hiring an assassin didn't work. Jonathan could always hire another one, but he could lose a lot of money if the next one failed too, and the one after that.

No, he decided the way to get rid of the gunman wasn't through violence, but trickery.

His plan was elaborate, but he felt it was necessary.

He figured once Lura was at Ginny's, she would write to the gunman and he would meet her there. They would be married. Eventually, once the child was born, they could return. But that was the problem. Jonathan didn't want them returning.

If Jonathan's plan worked, by the time Lura wrote her letter, the boy would be long gone.

To be on the safe side, he would pay a visit to the town's postmaster, Harold Watkins. A young but ambitious man from back East. Jonathan and Harold shared a glass of brandy every so often, and Harold held a position on the Town Council. Jonathan had contributed to Harold's campaign, and he thought for a fee, Harold would watch for any letters addressed to Johnny McCabe and intercept them. After all, Jonathan had helped count votes at the last election, making certain Harold won. Also for a fee.

Harold had his eyes on the California State Senate. Men like Harold knew the realities of the favors that had to be done to ensure success. And Jonathan understood the importance of putting himself into a position to work with men like Harold.

There was one letter Johnny McCabe was going to receive, though.

Jonathan locked the office door, then sat at his desk. He reached into a drawer and pulled out a folded sheet of paper. He unfolded it. It was a letter Lura had started to Ginny back over the winter. Lura had spilled tea on it and thrown it away. Following an impulse, Jonathan had fished it out of the trash later in the day. He kept a sample of Sabrina's handwriting hidden at the office and had decided he probably should keep a sample of Lura's too. Just in case he ever needed it.

It looked like the need had arisen.

He had always been good at copying a signature. He might not be able to copy her handwriting exactly, but it should be close enough.

Then a thought occurred to him. Was the gunman literate? Many men here on the frontier couldn't read or write. They signed their name with an X.

If not, then maybe he could find someone to read it to him.

Jonathan pulled a blank sheet of paper from the drawer. A bottle of ink and a pen were already on the desk.

He dipped the pen into the ink, and was very careful to make the words he wrote look like Lura had written them.

# 14

THEY HAD been working out of the cattle camp for three weeks, and for the last couple of days had found no more stray cattle.

Johnny sat in the saddle at the top of a low, grassy hill. The land out beyond was grassy, with an occasional scrub oak. It stretched out for a mile before rising in a small, rocky ridge.

Matt sat to one side of Johnny, and to the other side was McCarty. The ranch owner had ridden out a week earlier to see how things were progressing.

On the grassy stretch, three hundred head were grazing.

Johnny said, "I think we've found as many as we're going to. Including the beeves out there, we have about twelve hundred head."

McCarty shook his head. "That's going to set us back a little. But there comes a time when you've got to just go with what you have."

"We can rebuild. It's going to take a while, but we can."

McCarty nodded, and squinted as he looked off at the cattle in front of him. "And that we will. We've done it before. And you know what?"

Johnny looked at him.

McCarty said, "I can't think of another man I'd rather have at the helm of my ranch, rebuilding this herd."

"Thank you, sir. That means a lot."

"I still want to move forward with your idea of getting more into horse ranching."

Matt said, "Have you thought about timber, sir? There must be millions of board feet in the hills not all that far east of us."

McCarty shook his head with a shrug. "I'm a cattleman, son."

"True enough. So you hire a man who knows

lumber."

Matt had McCarty's interest now.

Matt said, "The mining industry doesn't seem to be slowing down, any. They'll need timber for reinforcing their tunnels. They also need lumber for homes and for firewood. There is also some shipbuilding in San Francisco. I say, why not diversify?"

"Do you know anything about timber, yourself?"

Matt shook his head. "Not really. I heard talk when I was at sea. I listened to timber men talking in seaports more than once. Our father said that a man can learn a lot by keeping his mouth shut and listening. That's what I do when I'm around experienced men in any industry."

McCarty was nodding with approval. "I think my daughter picked a good man. When we get back, let's talk more about that project. The logistics, and such. I think I might want to put you in charge of it."

Matt blinked with surprise. "Thank you, sir."

McCarty looked back at the cattle. "My father gave some words of advice, too. He said if a man wants to succeed in business, he has to surround himself with good men. That's what I'm doing."

They rode back to the cow camp at noon to find Mose roasting a haunch of beef over the fire.

He said, "I butchered a steer this morning."

"That's fine," McCarty said. "The men have to eat."

Johnny said, "Mose, we're calling it quits. Once the men have come in and eaten, break camp and we'll head back."

"Yessir, Boss," Mose said.

Johnny and Matt swung out of the saddle and headed for the coffee pot.

Matt said, "When we get back, after I've visited a little with Verna, I think I'm going to sleep for an entire day. My back is going to love sleeping in my bunk."

Johnny took a sip of coffee. "I'm going to take a long, hot bath and then head into town and see Lura."

Joe had arrived ahead of them and already had a cup of coffee going. He walked over to Johnny and Matt and said, "There's somethin' I've gotta tell you, Johnny."

"I'm listenin'."

"That man who tried to kill you, he had some money on him."

Johnny said, "He said something about being paid to kill me. That's probably where the money came from."

"Matt and me—we've been trying to figure out what to do with it. We wanted to spend it on somethin' important. Well, I think a good important thing would be for you to buy a nice ring for Miss Lura. She deserves it, like you said."

He dug into his vest pocket and pulled out the roll of bills, and handed it to Johnny.

Matt said, "Joe, I can't think of a better way for that money to be spent."

Johnny set his cup down on the iron rim of a wagon wheel and flipped through the bills. "Boys, this here's two hundred and fifty dollars."

Joe said, "Ought to buy a right nice ring."

Matt took a sip of coffee. "There was no identification on the body. No way we could know where to send the money. We could have given it to Marshal Brannigan, but it would probably have just gone to the town so the town government could find a way to misspend it."

"Now it can go to somethin' good."

They were back at the bunkhouse by dark, but Johnny found he was so tired his bones were aching. Fully dressed and with his boots still on, he dropped face forward onto his bunk and was asleep.

Come morning, he began heating kettles of water on the stove and dumping them into the tub. This ranch was much smaller than the Broken Spur and didn't have a bath house. The men had to do their washing in a corner of the bunkhouse.

Johnny soaked in the water a while and then

shaved, and by the time Matt was stirring to life in his bunk, Johnny was in his Sunday trousers and a white shirt, and was fixing the knot on his string tie.

He then grabbed his gunbelt and buckled it into place.

Zack was sitting at the table with a cup of coffee. "You're gonna wear that rig when you're all dressed up like that?"

Johnny nodded. "Lura said she didn't mind. After that man who tried to shoot us, she said she thinks she'd feel safer if I had my guns on."

Joe said, "When are you gonna go shopping for that ring?"

"I'm going to take a couple of days off sometime in the next couple of weeks and take a ride out to Stockton and see what they might have. Maybe you and Matt can come along."

"I don't know much about jewelry, but I'll be glad to ride along."

Matt raised one hand in the air and made a sound that might have been, "Me too."

Matt was not one to wake up quickly. He seemed to rise to consciousness begrudgingly, one blink of the eyes at a time.

"I'll see you tonight, boys." Johnny grabbed his hat and jacket and was out the door.

Bravo had worked hard for the past three weeks so Johnny decided to let Bravo have the day off, and he picked out a buckskin with a patch of white between the eyes.

His rifle was still in the wagon, and that's where he left it. He swung into the saddle and was off to town.

In a cow camp, one day was pretty much like another and it was easy to lose track of what day it was, but he had checked a calendar in the bunkhouse and found it was a Wednesday. This meant Lura would be teaching school. Summer school was over and the new schoolyear had begun, and she had told him before he left for the cow camp that the town had hired her to teach full-time. He figured this would probably be not only her first year of teaching, but her last, because they would be married soon and would be starting their life together.

He figured if he timed it right, he would arrive in town at noon and could sit and talk with her while her students were having lunch. Then maybe he would wander his way down to the Cattleman's Lounge, have a beer and chat with Slim and Artie while he waited for the school day to finish.

As he rode along, he thought about where they might live. He didn't want to rent, he wanted them to have their own house. It would have to be close enough to the ranch so he could continue his duties as ramrod. There was nothing on the trail between Greenville and the Bar M, so they would have to build. He would check at the land office and see if any of it was available for homesteading.

He got to the school and saw the children playing outside. He swung out of the saddle and walked up the stairs. He actually felt a little tingly inside at the thought of seeing the woman he loved so much. When you're in love, three weeks apart can be a long time.

He pulled off his hat and opened the door and was surprised to find an older lady sitting at the desk. She had a round face, and gray hair that was pulled back in a bun.

"I was expecting Miss Marker," Johnny said.

"Oh, I'm sorry," the woman said. "I'm Mrs. Henderson. Miss Marker isn't here anymore."

"Not here anymore?"

"No. Her father delivered her resignation the week before last."

Johnny actually took a step backward. "Resigned?"

"Yes. Are you the young man she was seeing?"

"Yes, ma'am. Do you know where she is? Is she home?"

"No one has seen her since she resigned. People are saying she left town."

"Left town?"

He didn't know what to think. He felt like the bottom was falling out of his stomach, but he also felt like he was caught in some sort of strange dream.

"Thank you," he said.

He ran down the stairs, putting the hat back on his head. He didn't bother to push his foot into the stirrup, but instead grabbed the saddle horn and leaped up and into the saddle.

He reined up in front of the Marker house. He left the rein trailing, and took the two steps up to the front porch in one long, running step.

He knocked at the door and her mother answered.

He pulled off his hat.

"Ma'am," he said.

"Mister McCabe. Wait here a moment."

Mrs. Marker stepped back into the house and returned a few moments later with an envelope. On the front was the name *Johnny* in a flowing hand that looked like Lura's.

Mrs. Marker said, "She asked her father to give you this, but since he's at the office, I thought I would."

"Mrs. Marker," Johnny said, "what's going on?"

"Just read the letter."

"Where is she?"

Mrs. Marker looked truly sad. "She asked us not to say. I'm so sorry."

She shut the door.

He stepped down off the porch and tore the envelope open.

# 15

JOHNNY CAME charging back into the ranch yard. He pulled the horse to a sliding stop that sent a cloud of dust into the air, and he was swinging out of the saddle before the horse had fully come to a stop.

Moses Timmons stepped out of the stable. He said, "Johnny?"

"Just saddle Bravo. And get my rifle."

"What's wrong?"

"I ain't used to giving orders twice."

Johnny strode to the bunkhouse. The large roweled spurs on his boots jingled as he drove his heels into the dirt.

Zack was near the front door, leaning his back against the wall and smoking a cigarette.

"Johnny?" he said.

Johnny pulled the door open without a word and stormed inside. Zack followed.

"Johnny," he said. "We thought you'd be in town all day. Didn't expect to see you until sometime after dark."

Johnny pulled the knot loose on his tie and tossed the tie away. Then he ripped his shirt open, sending the buttons flying and the shirt landed on the floor. He pulled on his range shirt and buttoned it up, and grabbed his vest.

"Johnny, what's wrong?"

Johnny stopped and was about to say something but then didn't. He grabbed his bedroll that he had stuffed under his bunk, and his jacket. He reached for his saddle bags and draped them over his shoulder.

Leaving his shirt where it had landed, he walked past Zack and out the door.

Zack hurried to catch up with him.

Johnny said, "I'm gonna take the first bottle of tequila I find and drink it to the bottom. And anyone who gets in my way, I'll cut 'em down."

"Johnny..."

Johnny stopped at the stable and called out, "Mose! Got that horse saddled yet?"

Mose came from around the corner, leading Bravo. The horse wasn't saddled yet.

"Never mind," Johnny said. "I'll do it myself. Get my rifle."

Mose looked at Zack. Zack shrugged, so Mose went off to his wagon and came back with the Hawken and the pouch with the lead balls and the powder horn.

"Johnny," Zack said, as Johnny went to work saddling Bravo. "You and I been through a lot together. We're like brothers. There's nothing you can't tell me. You know that."

"Ain't ready to talk. I might never be ready to talk."

"Look, Matt's off at the house, talking with Mister McCarty about his lumber idea. Want me to get him?"

"I don't really care what you do. I don't think I care about anything, anymore."

Once Bravo was saddled, Johnny tied his bedroll and saddle bags to the back of the saddle, slid the rifle into place, slung the pouch and the powder horn over the saddle horn, then mounted up.

"Where are you going?" Zack said.

"Like I said. First bottle of tequila I can find."

He touched his spurs to Bravo and they were off.

Zack stood and watched Johnny ride away, pushing Bravo to a full gallop before they were even out of the ranch yard.

Matt was walking over from the house.

Matt said, "What was that all about?"

Zack shrugged. "I wish I knew. He stormed into the bunkhouse and pulled off his Sunday-go-to-meetin' clothes, changed and grabbed his soogan and was out the door."

Matt and Zack went to the bunkhouse, and Matt scooped up Johnny's white shirt from the floor.

"So strange," Matt said. "Something must have

happened in town."

"Maybe I'll saddle up and ride into town myself, and talk to Miss Lura. It might be none of our business and Johnny might be riled with me, but I've never seen that look on his face before."

"Me neither. Not in the whole time we grew up together."

Matt realized there was a piece of paper in the front pocket. Half folded, half crumpled. "What's this?"

He took it out and opened it up.

He said, "Maybe this will tell us what's going on."

In flowing hand were the words,

*Dearest Johnny,*

*It breaks my heart to have to tell you this way, but I've decided to leave town. Our romance has been such a whirlwind but it left my head spinning. A little time apart has let me clear my mind, and in my renewed clarity, I realize that what we have is not right for us. I am so terribly sorry to say we don't belong together.*

*I'm leaving town and I may not ever be back. Please don't come looking for me.*

And it was signed, *Lura.*

"Son of a gun," Zack said, standing beside Matt and reading the letter.

Joe stepped in the door. "They say Johnny just came riding in like a madman, packed his bags and rode on out. All without a word."

Matt handed him the letter.

Joe read it and said, "I don't believe it."

"I'll admit, I'm shocked," Matt said. "The way those two look at each other. The only couple I've ever seen look at each other that way is Ma and Pa."

"Sure didn't expect this." Joe dropped the letter on the table. "So, what do we do, now?"

Zack rubbed his chin and paced for a moment. The cigarette he held between his thumb and fore finger was burned down to a stub, so he opened the stove and tossed it inside.

He said, "If I was in his place, he'd ride after me. I

know he would."

"But," Matt said, "we don't even know where he's going."

"What he said was he was going to find the nearest bottle of tequila. That means he's going on one of his historic benders."

Joe and Matt looked at him.

Zack said, "If Johnny has reason enough, he can go on a bender that'll leave a town talking for weeks."

Matt said, "He mentioned something about that, once."

"Hearing about it doesn't do it justice." Zack went to his bunk and grabbed his gunbelt.

Matt said, "How will you find him?"

"Follow his trail." His bedroll was still rolled from the cow camp, so he tucked it under his arm and grabbed his saddle bags.

Joe said, "I'm goin' with you."

"Me too," Matt said.

Zack shook his head. "I don't think that's a good idea. Without Johnny here, this ranch will need leadership. You're practically Mr. McCarty's son."

"True," Matt said. "I hadn't thought of that. All right, you two go after him. Bring him back."

"Might be a few days."

"Quint and I can handle things. Just find him and bring him back."

Joe had taken off his range shirt and vest, and was pulling on the buckskin shirt he had been wearing when the brothers had returned to Pennsylvania, what seemed to Matt like so long ago. Joe buckled on the belt that held the sheath to his knife and then tucked his revolver into the front of the belt.

Mose saddled two horses for them. Joe tucked his Enfield into the scabbard, and he and Zack mounted up.

"Find him," Matt said.

"We will."

Matt watched the two of them ride away.

Quint walked up and said, "Is Johnny gonna be all right?"

Matt shook his head. "I don't really know."

"How about you? You're lookin' a little pale."

"I'll be all right. But I was just struck with the feeling that I may never see any of them again."

## PART TWO

## *The Bender*

### 16

Montana
April, 1882

BREE SAID, "That must have been a hard time for you."

Johnny nodded. "It was a dark time. I don't really remember much of it. Tequila can do that to you. I was known for what Zack once called *historic benders*. Nothing I'm proud of. But that was the last one. I never touched tequila again after that."

"You thought Ma had written that letter?"

Johnny nodded. "I had seen her writing a couple of times and it never occurred to me to look at it closely to see if it was a forgery."

Bree shook her head. "I've never met them. My grandparents."

"It might be best that you never do. They were still living in Greenville a couple of summers ago but I didn't bother to see them. I didn't see what the point would be."

They stripped the saddles off the horses and Johnny said, "You know what? We should heat up some coffee."

She grinned. "You brought coffee fixin's with you?"

He nodded. "I figured since we tend to spend the day in the mountains, we might want to stop and have a fire."

They gathered some dead pine branches that had fallen from higher up, and on a flat slab of rock, they built a fire. Johnny put a kettle of coffee on to start boiling.

Bree said, "You know where Charles and I are

thinking of building our home?"

Johnny shook his head.

"Remember that old shack where Josh fell into that shaft, years ago?"

Johnny chuckled and nodded. "Haven't been back there in a long time. That was when you shot that bear. How old were you? Ten?"

She nodded with a big smile. "Sure was."

"You know, you kids talk about some of the things I've done as being the stuff of legend."

"Gunman of the Rio Grande."

"But what you did was as big as anything I've ever done."

"It runs in the family."

He put his arm around her shoulders and pulled her in for a quick hug. "So you want to live in that old shack?"

"No. We're going to take it down and build a cabin there. If there's anything useful in the shack, we might use it. Like a stove, maybe, if it's not rusted out. We want to build a small horse ranch."

Johnny nodded. "You've talked about raising horses since you were a little girl. I don't see why we can't deed some acreage over to you. Since all of our names are on the place, we'll have to ask everyone, but I don't think anyone'll say no."

"Charles has been talking to Jack's friend Darby. He might want to work for us part time, for a small share of what we get from the horses. We can sell horses to the army and maybe get a contract with the stage company. And even sell to the Circle M."

"That'll be between you and Josh. He runs the place, now. But for when Josh visits, you might want to fill in that old shaft."

She laughed. "So, when you rode off the old McCarty ranch, how long was it before Uncle Joe and Zack caught up with you?"

"I didn't want to stop in Greenville, because I didn't want to see anyone I knew. So I rode all the way to the town of Camanche, which was a couple of hours or so down the road. That was where they found me, sitting at the saloon and pouring down tequila. I wasn't in good shape when they did."

# 17

## California
## October, 1858

"THERE HE IS," Joe said. "In the corner."

Johnny was sitting alone at a table with his back to the wall. A bottle was on the table, and a glass. He wasn't bothering with the glass. He lifted the bottle and took a drink.

They watched while a couple of men walked over. Dressed like cowhands, but their shirts didn't look like they had been changed in a few weeks. They had whiskers that were growing wild, like men who hadn't shaved since they had put their shirts on.

"They look like trouble," Zack said. "Come on."

Zack and Joe headed across the floor, but the two saddle bums got there first.

"Hey, mister," one of them said. He had a cigar in his mouth that bobbed when he talked. "We saw that wad of cash you pulled out when you bought that bottle. How about you buy us a drink?"

"Leave me alone," Johnny said, without looking up at them.

Zack said, "Mister, back off and leave him alone."

The man looked at Zack and said, "This ain't your fight. *You* back off."

Johnny sprang to his feet, drawing his gun as he did, and shot the cigar out of the man's mouth. The man stood with his mouth open and looked at Johnny. He put a hand over his mouth and then looked down the floor, where the cigar had landed.

Johnny cocked his gun. "Anything else you want shot off?"

The man said, "You could'a killed me. That bullet was only a couple inches from my face."

"If I wanted you dead, you'd be dead. But all I want is to be left alone."

The men backed off. They actually backed up a few steps, then turned and tried not to make it look like they were hurrying as they crossed the floor to the door.

The barkeep called over, "Should I send for the marshal?"

Zack shook his head. "We got this under control."

Johnny eased the hammer back, and then returned the gun to his holster and sat down. Smoke from his gunshot was drifting about overhead.

Zack said, "Mind if we join you?"

Johnny said nothing.

Zack looked at Joe. "I don't think he minds."

Joe said, "Hard to tell."

They sat. Zack reached down to the floor and came back with the cigar. It was bent, but was mostly intact and still burning. He straightened it out as much as he could and took a draw from it.

Johnny said, "What're you boys doing out here?"

"What're we doing out here?" Zack said. "If it was one of us, where would you be?"

"I wouldn't be bothering you if you wanted to be left alone."

"Oh, sure you would." Zack let out a puff of smoke.

Joe said, "We seen the letter."

Johnny shrugged and took a pull of the tequila.

Zack pulled the letter from his vest pocket and handed it to him.

He said, "We didn't know if you'd want it."

Johnny looked at the letter. Then he said, "Hand me that cigar."

Zack did.

Johnny held the letter in front of him and touched the end of the cigar to one corner. Flame began reaching up the side of the paper.

Johnny set the paper onto an ash tray on the table and handed the cigar back to Zack.

"Up in smoke," Johnny said. "Just like what I had with Lura."

# 18

ZACK REACHED for the bottle. He took a pull and said, "Haven't had tequila in a while."

Johnny said, "I haven't had any since I left Texas."

Zack offered the bottle to Joe, who shook his head.

Joe looked back at the bar. "Hey, barkeep. I'd like a beer."

The bartender said, "Then come on over here and get one."

Joe went to the bar and came back with a bottle of beer. The label read *Blatz,* in cursive script.

Zack said, "So, are you spending the night here in town and then heading back to the ranch tomorrow?"

Johnny shrugged. "I don't know what's next. Maybe Texas. I'm sure Maria Carrera would take me in. Maybe I should have stayed in Texas with her. I could have been ramrod of her father's ranch. The two of us together could have been a good thing."

Joe said, "At the time, you said it wouldn't be right for you. I remember you gave a little talk about destiny and such things. Sounded a lot like Matt."

"Fine destiny this is." Johnny had the bottle back in his hand and took another mouthful.

"You should go easy on that," Zack said.

"Going easy is not my plan. I intend to put a lot more of this away."

"We know you're hurtin'," Joe said. "But don't be stupid."

"Being stupid seems to be what I do best."

"Johnny," Zack said. "Don't be too hard on yourself. What you thought she was feeling, she wasn't. I know it's hard. I've been through it."

"We all have," Joe said.

Johnny said to Joe, "That Cheyenne girl."

Joe nodded.

Johnny said, "How'd you handle it?"

"I left the Cheyenne village, and I just rode. I wandered for a time. Months, I guess. I didn't really keep track of the time. Eventually decided to head home."

"Maybe that's what I'll do. Wander. Maybe I'll go back to south Texas and start wandering through those border towns again. Drink tequila and get into trouble."

"Well," Zack said, "whatever you do, you're not doing it alone."

"Suit yourself."

Johnny sounded angry, Joe thought. And hurt. And so sad he was way beyond the point of crying. Joe knew Johnny would say things that sounded cruel or angry, things he didn't really mean. Joe had ridden the path Johnny was on now, and understood all too well.

They took a hotel room that night. Johnny paid from the roll of cash Joe had given him.

Johnny said, "This was gonna be used to buy her a ring. Not anymore."

Johnny took the bed, and Joe and Zack slept in their bedrolls on the floor.

Come morning, they were saddled up and riding. A trail led south out of Camanche, and they took it.

"So," Zack said. "Do you have any destination in mind this morning?"

Johnny shook his head. "Just riding."

He reached back and fished a bottle of tequila out of his saddle bag. He had bought an extra one the night before.

"Kind of early for that, isn't it?"

Johnny shook his head. "The way I feel, sunrise is not too early."

He pulled the cork and took a pull from it. Even feeling the way he was, though, he held the bottle in his left hand so his gun hand could be free. He didn't need a hand for the reins. Bravo knew where he was going.

By afternoon, they found themselves riding down the main street of the town of Coulterville. Ahead of them was a three story building with wooden clapboards, and in large green letters on the wall were the words JEFFERY HOTEL. On the bottom floor was the Magnolia Saloon.

They swung out of the saddle and left their horses at a hitching rail. The bottle of tequila was about a quarter full. Zack had helped a little but Johnny had done most of the work, and yet Johnny managed to walk a straight line as he climbed the stairs to the barroom.

There was a long, mahogany bar along one wall. Beyond the bar was an open doorway that led to a billiards room.

"Looks like prosperity," Johnny said. "That's what I like. Lots of prosperity."

He leaned an elbow on the bar. "You know what else I like? Tequila."

The barkeep shook his head. "Fresh out. We're expecting a new shipment on tomorrow's stage."

Johnny looked at Zack. "Can you imagine? What a hardship. All right. Whiskey. One for each of these gentlemen, too."

Joe said, "Thanks, but I'll take a beer."

The barkeep was about Johnny's age, and was in a white shirt with suspenders and a bow tie. He placed a glass in front of Johnny and another in front of Zack and said, "You boys looking for work around here?"

"No," Zack said. "We're just passing through."

The bartender poured a couple of ounces in each glass, and Johnny said, "Leave the bottle."

"I'll have to see some money, first."

Johnny chuckled. "Three ruffians come in looking like us, I'd ask for money upfront, too."

Johnny pulled out a ten dollar bill and set it on the bar.

The bartender blinked with surprise. "Ten dollars?" His voice had gone up an octave. "The entire bottle only costs eighty cents."

"Consider it a tip."

Johnny downed the whiskey. "Kind of pales compared to tequila, doesn't it?"

He didn't wait for an answer. He grabbed the bottle and headed for a table in a corner.

Joe had a bottle of beer with a label that read, *Yoerg's*. The barkeep had said it was all the way from Minnesota.

"This is a nice place," Zack said. "Better'n I expected after the saloons in Camanche and Greenville. There shouldn't be any trouble here. As long as you don't go shooting the cigars out of anyone's mouths."

As it grew dark outside, Joe took their horses to a livery and saw that they were taken care of. When he came back, the barroom had more customers. Some at tables, some bellying-up to the bar. A billiards game was in progress at the next room.

Two women were sitting at the table with Johnny and Zack. Joe got another bottle of Yoerg's and went back to the table.

Zack's hat was tipped back and he was aiming a wide smile at one of the girls. "I'll tell you something, sugar. You're lookin' at two honest-to-goodness Rangers. All the way from Texas. Yessirree."

She was smiling and looking at Zack like he was the most famous actor from the stage, stepping down to mingle with his adoring public. Though Joe knew it was probably more because of the money Johnny was throwing around than because of Zack's smile.

The girl sitting with Johnny looked like she was ten years older than he was, with eyebrows that were carefully sculpted and enough grease paint that she could have belonged on a stage, herself.

She said to Johnny, "If you'd like, we can take a walk. We have to work out of the hotel down the street. They let us meet customers here, but we can't use the rooms upstairs."

Johnny wasn't looking at her. His eyes seemed fixed on the table, but Joe didn't think he was actually seeing the table. He was looking off at the life he thought he had been building with Lura. If he was feeling what Joe had felt when the Cheyenne girl threw him over for another man, then he was feeling a sort of combination of hurt, anger, and even fear that Joe didn't think had a name.

Johnny said, "Not tonight. I'm not ready. Been through a hard loss recently."

"A girl? Did you love her?"

Johnny nodded.

"Did she love you?"

"I have to say, no. But I thought she did."

Johnny emptied his glass. At least he's using a glass tonight, Joe thought.

"Well," the girl said, "maybe I can help you forget her for the night."

Zack was still grinning. "Hey, Johnny. A girl's gotta work, right?"

Johnny pulled out a ten dollar bill.

"I only charge a dollar," she said.

He pulled out another and gave them both to her.

"Twenty?" she said.

"Take the night off."

Johnny bought another hotel room. Like the night before, Zack and Joe slept in their bedrolls on the floor.

Zack said, "We should at least flip a coin to see who gets the bed."

But Johnny was already asleep.

Joe said, "A man puts away the drink he's been putting away for the past couple'a days, he's gonna sleep."

Come morning, Johnny said, "I've had enough of this. I'm heading for the mountains."

# 19

THEY WEREN'T following any trail, just wandering in a general easterly direction. Pine trees stood tall around them. Occasionally they would catch a glimpse of a ridge in the distance.

Zack said, "You know, maybe you ought to do some hunting. Make one of those impossible shots you were always doing back with the Rangers. Use that rifle of yours and bring down a deer. If we're gonna be out here for a couple of days, we're gonna have to eat."

"I'm not in the mood for hunting. One of you go ahead if you want to."

Joe looked at Zack but didn't say anything. He was starting to think Zack didn't fully understand the situation.

After a while, Joe started lagging behind a little. When Zack looked back at him, Joe lifted his head and indicated for Zack to come back.

Zack began lagging too, and Johnny didn't seem to notice. Or he did but didn't care. He continued to ride on alone.

Joe said to Zack, "You ain't been through what he's goin' through."

"Well, no," Zack said. "Not quite like that. I had a girl back in Texas once. I really liked her but she left me for someone else. I remember it hurt."

"Ain't the same thing."

"I suppose not. I couldn't say I was in love. I don't know if I've ever really been in love. Not like him and Miss Lura."

"He ain't gonna be in the mountains for just a couple of days."

"What do you mean?"

"What I mean is, he may not know where he's goin', but I know one thing. He ain't goin' back."

"Then, where's he going?"

Joe shrugged. "At the moment, he's just ridin'.

Sometimes just ridin' is the best thing you can do."

Zack nodded. "Then, who's gonna run the ranch? He's the ramrod."

"I guess Matt and Quint will run it. Matt's gonna be Mister McCarty's son-in-law. He's gonna inherit the ranch, someday. He might as well run it."

Johnny took pulls from the bottle of tequila as he rode along. At one point, he saw a pine tree ahead and a branch that hung about twenty feet from the ground. He pulled his gun and shot it. The branch shook.

He fired again and the branch snapped and fell.

"What did that prove?" Zack said. "Wasting ammunition shooting at a branch."

Johnny shrugged and slid the pistol back into his holster.

Joe said, "It proves tequila and guns don't mix."

By afternoon, they crossed a trail of fresh deer tracks.

Zack said, "You sure you don't want to go shoot us some deer meat? That would taste awful good tonight, over an open fire."

Joe said, "A deer would be too much for us to eat tonight. We got no way to carry it with us. The meat would spoil."

Johnny was looking off to the left. Joe followed his gaze and saw two wild rabbits about fifty feet away in the grass. They had been nibbling on something and were now looking at the riders.

Johnny had the tequila bottle in his left hand, and with his right he drew, cocking the gun as he moved, brought the gun out to full extension and fired. One rabbit went down. The other darted off in a zig-zag pattern. Johnny cocked and fired again, and the rabbit flipped over and was down in the grass.

Johnny said, "There you go. An impossible shot. Two of 'em. You want 'em, go get 'em."

He took a pull from the bottle, and continued riding along.

By nightfall, they had a fire going and both rabbits were roasted and eaten.

Johnny unrolled his bedroll and stretched out on it, and within moments was asleep. He had finished off the tequila and Joe figured he would sleep the night.

Joe said, "We made good time today, even though we weren't riding fast. We made a fairly straight line, going directly east."

"Maybe that's what he wants," Zack said. "To put as much distance between himself and California as he can. Like you said."

Zack threw a stick on the fire. "I would sure like a taste of coffee. We didn't bring any with us."

"I don't think we figured we'd be gone this long. We were gonna find Johnny and bring him back to the ranch. I should'a known better."

Joe dropped cross-legged in front of the fire. "We find us a trading post, we should buy some supplies."

Zack sat by the fire. He looked at the way Joe was sitting and decided against it, and instead sat with his knees bent in front of him and his arms resting across them.

Zack said, "There must be a trading post on the other side of the mountains. There's some prospecting going on."

Joe nodded. "From talk I heard, there's a small settlement at Washoe Flats. If we're as far north as I think we are, we should come out about there. There's also the small town of Eagle Station, a few miles south of Washoe. The town's growin', and folks are startin' to call it Carson City. But if you get him near a saloon, he might blow all the money on tequila."

Zack looked back at Johnny and said, "He keeps drinking like this, it'll kill him."

"Maybe that's what he wants."

# 20

JOHNNY ROSE slowly to consciousness to find the sun already in the sky. He tried to sit up but found his head was pounding.

He said, "I slept past dawn. I hardly ever do that. Is the coffee hot?"

"We ain't got any coffee," Joe said. "Remember how fast you left? We've gotta get us some supplies if we're not goin' back to the ranch."

Johnny nodded and found nodding hurt his head.

He pulled the wad of bills from his vest pocket. "This should be enough to cover supplies."

Johnny then sniffed the air. "What's that smell?"

He realized Joe was in front of the fire, fussing over something.

"Trout for breakfast," Joe said. "There's a stream off through the woods. I did some fishin' this morning."

"I don't need fish. I need coffee, to stop my head from hurting."

"We got some fresh, cold water in our canteens now. That's all there is. No coffee. You drink like you've been doin' for the past couple of days, you gotta expect your head to hurt."

They came out of the mountains and into the foothills of Utah Territory. The land about them was flat and then would rise in small ridges that were gravelly in places, and in other places there was chaparral and scattered pines.

By night they were in Washoe. Not really a town, just a scattering of huts that were made of tent canvas cut into long sheets and stretched over a two-by-four frames.

One such building had a slab of wood nailed in place over the door, and the words GENRL STORE painted on it.

There was one structure made of solid wood, and

that's what Johnny rode for. Joe and Zack rode along.

The building was a single floor, with a false front that rose above the roofline. The walls were made of planks nailed into place upright.

The interior was a far cry from the elegance of the *Magnolia*. A dirt floor, a bar that was made of planks nailed to a rectangular frame. Two working girls sat at a table. One was chunky and wearing a dress a couple of sizes two small. The other had hollow cheeks and dark, deeply set eyes. They gave bored glances at the boys, then went back to talking.

"Wait'll they see the wad of cash Johnny has," Joe said. "Then they won't be lookin' away."

Zack said, "If it's all the same, I'd rather they did."

"The way he's spending, though, the money ain't gonna last long."

Johnny asked for a bottle of tequila but had to settle for whiskey. He took the bottle and went to a corner. Joe and Zack went with him. Joe decided not to bother with a beer. He had never been one to drink too much. Three bottles of beer in two nights was a lot for him.

"So," Zack said, "what're you gonna do? Sit in the corner and drink the bottle down?"

"That's the plan," Johnny said.

"While you do," Joe said, "I'm gonna take a walk down to the general store and see about buying us some supplies."

"You do that," Johnny said. "I'm gonna sit here and drink whiskey."

The afternoon went pretty much like the previous evenings. Except this time, they didn't stay at the saloon well into the night. The accommodations in this town weren't as appealing. The only hotel was where the girls plied their trade, but it was really just three tents sewn together with cots, and flaps of canvas hanging from the canvas ceiling for privacy.

"I ain't stayin' there," Joe said. "And I don't want to set up camp after dark. Let's get riding."

Johnny agreed, and they rode out and as dusk was settling across the land, they set up camp in a wooded ridge a half mile outside of town.

Zack said, "This has got to stop. You can't drink your way all the way to Texas."

"I can try," Johnny said.

Joe said, "Is that where we're goin'?"

Johnny shrugged. "I don't rightly know. I'm just drifting. Like a leaf on the wind."

"What would Ma say? What would Pa have said?"

Johnny looked at him. Joe could tell Johnny was getting annoyed. "When that Cheyenne girl ran out on you, did you have anyone saying that kind of thing to you?"

"I wish there had been. Maybe I wouldn't have wandered like I did for months. I could have stayed with the Cheyenne. I had a life there. But I walked away from it all."

"Maybe you should go back to it." Johnny walked away.

Joe sat down by the fire and got out his Cheyenne pipe.

Zack watched until Johnny was gone from the circle of firelight.

He said to Joe, "He didn't mean it."

Joe nodded. "I know. Remember, I've been where he is."

Joe didn't look into the fire. He had learned with the Cheyenne that you didn't do that at night.

He was wondering if he really should be here. Not because of what Johnny said, but because just a few months ago he and Johnny had both decided to stay on the McCarty ranch because they didn't want to be far from Matt, in case Matt needed them. Matt wasn't aware that Verna was potentially capable of murder, and he was too in love with the woman he thought she was to listen to reason. And now Matt was alone at the ranch.

Joe wondered if maybe he should head back to the ranch and let Zack stay with Johnny.

But then he decided against it. Of his two brothers, Johnny was the one who needed him the most right now.

After a time, Johnny came back. He slapped Joe on the shoulder and said, "I didn't mean what I said."

Joe nodded. "I know."

"I'm gonna get some sleep. Tomorrow maybe we'll figure things out."

But come morning, Joe and Zack found Johnny was gone.

# 21

IT WAS near midnight when Johnny rode down the main street of Carson City. He rode past a slapped-together wooden building with an uneven roofline. Mounted over the door was a hand-painted sign that read SALOON. It looked to be open. It would be his destination once he took Bravo to the livery.

Odd thing about what he was going through, he thought. There were times when he felt almost like his old self. And then the whole thing would come crashing down on him again. And when it did, he found he couldn't breathe. He wanted to cry or scream. None of it seemed real. It was like it all had to be part of some bad dream.

The saloon had no swinging batwing doors like in some saloons, just a regular door like what you would find on a house. He turned the knob and walked in.

There were a couple of girls at a corner table, and a bartender was puttering about behind the bar. Otherwise, the room was empty. It was a slow night.

Johnny walked up to the bar. The bartender was about thirty with a thick mustache and bushy sideburns.

Johnny said, "Do you have tequila?"

The man shook his head. "Whiskey and beer is about all we have."

Johnny said, "Whiskey, then. I'll take a bottle."

From his vest pocket, Johnny pulled a fistful of silver dollars. Change from the saloon the night before. He dropped them on the bar and said, "Keep the whiskey coming until I fall over."

He took a bottle and went to a table and sat down.

The women at the table looked over at him. Apparently they worked here. Johnny hoped they would leave him alone. He wanted to drink his way into oblivion, and the best way to do that is when you're alone.

But one of them came over. Maybe mid-twenties. She had dark hair and dark eyes. Looked a little Indian. She was pretty enough and back when Johnny was getting himself into trouble in border towns, she would have had his attention.

He said, "I'd just like to be left alone."

She slid out a chair. "Sometimes when you want to be left alone is when you really shouldn't be alone."

She sat and said, "My name's Rosie. Girl over there in the corner is Annie."

Johnny looked over. A woman about Rosie's age with light colored hair was sipping on a cup of coffee.

Johnny said, "I don't want to seem rude, but I'm not interested."

"I just thought maybe you might want someone to talk to."

Johnny looked at her.

She said, "I can see the pain in your eyes. I could the moment you walked in. In my line of work, you see all kinds, and you get to recognize real pain when you see it."

Johnny tipped the bottle for a drink.

Rosie said, "Sometimes it's easier to talk to a stranger."

Johnny took another belt of the whiskey.

She said, "You really should go easier on that."

"I'm just getting started."

"Then, you can share it with me."

Johnny gave a shrug, as if to say he didn't really care. She tipped the bottle for a swallow.

She reached a hand over to Johnny's. She said, "You're not alone."

"I sure feel it."

"Well, you're not."

Johnny looked at her again. He didn't know what it was about her that made him say it, when he really just wanted to be left alone. But he said, "Her name is Lura."

## 22

THEY DIDN'T realize Johnny was gone at first.

Joe woke up with the eastern sky lightening. Johnny was usually the first one awake, so it didn't strike Joe as odd that Johnny wasn't in camp. He figured Johnny had gone off to gather some wood for the morning fire.

Joe stretched and then grabbed his revolver from where he had set it on the ground beside him, and tucked it into his belt. He climbed to his feet and was thinking he wished Johnny would get back with the wood. He had a hankering for some coffee.

It was then that he noticed only two horses were where three had been picketed the night before. Joe glanced over to where Johnny's bedroll was spread out and saw Johnny's saddle was gone.

Joe kicked Zack's foot and Zack was startled into consciousness.

"Wake up," Joe said. "I think we got a problem."

Joe gathered some wood and began nursing a fire to life.

Zack said, "He's long gone."

Joe nodded. "Slipped off sometime in the night."

"What do you suppose happened?"

Joe shrugged. "He might have been layin' there awake and thinkin' about Lura, and it all started weighin' heavy on him and he just had to ride. Sometimes bein' in motion makes you feel better."

"So, he's just gone?"

Joe shook his head. "We'll find him."

"How? I cut for sign outside of our camp. His trail ends about a thousand feet to the south."

"He don't want to be found."

The fire was going, so Joe dumped some water from his canteen into the kettle.

Zack said, "So what're we gonna do?"

"We're gonna find him. After we have some coffee."

"How are we possibly gonna find him?"

"There ain't a man alive can hide his trail from me if I want to find it."

Zack shook his head with a grin. "You keep saying things like that."

"'Cause it's true."

After their coffee, Joe saddled his horse and tied Johnny's bedroll to the back of his horse with his own.

Zack said, "Where do you suppose he went? Carson City?"

Joe swung into the saddle and said, "Most likely. Let's go find out."

It was mid-morning when Joe and Zack rode into Carson City. They found Bravo at the livery.

"So, what now?" Zack said.

Joe shrugged. "Start checking out the saloons."

Carson City was small, and there were only two saloons. The first one they came to wasn't open yet—the front door was locked. Zack knocked and a man opened the door.

Zack said, "We're looking for a man."

The man nodded. "I have a feeling I know who you're looking for. Come on in."

They stepped in and the man shut the door and locked it.

He said, "My name's Lewis. I'm the bartender here."

"Zack Johnson. This here's Joe McCabe."

Lewis nodded. "He came in last night, around midnight. Had a look in his eyes that was like nothing I've ever seen before. I don't think I'll ever forget it."

Joe said, "Where is he now?"

"Upstairs."

Annie had walked in from a room out back while they were talking. She said, "Come on. I'll take you to him."

"My name's Annie McGraw," she said, as they

followed her up the stairs.

"I'm his brother," Joe said. "This here feller rode with him in the Rangers."

"He's in a bad way. Are you going to take care of him?"

"We'll do the best we can, ma'am," Zack said. "But sometimes taking care of him is like trying to throw a rope on a tornado."

Joe snorted a chuckle. "Ain't that the truth."

The floor of the corridor was made of raw, unfinished planks, and it was uneven. It creaked underfoot when they walked.

Annie stopped at a door and knocked. There was no answer.

She said, "Rosie?"

The door opened. A girl with dark hair that fell down over her shoulders in chaotic-looking waves and curls was there, wearing a robe. She looked like she had put down a little too much whiskey the night before, and her head was letting her know.

Annie said, "Rosie, this is Johnny's brother and a friend of his. They're here looking for him."

Rosie nodded, doing it easy like the motion hurt. "He's in here."

She stepped aside, and Zack and Joe went in. The room smelled of whiskey and perfume.

Johnny was in the bed, looking a little gray. More like he was dead than asleep. He had no shirt, and the sheets were pulled up to his chest. His clothes were tossed about on the floor.

His gunbelt was on the floor, but one gun was on a small, rickety-looking wooden table that served as a nightstand. Despite the state of mind Jonny was in, he kept a gun within reach.

Zack was about to call out Johnny's name to wake him up, but Joe held a hand up to for him to wait. Joe then went to the night stand and got the gun.

Zack nodded. Then he said, "Johnny."

Johnny didn't budge. Joe thought he could see

him breathing, but otherwise would have thought his brother had expired.

"Johnny!" Zack said louder.

No budge from Johnny.

Zack reached over and pulled the pillow from under Johnny's head. The back of Johnny's head hit the bed. Johnny gave a little sputter, and his eyes opened and blinked, and then shut again.

Zack slapped at the blankets where he thought Johnny's foot was. "Johnny. Wake up."

Johnny was awake—sort of. Eyes unfocused, he was reaching for his gun. Joe was amazed that even in this state of mind, Johnny's hand landed right where his gun would have been.

"Johnny," Joe said. "You gotta wake up."

Johnny sat up in bed. He buried his face in his hands. He made a sound like, "Uhhhh."

"Johnny, sweetie," Rosie said. "This is your brother and a friend of yours. They're looking for you."

Johnny said, "I think I'm dyin'."

Joe grinned. "No, you ain't. You're just gonna feel like it for a while."

Zack said to Annie, "Is there any place around here where we can get coffee?"

"Yeah, there's a pot downstairs."

"We're gonna need a lot of it."

She nodded toward the door. "Come on."

An hour later, Johnny was dressed and was able to walk, as long as he placed his feet down carefully. He wasn't very steady and to get downstairs he needed one hand on the railing and the other around Joe's shoulders.

Johnny said, his voice a little shaky, "I left Bravo down at the livery."

Joe said, "Bravo's saddled and waiting for you outside."

"I think I'm still drunk but hungover at the same time."

"It's amazin' you're even breathin'."

They got to the first floor and started toward the door.

Zack went to Lewis and said, "Do we owe you anything for last night?"

Lewis shook his head. "Hold on. I have something for you."

He went behind the bar and came back with a fistful of silver dollars.

He dropped them in Zack's hand and said, "He gave these to me last night. Told me to keep the whiskey coming until he fell over. That's about what happened. I kept what he owed me but there's the rest."

"A lot of men would've kept it."

Lewis shook his head. "Not me. I could see he's hurting real bad. It wouldn't be right to take advantage."

Zack headed outside and saw Johnny was on Bravo. He was hunched over in the saddle and looked like he might pitch over if Bravo took a wrong step.

Zack said, "How'd you get him in the saddle."

"Weren't easy," Joe said.

They made camp outside of town. Joe built a campfire and got some coffee going.

"Drink water, too," Zack said. "I remember you saying that old Chinese man in Texas told you that. I found out he was right. It works."

Johnny took water from a canteen, then ran to the edge of camp and all of the water came up.

Zack said, "I didn't know he could move that fast."

Joe shook his head. "It's gonna be a long morning."

By afternoon, Johnny was able to walk with full steadiness. He was caught between wanting to keep his hat on to shield his eyes from the daylight, which he still found painful, and how heavy his hat felt on his painful head. But he had a cup of coffee in one hand and was able to keep it down.

He set the coffee on the ground and got out what

was left of the bills, and the silver dollars.

He counted it and said, "You know, I don't think she charged me last night."

Zack said, "A saloon woman who doesn't charge?"

Johnny shrugged. "We talked for a long time. Talked over whiskey. I talked all about Lura, even though I hadn't intended to. I talked and she listened. And she talked about her hard times."

"What kind of hard times?"

"I don't really remember. I don't remember much after we opened the second bottle. I don't even remember going upstairs."

Zack nodded. "Whiskey can do that."

Johnny put the money back into a vest pocket. "I can't do any more of this."

"Count money?"

"What I've been doing these last few days. Drowning myself in whiskey or tequila."

Johnny stopped and looked off at the ridge in the distance. "I don't know what the future holds, but I'm not going to find it in the bottom of a bottle."

"The way you've been going," Zack said, "you're not going to have a very long future."

"Maybe I haven't been wanting to live, the way I feel." Johnny grabbed his cup and took a sip of coffee. "Maybe I still don't. I don't know. But I'm a survivor. Survivors don't quit. We keep on going, we keep on breathing, no matter how much it hurts."

Joe was at the campfire, roasting some partridge.

Johnny said, "My appetite's coming back. That smells real good."

Joe said, "So, after you've eaten and had a good night's sleep, do you want to head back to the ranch?"

Johnny thought about that for a moment. "No, I don't think so. I don't want to be in the area where she and I had our...whatever it was we had. Romance, I suppose. I don't want to be reminded of her."

"Then, where are we going?" Zack said.

Johnny thought about that a moment, too. He

stood with a cool breeze touching his face. "The mountains. I miss the mountains. Joe, Matt and me spent a few weeks in the mountains last year, after we left Texas."

Joe said, "You want to go back to that little valley?"

Johnny shook his head. "North. I think I want to go north. You said those mountains stretch all the way up to the Canadian border."

"Past it."

"Then, let's go see some mountains."

Zack said, "It's gonna be cold. It's October now. Winter will be hitting those mountains, if it hasn't already."

"I don't mind the cold. Maybe it's what I need."

Joe nodded. "All right. Then tomorrow morning, we head north."

# PART THREE

## *The Lakota*

### 23

Montana
April, 1882

JOHNNY AND BREE MOVED carefully through the woods. They had each pulled a pair of buckskin boots from their saddlebags and slid them on. Johnny had his Sharps rifle in one hand, and Bree her Winchester. It was often called a Yellow Boy because of the brass receiver.

The forest was pine, with trees a few yards apart. Walking quietly was easy, as long as they avoided any dry sticks that had fallen to the pine straw underfoot.

They came to a small clearing. Bedrock was too close to the surface for trees to take root, but there was grass and a scattering of junipers.

In the middle of the field was a brown bird. About the size of a small turkey.

"All right, Punkin," Johnny said, "let's see you take the shot."

The bird was pecking at something on the ground, and its head disappeared below the height of the grass. Bree jacked a round into place, and the bird burst into a noisy, explosive flight.

She brought the rifle to her shoulder and fired, and the bird went down in a small cloud of feathers.

"Good shooting," Johnny said.

"I learned from the best."

They brought the bird back to the cliff. Thunder had wandered a bit but Midnight was still where they had left her.

Johnny gathered some dried pine branches while Bree prepared the bird using a bowie knife she kept in her saddle bags. Once a fire was going, they improvised a spit and began roasting the bird.

Johnny said, "Partridge can be tasty when it's cooked over an open fire like this."

"Aunt Ginny says it's actually called a ruffed grouse. She says it's incorrectly called a partridge."

Johnny grinned. "Well, I suppose she would know. But up in these mountains, as far as I'm concerned, it's a partridge."

Bree smiled.

When the bird was ready, they sat cross-legged by the fire. The sky overhead was a clear blue and the wind had a crispness that mountain winds often had, which Johnny had learned to love.

Bree said, "So you never touched tequila again after that last bender?"

Johnny shook his head. "Not once. Not that I'm opposed to it, and I do take an occasional drink of scotch. But I just think the taste of tequila would bring back too many unpleasant memories."

She nodded and chewed into a drumstick. "So, that bender was how Dusty came to be."

Johnny nodded. "I don't really remember anything about that night. I remember sitting down at the table with a bottle of whiskey and the saloon woman sitting down with me. I don't even really remember waking up the next day. I remember Joe helping me down the stairs and then getting me onto a horse. I put that time behind me and thought about it as little as I could after that. I guess I was just embarrassed. And then Dusty rode into our lives."

"And after that, you and Uncle Joe and Zack came north to this valley?"

Johnny nodded. "We rode east first, to Fort Bridger. There I spent some of the money and we stocked up on provisions. Then we headed north."

Johnny thought for a moment. "Did I ever tell you about the band of Lakota your Uncle Joe, Zack and I met on the way? And the woman they had with them? A captive?"

Bree shook her head, suddenly intrigued. "No. Was that the first time you had any doings with the Lakota?"

"That it was."

"Tell me all about it."

## 24

Rocky Mountains, Northwest of Fort Laramie
November, 1858

THERE WERE four inches of snow on the ground. Johnny had bought a buckskin shirt at Fort Bridger, because Joe had said if you dress in layers, with buckskin as your outer layer, then you can be quite warm. Johnny pulled the buckskin on over his range shirt, and he realized Joe was right.

While they were at Bridger, Zack wrote a quick letter to Matt. It had been Joe's idea, but he wasn't so good with putting words on paper so he asked Zack to do it.

"Look alive," Joe said as they rode along. "This is Cheyenne country. And Lakota. It's best that we see them before they see us."

Joe was riding with his Enfield across the front of his saddle. Johnny pulled his Hawken from the scabbard and rode with it in one hand.

Zack didn't have a rifle. He had used a Colt rifle when they were with the Rangers, but he had sold it to a settler. He had never liked the way it fired. The blow-by was too near his face. That was one thing Johnny didn't miss, either.

They were riding through a wide pass between two long ridges. The ridges were covered with pines, but the pass was flat and barren, with only an occasional short pine or a juniper.

They rode single file, with Joe in the lead, Zack in the middle, and Johnny pulling up the rear.

The land was a blanket of white, and the sky overhead an impossibly deep blue. The air was cold but not unbearably so. Johnny's hat was pulled down over his head and he felt not quite warm but warm enough in his buckskin shirt.

They followed the pass out to a more open area, and that was where they stopped to rest the horses. The wind was strong and had blown away some of the powdery snow, and the horses pulled at strands of grass with their teeth.

"Fort Laramie is about four hundred miles that way," Joe said, pointing with one hand toward the southeast.

Johnny squinted against the sun, and the wind felt cold on his face.

"The land is harsh," he said. "But it takes ahold of your heart and doesn't let go."

"In the spring, this whole area will be rich with green grass. This is one of those areas I mentioned back in our little valley, where a man could run cattle. Except for the Indians. The Cheyenne and Lakota probably wouldn't take too kindly to it."

Zack was in a heavy, wool coat and the collar was turned up. "Never been this far north before. I'm not sure I'd pick an area like this to build a home."

"So," Joe said to Johnny. "Want to head to Laramie? Or go further north?"

Johnny looked to the north. A ridge stood in the distance. He estimated it to be maybe five miles away.

"I think I'd like to keep going north. Maybe find a place kind of like our little valley. Settle in for the winter. Maybe find some of that peace of mind I had there."

Joe nodded. He understood. "Something about the cold, it somehow clears the mind. Washes away your troubles."

They mounted up and continued on.

They rode around toward the eastern face of the ridge that had been ahead of them. When the ridge was to their left, Joe held up his hand and they stopped.

"Got company," he said.

Johnny squinted against the brightness of the snow-covered landscape. He could see some faint dark shapes off a ways. Maybe two miles. He would have thought they were trees.

Zack said, "I see 'em. Looks like five riders."

Johnny had never been quite as good at seeing long-distance as some folks. But when he squinted and watched them for a while, he could see the shapes were moving. He decided that if he should ever ride this country alone, he would stay more to the wooded ridges.

Zack said, "Do you think they see us?"

Joe was silent a moment, watching. Then he said, "Yep."

"So, what do we do? If they're anything like the Comanche and Kiowa Johnny and I fought in Texas, they're too small to be a raiding party."

"Or a hunting party. But they see us. They've turned their horses toward us."

Johnny said, "Let's go ride up to 'em. If we show we're afraid, we'll give 'em the upperhand."

Joe nodded. "That's the way of it."

"If they're Cheyenne, then you should be able to talk to them."

"If they're Lakota, I probably can too. They share a lot of their customs and ways with the Cheyenne."

Zack said, "I don't think I've ever heard of the Lakota."

"White men call 'em the Sioux."

Joe started forward, and Zack and Johnny fell into place behind him.

Joe looked over his shoulder to them. "Keep your rifle out. Zack, push back your coat so they can see your guns. Not threatening, just a show of strength."

Johnny kept his Hawken in hand, but he switched it to his left hand. The buckskin shirt was short enough that he could reach his pistols, and if it came to a fight at close range, he would be using them, not the rifle.

Joe said, "There are five riders, but only four are warriors. One's a woman. Looks to be a white woman."

They kept their horses to a walk as the Indians approached.

The woman's hair was a light brown, and it was flying wild. Like it hadn't seen a brush in a day or two. Her dress had a blue checkered pattern, but one seam was torn at the shoulder and it looked like there were dirt stains on the front. Her wrists were tied together in front.

"This doesn't look good," Zack said.

Johnny kept his eyes on the rider in front. He had the reins to the girl's horse. He looked like the leader.

Johnny said, "Just keep ready."

They reined up, and the Indians did so, too.

The one in front said a word in a language that Johnny didn't recognize. It sounded like, "Mizazapa Nape."

"Lakota," Joe said back to Johnny and Zack. "He's giving his name. Iron Hand, or...I'm not really sure."

Joe gave a hand sign, and then gave his name. "Josiah." Then he indicated Zack and Johnny and gave their first names.

Iron Hand looked tall. He was in a white man's shirt that was hanging unbuttoned, despite how cold it was. His chest muscles were well defined, and he had a strong neck. Around his shoulders was a wolf pelt. He was in canvas pants, like a cowhand would wear, and knee-high rawhide boots. His hair was black and in a braid that fell down along his back. A leather headband was tied about his temples, and four feathers were tucked into the back of it. Looked like eagle feathers.

The other three men were dressed more like what Johnny thought of as standard plains Indian clothes. Loin cloths, buckskin leggings, buckskin shirts.

The leader seemed comfortable in white-man clothes, Johnny thought. And they fit him. They weren't something he took in a raid.

Johnny said, "He might speak English."

Joe said to Iron Hand, "You speak English?"

The man nodded and gave a grin. But it wasn't a happy grin. It was one of amusement and just a hint of condescension.

"Your boots," he said. "Your sheath. Cheyenne."

Joe nodded and said, "Yes. Cheyenne. I spent some time among them. The Lakota were always good friends."

Johnny nudged Bravo ahead until he was beside Joe.

Iron Hand spit to the ground. "The Cheyenne are weak. They are nothing without Lakota."

Joe's eyes were on the girl. Her eyes met his, and she said, "Please. Help me."

Iron Hand reached over and back-handed her across the mouth. She fell out of the saddle and landed in the snow.

"Hey!" Joe shouted and jumped out of the saddle.

"Leave her!" Iron Hand shouted at Joe, and reached for a knife on his belt.

Johnny said to him, "Leave that knife where it is."

Iron Hand sneered at him. "Or you'll do what, white man?"

Johnny's gun was in his hand and he fired. The bullet snapped one of the eagle feathers in half.

Iron Hand blinked with surprise. Johnny already had his pistol cocked again.

Johnny said, "Let go of that knife or the next one is between your eyes. And I know you speak English well enough to know what I'm saying. You've spent time among the white man."

Zack brought his horse up beside Johnny's, and he had a pistol in his hand, too. His eyes were on the other three.

They were eyeing him warily but made no move for any weapons.

Joe was on his knees beside the girl, helping her up to a sitting position. Blood was running from one side of her mouth to her chin.

"Please don't let them take me," she said. Joe thought he noticed a British accent.

"They won't," he said. "I promise."

He got to his feet. "Let me talk to him. Maybe we

can make a deal with him."

Johnny said, his eyes on Iron Hand, "No deals. I think maybe he and I speak the same language. The girl comes with us."

Iron Hand said, "Not without a fight."

"She comes with us, whether you're alive or not."

Joe nodded. *Yep, Johnny speaks his language.*

He decided Johnny was in his element, so he knelt down by the girl again. He pulled a bandana from a pocket in the side of his buckskin shirt and gave it to her to dab at the blood.

Iron Hand sneered at Johnny. He said, "White man is brave with his gun in his hand. But are you brave enough to face me with my weapon of choice?"

Johnny was grinning. "You name it."

Iron Hand tapped the handle of his knife.

Zack said, "Johnny, what're you doing?"

"What I do best."

"You're gonna get yourself killed."

Johnny said to Iron Hand, "You've got yourself a challenge."

They both dismounted. Johnny let Bravo's reins trail.

"Johnny," Joe said. "If you get yourself killed, I'm gonna be madder'n heck at you."

Johnny holstered his pistol and then unbuckled his gunbelt, and he draped the gunbelt over his saddle.

Iron Hand draped his wolf skin over his own saddle and then drew his knife.

He said, "Where's your knife, white man?"

Johnny shook his head. "Don't need one."

He set his hat on his saddle also, and then stepped away from Bravo. He moved in a sort of side-stepping boxing stance and he kept his hands open, ready for Iron Hand's attack.

He had learned how to box and wrestle from his father. And then he had learned some principles of Chinese fighting from a man he had told Matt and Joe about. A Chinese farmer he had met in Texas.

One thing the Chinese man had taught Johnny about fighting with a weapon is when you hold a weapon, it becomes your entire focus. When your hands are empty, then your entire body can become a weapon.

Iron Hand charged at Johnny, lunging with the knife.

Johnny side-stepped him, and Iron Hand's momentum took him past Johnny, and Johnny gave him a push. Iron Hand went face-first in the snow.

Iron Hand got up. His eyes were dark with fury.

He charged at Johnny but then pulled up short and began swiping at him with the knife. Short, horizontal slashes. Johnny stepped back with each swipe, avoiding the blade by inches.

Iron Hand then lunged at him again, but Johnny grabbed Iron Hand's knife hand with both of his hands, pulled Iron Hand toward him, then freed up a hand and drove his elbow into the warrior's face.

Iron Hand staggered back, which caused his right arm to fully extend. Johnny yanked it hard and pushed the flat of his free hand into the back of the man's elbow and hyper-extended it. That got a yelp out of Iron Hand, and the knife fell into the snow.

Joe was on his feet now and had drawn his own gun to help Zack cover the other three.

Iron Hand had his left hand wrapped around his right elbow. He was glaring at Johnny but not charging at him.

He said, "You don't fight like any white man I have ever seen."

Johnny said, "You're not like any Indian I have seen. They all had honor."

That pulled the trigger. Iron Hand charged at him, swinging a fist. *He had indeed spent time with the white man*, Johnny thought. You didn't normally see an Indian warrior fight with his fists. Indian fighting was based largely on wrestling. They often didn't strike with the fists because an injured hand could disable a warrior. They preferred to wrestle.

Johnny ducked the fist and then drove one of his own into the man's midsection. A certain place just below the breast bone. The Chinese man had talked about it, and so had his father. Iron Fist huffed as the wind was driven from him.

Johnny side-stepped and drove a punch into the floating ribs and then stepped away. Iron Fist was having trouble breathing, and he dropped to one knee. Blood was streaming from his nose, from Johnny's elbow strike.

"Get up," Johnny said. "I'm just getting started."

Iron Hand got to his feet, but then he staggered a little. His right arm was hanging limp at one side.

Johnny said, "Where we come from, you treat a woman right. A man with honor should know this."

Iron Hand charged at him. He apparently wasn't as staggered as Johnny had thought.

Johnny tried to side-step again, but Iron Hand caught him with his left and pulled him down.

They rolled over in the snow once and then again. Iron Hand was now on top of Johnny. He drove his left fist into Johnny's face once and then twice. Johnny blocked a third punch with his forearm, and drove a short punch at Iron Hand's face.

Iron Hand rolled away from him, but they were now near where the knife had fallen, and he grabbed it with his left.

He began a hard, downward strike with the knife. Johnny brought his arm up to Iron Hand's wrist to block him, and then got both hands on his wrist and did what the old Chinese man had called a wrist lock. Bending the wrist the wrong way so the hand lost its strength, then he pulled the knife free.

Joe said, "You're gonna have to kill him, or he'll keep hunting you until you do."

One of the other Lakota men nodded. "Kill him. Must."

Johnny had begun this fight because of his own anger at seeing a woman abused. He hadn't intended it to be a fight to the death, but now he saw it was unavoidable.

He drove the knife into the upper abdomen of Iron Hand. Where he had punched him a few moments earlier. He drove the knife to the hilt and then lifted, pulling the blade upward until it hit the breastbone.

Iron Hand's eyes went wide with surprise.

Johnny pulled the knife free and stepped back, out of Iron Hand's reach. He had learned in the Rangers you don't leave a knife in a man. Even mortally wounded, a man can still be deadly, and a knife left in a man was a knife he could use against you.

Blood was pouring fast from the wound. Johnny had dug deep and though he had missed the heart, he had got some major blood vessels that feed it.

Iron Hand dropped to his knees. He looked at Johnny with hatred in his eyes. Blood ran down to his belt.

Then his eyes rolled back in his head and he fell face forward to the snow.

Johnny looked first at Joe and Zack, then to the riders. He said, "It's finished."

Johnny was winded. He had taken two punches to the face, and his nose was dripping blood and one eye had swollen shut. He leaned one elbow on Bravo's saddle and caught his breath.

He looked at the knife in his hand. The blade was red with blood.

A bowie knife. Johnny thought he might keep it.

Joe was talking with the three remaining Lakota warriors. They were nodding their heads and talking in what sounded to Johnny like jabber.

Joe said to Johnny, "They're glad you killed Iron Hand. They say he was cruel and without honor. But he was strong and no one had ever beaten him in a fight. They didn't believe it could be done. They say we can keep the girl."

Zack said to Johnny, "Did you enjoy yourself?"

Johnny nodded and found himself smiling. The

first real smile he had given since Lura. He said, "You know, I really did. Maybe this is what I needed."

# 25

## Texas, Three Years Earlier

JOHNNY COULDN'T guess the age of the man from China. It was hard to tell. He looked ancient, but moved like a young man.

He would have Johnny try to push him down, and when Johnny did, the man would side-step so casually he didn't look like he was even fighting. Then he would grab Johnny's wrist with a hand that was impossibly fast, and give Johnny a pull. Between the pull and Johnny's own momentum that he built up pushing him, Johnny would wind up face-down in the grass.

The man had a small sod hut he built on the flat Texas prairie. The wind blew and the sun baked down. A small barn stood off to one side.

The man had made a garden of herbs and vegetables, and he hauled water with a bucket every day from a water hole a quarter mile away to water his crops and to heat for tea.

"What do you do for a living?" Johnny said one day over tea.

"I live."

Johnny grinned. He thought the man was being funny. "No, I mean, what do you do for money?"

"If I need money, I go into town and sweep saloon. Or work in livery stable. But don't need much money."

The man gave his name as Wong. Nothing more.

Johnny said, "Why do you live out here all alone?"

Wong took a sip of tea. "You Ranger."

Johnny nodded.

"You can arrest people."

Johnny nodded again. "Rangers have that authority, yes."

"If I tell you I kill a man in China and I'm on the run, will you arrest me?"

Johnny chuckled. "No."

"Then I kill man in China and I'm on the run."

Johnny laughed. But then he stopped. Wong wasn't laughing.

Johnny had first met Wong one day when he had a weekend furlough from the Rangers. Wong was in a saloon and a cowhand with too much whiskey and too much bad attitude tried to push Wong aside. Wong did his side-step maneuver and the man cracked his head against the wall.

Johnny said, "Can you show me how to do that?"

Wong gave him a long look, then said, "I live in small grass house north of town. Five mile. Come see me."

So Johnny did.

Johnny had been with the Rangers for a year and had already killed a dozen men. He had also been in a couple of saloon brawls and had emerged the victor. His father had taught him how to box and he was a fair hand with his fists.

But he found he couldn't lay a hand on Wong.

Johnny had tried to push Wong and landed face-down in the grass. He got to his feet and said, "How'd you do that?"

"You do that. You throw yourself down in grass. I just help."

"You're mighty helpful."

Wong nodded with a smile. "So they say."

Johnny made like he was stretching a shoulder that he might have wrenched when he fell, but then charged at Wong. Didn't do him any good. This time Wong did some sort of maneuver that happened so fast Johnny couldn't even follow it. But it ended with Johnny fully in the air and landing hard. It almost knocked the wind out of him.

"You not know how to fall," Wong said. "I should have expected. People in America don't know how to fall. If you keep learning from me, you will do lots of falling."

Johnny got to his feet, a little shaky at first.

He said, "How do you learn how to fall? Seems to

me that's something that just happens to you."

"It can just happen, or you can take control of it."

Johnny had no idea what Wong was talking about.

Johnny began spending some of his weekend furloughs at Wong's house, and Wong taught him first how to fall properly—rolling or slapping at the ground with a hand or both a hand and a leg to absorb some of the force of the fall.

"And never let head hit ground. No matter what, always keep head safe."

Johnny learned to fall. It got so when Wong tossed him around, he could land with no injury at all, and more than once he landed with a head-first roll that brought him back to his feet.

Then Wong taught him to do what Wong called *yielding*. Don't try to match opposing force with opposing force, but to instead move away from it so the attack has nowhere to land.

"The same way you duck a punch," Johnny said.

Wong slapped his hands together. "Yes."

After a few weeks of training, Wong said, "Push me down."

Johnny went to push, but he didn't lean into it. He kept his weight evenly balanced, his feet about as far apart as his shoulders. Wong yielded from the push, and both stood facing each other.

"I still couldn't push you down," Johnny said.

"No. But you still on your feet. You didn't win, but you didn't lose. In China, losing a fight can sometimes mean death."

"Same here."

That night, Johnny found out Wong liked to drink whiskey sometimes, too. They sat outside his sod hut with a starry sky overhead and handed a bottle back and forth.

"Mister Wong," Johnny said, "why'd you agree to teach me?"

"When I look at you, I look at your eyes and feel

your energy. I feel you a good man."

Johnny shook his head. "No, I'm afraid I'm not a good man."

"You a rough man, in a rough business. But that not mean you a bad man."

Johnny let that sink into his mind for a minute.

"Mister Wong, I want you to know, you're always welcome at my fire."

It was a month later that Johnny got another weekend furlough, and he rode out to the sod hut. He had a bottle of whiskey to share with Mr. Wong, but he found the hut empty. Wong had very little for belongings, but they were all gone. A small horse Wong rode was gone, too.

Johnny rode into town and asked questions. Finally it was the town marshal who said, "A bounty hunter came riding through. Had a reward poster for a Chinaman by the name of Zhao Jing. Wanted for murder, in China. They say he's dangerous. I told him the only Chinee we had around here was that old man Wong, living outside of town. A couple of days later we found the bounty hunter dead, and Wong was gone."

"Dead? What happened to him?"

"His neck was broken. But there were no signs that he was in a fight. We don't know what happened to him. It was nothing that old man could have done."

Johnny wanted to say, *Don't be too sure.* But he said nothing.

Johnny went back out to the sod hut and sat in front of it, and he took a drink from the bottle.

He said to the wind, "I won't forget what you taught me, Mister Wong."

Somehow, he thought Mr. Wong might have heard him.

## 26

## The Rockies
## November, 1858

THEY MADE camp in a flat area partway up a wooded ridge. Their back was to a thick stand of pines, the trees blocked most of the wind.

The three Lakota wanted to join them.

"Do you think it wise?" Johnny said to Joe.

Joe nodded. "I think they're all right. They seem genuinely happy that Iron Hand is dead. Like they're relieved."

The Lakota left Iron Hand's body lying face-down in the snow. A true insult, Johnny knew. No funeral ceremony at all.

The warriors had a couple haunches of elk meat wrapped in oiled buckskins, and once a fire was built, they roasted it and offered some to their new friends.

The woman's name was Katarina Waddell.

Joe said, "That's a purty name."

Despite all she had been through, she managed a grin. She said, "It's Russian. My grandmother was Russian, and I'm named after her. Most people call me Kate."

Joe had dropped his saddle on the ground near the fire so she could use it. Wouldn't do for a lady to have to sit on the bare ground.

She had no coat and had been shivering with cold, so Joe unrolled his bedroll and draped it about her shoulders.

He said to her, "I won't let nothing happen to you. You're safe."

She nodded. "I'm so grateful. But there's nothing I can do to repay you."

*Yep,* Joe thought. *Definitely British.*

He shook his head. "Ain't no need. You don't help a lady for payment. You help a lady 'cause it's the right thing to do."

Zack was making coffee. Johnny was sitting on his own saddle near the fire. His nose had stopped bleeding, but it was swollen.

Zack said, "I think you might have a broken nose."

Johnny said, "I'm not surprised. He was strong and fast. He would have given Coleman Grant a run for his money."

"Who's Coleman Grant?"

"That's a long story."

The Indians were talking and kept glancing over to Johnny, and they were smiling and laughing.

Joe said, "I cain't get every word, but from what I gather, they're right pleased you took down Iron Hand. He was known far and wide as a mean one. They say this will go down in legend, and you will always be respected by the Lakota as the story travels."

Johnny shook his head. Carefully, because his nose hurt. "I can't get away from that *legend* business, can I?"

Zack grinned, "You keep doing the kind of thing you did today, and you can't avoid it. You bring it on yourself."

Once the meat was ready, Joe cut some off for Kate, and he poured her some coffee.

He said, "We ain't got any silverware or plates, but I can maybe find a flat piece of wood."

She shook her head. "Thank you kindly, but I can eat it just as it is."

She chewed into the elk almost with desperation.

Joe said, "You're really hungry."

She nodded. "I haven't eaten in almost two days."

She said that she had been part of a wagon train, bound for Oregon. Eighteen wagons. An axle on one family's wagon had broken, and her family stayed behind while her father helped repair it. That was when the Indians had attacked.

From what Kate described, it was Iron Hand who

had shot her father and the other family's father. The other three warriors had held back.

"They weren't wearing paint," she said. "According to what our guide had said, they won't attack if they're not wearing war paint on their faces."

Joe nodded. "A battle is often a big ceremony for them. But apparently not Iron Hand."

"He grabbed me. He pulled me onto his horse in front of him and whisked me away."

She chewed down some elk and then reached for the coffee.

She said, "I have heard of some of the horrid things Indians can do to women prisoners, but he did nothing like that. But he made it clear I was to be his wife when we got back to their village. I am so grateful you came along."

Joe nodded. "The Good Lord puts us where we're meant to be."

She smiled. "So, you're a Christian, then?"

He nodded. "Sort of. I guess I'm kind of a mix of things."

"Well, whatever you are, you have my eternal gratitude."

Zack was on his feet, holding a .40 caliber Sharps carbine he had found in the scabbard in Iron Hand's saddle.

"This is sure a beauty," he said. "Looks like an 1853 model."

The warriors had insisted Zack take it. They were also going to leave a horse so Kate could be taken back to the wagon train.

With the fire roaring and a blanket wrapped around her, she said, "I finally feel warm. For the first time in two days. I didn't have a coat, and at night, I had no blankets. Last night, I thought I was going to get frostbite in my feet."

She told her story, of how her family and another had left their farms in northern England and taken a ship to America and then joined a wagon train bound for Oregon.

She said, "We didn't own the land we farmed. We were what you call in this country *share croppers*. But with rich farming land available in Oregon, my mother and father and the parents of a neighboring family decided we should all pack up and head to America."

Joe said, "It's really late in the year for a wagon train. You folks should have been well into Oregon by now, with your cabins built."

"We had some problems, including a late start. We also have a guide who seems more interested in whiskey than getting us to our destination."

"We're only about a day's ride north of the trail, and I can't imagine those wagons have gone very far. We can get you back to them."

"I would be so grateful. But I hate to be a burden."

"You ain't no burden a'tall, ma'am."

"Please, call me Kate."

He smiled. "And you call me Joe."

"Joe. It's a deal."

They talked a bit more, of her life on the farm in England, and of his childhood in Pennsylvania.

Then she said, "I'm sorry, but I am so sleepy."

"You've been through a lot."

He spread the blankets in front of the fire and once she was lying on them, he wrapped them about her. He put his saddle bags under her head for a pillow.

"You're taking such good care of me," she said.

He nodded. "You've been treated real rough for the past couple of days. Now it's time for you to be treated good."

She gave him a big smile. "Where will you sleep, now that I'm using your bedroll?"

"Oh, I ain't gonna sleep, ma'am. Kate. I'm gonna be standin' guard all night."

"Oh, Joe, I can't ask you to do that."

"You ain't askin'. I'm volunteerin'. I meant it when I said I won't let nothin' happen to you."

"You're an angel, do you know that?"

He laughed and looked away, suddenly embarrassed. "I been called a lot of things before, but nobody's ever called me that."

"Well, maybe it's time they started."

Once she was asleep, Joe wandered over to Johnny, who was standing a little away from the fire.

"Just keeping a watch on our Indian friends," Johnny said. He had a cup of coffee in one hand.

"I think we can trust 'em, but it might be good not to trust 'em too far. Just in case."

"I heard what you said to Miss Kate. You don't have to stand guard all night. We can take turns. You can use my bedroll when it's my turn to guard."

Joe nodded. "Much obliged."

"So," Johnny looked at him with a grin. "I thought you were gonna kiss her, the way you were going."

"It ain't polite to spy on people."

Johnny laughed. "I wasn't spying. It was just hard to avoid listening. This camp isn't very big."

Joe looked over at Kate. She was breathing like she was already in a deep sleep.

Joe said, "It wouldn't have been right to kiss her. She's been through too much. I don't want to take advantage. But I've gotta admit, I wanted to. I ain't kissed a girl since that Cheyenne girl. But maybe it's time."

"I'll stand first guard. I'm not sleepy. You go and take my bedroll." Then he said, "I wouldn't want an angel to get cold."

Joe glanced over at Zack, who was sleeping back a ways from Kate.

Joe said, "Don't you go sayin' things like that. If Zack hears, I'll never live it down."

Johnny slapped him on the shoulder. "He won't hear it from me."

## 27

THE FOLLOWING DAY, Joe rode beside Kate. She still had one of his blankets wrapped around her.

Johnny rode ahead, taking the lead since Joe was occupied. Zack rode behind them.

The three Lakota had ridden on after breakfast.

After a time, Johnny held his hand up for everyone to stop. Time to rest the horses. Johnny dismounted and walked away and up a short grassy hill. He stood with his rifle in his hand, scanning the distance behind them with his eyes.

Zack walked up and said, "What do you think?"

"I think we should be careful and watch our back trail until we get to that wagon train."

Zack nodded. "I take it you don't totally trust those three Indians."

Johnny shook his head. "They were riding with the man who kidnapped Miss Kate. Maybe it's like they say, and they were afraid of him. Among their culture, a great fighting man often will have followers out of pure respect, even if they don't agree with him. But we both learned from our time in the Rangers not to trust too easily, especially when the men rode with our enemy not long ago."

Zack nodded again. He had the Sharps in one hand. "I was talking to Joe this morning, and he talked about that, too. How Indians respect a good fighting man. He was saying that's how they feel about you, now."

Johnny shrugged. "Let's hope any respect they might have for me is enough for them to leave us alone."

Zack let his gaze travel down to Joe and Kate. They were standing by the horses. She still had the blanket wrapped around her.

Zack said, "I think Joe's falling in love."

Johnny nodded. He said nothing.

Zack looked at him with curiosity. "Do you think

that's a bad thing?"

"He's going through the same thing I am, but he's been going through it for a lot longer. Like he said, he hasn't kissed a woman since then. I'd feel a little better if he went about this slowly."

Zack shrugged. "It seems to me every romance moves along at its own pace."

"If a romance is what it is. If she feels the same way about him. I'd hate to see him get hurt again."

They all mounted up and rode on.

Kate said to Joe, "You're not like any man I've ever met."

He grinned. "There are a lot of men like me out here. Mountain men. We're rough and not too civilized, I suppose."

"No, I don't consider you rough at all. I consider you one of the kindest, most caring men I have ever met."

"And you are one of the most beautiful and incredible women I have ever met."

She gave a big smile.

They stopped at a small stream to rest the horses again. Johnny broke out some jerky for everyone. He had bought a load of it at Fort Bridger.

The day was growing warm. Much of the snow had melted, and large patches of brown grass were visible. Kate folded up the blanket Joe had given her and left it on her saddle.

Joe said, "I'm gonna go fill the canteens."

He had two canteens on his horse and had been sharing his with Kate.

"May I walk along with you?"

"Yes'm. You don't even have to ask."

They walked, him with both canteens hanging from one hand.

She said, "What kind of life do you want, Joe?"

"I suppose the same kind as any man. A good woman and children. A nice home. I don't know if I'm civilized enough anymore to settle down on a farm, though. I was brought up civilized back in Pennsylvania, but I don't know if I could ever go back to it."

"You meet the right woman, and she won't care. She'll want you as you are."

He knelt down to fill the canteens. She knelt beside him.

She said, "I can fill one."

"All right."

He handed one to her and their hands brushed. She looked up at him, and their eyes met.

He began leaning closer to her.

But she said, "Joe, we can't."

"Why cain't we?"

"Because," she looked down for a moment. She had to say something that was apparently hard for her to say. "Because I'm engaged to be married."

He hadn't been expecting that.

She said, "A man in the wagon train. The eldest son of the family I mentioned. His name is Elias Compton. We grew up in England together. He asked me to marry him before we left for America. We have been planning to marry once he has a cabin built for us in Oregon."

Joe didn't know if he was feeling pain or shock. He felt embarrassed, and he felt sad. And he felt somehow empty.

He forced the words out, "You're engaged."

"Yes." She placed a hand on his. "I'm so sorry."

He looked away. "Let's get these canteens filled."

He pulled a cork and dipped it into the water.

She said, "I want you to know, if it wasn't for Elias, then I think I might be a woman who would want a mountain man for my husband. The right mountain man."

He looked at her. "But you love this Elias feller."

She nodded. "I do."

"But if not for him, then you think you might have been able to love me?"

Tears were welling up. "Not just *might*. I do."

Despite all of the conflicting emotions he was feeling, he now felt a little touch of warmth inside.

"But he come along first, and you gave your word that you'd marry him."

She nodded.

"Then, the right thing to do is to deliver you safely to him."

A tear ran for freedom down along her cheekbone, but despite it, she smiled. "You are a dear man. Has anyone told you that?"

"My ma, a few times."

"Well, I believe there's a woman out there for you, and you will hear it often from her."

He shook his head. "I hope you're right, but I'm a'feared you ain't."

He pulled the canteen from the stream and pushed the cork in place. Then he took the second canteen from her and pushed it into the water.

She looked at him sadly. "You deserve such happiness."

He shrugged but said nothing.

When both canteens were ready, they started back to the horses. He held both canteens in one hand, and she took his other hand on the way back.

He held on, knowing the short walk back to the horses was the extent of any life he would have with her.

## 28

KATE HAD LEARNED to ride in England, on the farm. She could handle a horse well, and they were able to make good time.

With sunset still an hour away, they reined up atop a long, low ridge. The wagons were below, their canvas tops rippling in the wind.

"There they are," she said.

One man stepped away from the wagons. He looked to be mid-twenties. He was in a coat and a cap that dipped low in the front and had a short brim. Johnny didn't know what that kind of hat was called, but had seen men from Europe sometimes wearing them.

Kate said, "That's Elias."

Elias waved and called out to her, his voice seeming almost lost in the distance. She waved back.

"Come down and meet them all," she said to Joe. "I'm sure they would love to meet you. You can all camp with us for the night."

Joe shook his head. "I cain't go down there."

Johnny backed Bravo up until he was thirty feet behind them. Zack did the same.

"Joe," she said. She reached over from her horse to put her hand on his. "I'm so sorry."

"Don't be."

"Am I allowed to feel sorry for what might have been?"

He gave an uncertain shrug of his shoulders. "I suppose."

Then he said, "Winter's settin' in, and the worst of it's still to come. You'll never make it to Oregon in time. Fort Bridger is only about fifty miles down the trail. You tell 'em I said to hole up there for the winter. The folks there'll help you. Then in the spring you can start out again. You'll make Oregon with plenty of time to set up cabins for the winter."

"I'll tell them."

She began to turn away, but found she couldn't. "No amount of words seem adequate to express how thankful I am to you. And how I feel about you."

He said nothing.

"I love you, Josiah McCabe."

He nodded. "I hope you know, I feel the same about you."

"I do."

She sat and looked at him a moment longer, then turned her horse and rode down the hill.

Elias ran toward her. She started to climb off the horse but he grabbed her and pulled her free, and they took each other in a long hug.

"I never thought I'd see you again," he said.

He lifted her feet off the ground and spun her in the air.

But she looked back up the ridge to the three riders sitting and watching.

"Who are they?" Elias said.

"Three of the greatest men I've ever met. They saved my life. I'll tell you all about it."

Joe couldn't hear what they were saying, but he saw the hug, and he saw Elias spin her around while he squeezed her.

Joe looked back at Johnny and Zack, and he said, "Come on. Let's ride."

"Where to?" Zack said.

"I don't care. As long as it's far from here."

Johnny turned Bravo and started back over the hill, with Joe and Zack falling into place behind him.

# PART FOUR

## *The Shoshone*

### 29

Montana
April, 1882

JOHNNY SAID, "It's been a lot of years since Mister Chen was called Mister Wong."

He took a sip of coffee. "When he first came here, he remembered what I had said to him, and he said, *I need a fire to be welcome at.* Then he said, *Even more than a fire, I need a place to stay and a job.*"

"You sent him to Mister Hunter."

Johnny nodded. "I went with him myself. Hunter hired him. Mister Wong heard I had settled in Montana and came looking for me. He said sometimes an old man just gets tired of running. But he had no desire to turn himself in because they would take off his head."

Johnny chuckled. "He said he didn't want to lose his head. He wasn't that old, yet."

Bree laughed. "That sounds like him."

"He asked me not to tell anyone. He didn't even want me to let on that I knew him. I haven't told anyone, not even Aunt Ginny. But I don't think he'll mind you knowing. After all, you're his student now."

Bree said, "I pretty much knew, anyway. He's dropped a few hints. He was talking about how fast I'm learning, and he said I was like my father. I asked him when he taught you, and he said sometimes an old man says too much."

They were standing on the cliff again, looking down at the valley.

She said, "You never mentioned that woman before. The one the Indians had captured. I wonder what ever happened to her?"

Johnny shrugged. "I never heard. I presume they followed Joe's advice and camped for the winter at Bridger and then continued on to Oregon in the spring. She's probably a mother now. Maybe even a grandmother."

"Poor Uncle Joe."

Johnny nodded. "We rode north. Joe wanted to put as much distance between himself and that wagon train as he could. I suppose he felt like he was running from his pain. I fully understood."

"Is that when you found this valley?"

He nodded. "They call these mountains the Crazies. A scout at Bridger had drawn us a map, and that was where I first saw the name. It was November and winter was fully on us. The snow was deep. We rode into these mountains hoping to find some place where we could hunker down until spring. We rode through the pass and into the valley. The pass we call McCabe Gap now. And that's when we found the Shoshone."

"You've talked about the Shoshone over the years, and your time with them."

He nodded. "And that's when I met the Shoshone girl."

Bree blinked with surprise. "You met a Shoshone girl? You've never mentioned her before."

Johnny grinned. "I suppose not. Let me tell you all about her."

# 30

## The Crazy Mountains
## Mid November, 1858

THE VALLEY STRETCHED nearly two full miles from the pass they had just ridden through to the other side.

Zack said, "This valley is huge."

Smoke was drifting up from some place toward the center. Smoke from more than one source.

"We ain't alone," Joe said.

"Indians?" Zack said.

"Most likely. There's some prospecting going on this far north, but not much. Very little fur trapping anymore."

Johnny said, "Maybe we should turn around and ride on. I don't want to cause trouble."

Joe glanced at the sky. The northwestern half was covered with heavy clouds that were flat in some places but swirling in others.

He said, "Won't have time. That there storm is comin' on us fast."

"Then, at least we should stay as far from the Indians as possible. Maybe on this side of the valley. Then once the storm's passed, we'll ride on."

They started down into the valley. Joe rode first, with Zack in the middle and Johnny last. All three rode with their rifles in their hands.

Joe cut to the right, and they rode along the edge of a pine forest that stretched up the slope of a ridge. The snow had drifted deep enough in places that their horses had to do some high-stepping to get through it.

Johnny saw a crow take flight from the edge of the woods five hundred feet ahead. He was about to say something, but Joe saw it too and held his hand up for everyone to stop.

Two riders came out of the woods.

One was an Indian girl. Johnny guessed her age

to be somewhere in her late teens. Her hair was in two long black braids and she had a strip of buckskin tied about her temples. She was in a buckskin dress and had a short buffalo robe wrapped about her shoulders.

The other rider was a boy of maybe ten. He was in a buckskin shirt and leggings, and his hair was hanging loose.

They glanced at the riders, and their eyes opened wide in panic. They tried to kick their horses into a gallop, but the girl's horse reared up and she slid off the back.

Then the girl's horse slipped in the snow and crashed into the boy's horse. Both horses went down and the boy fell free and rolled through the snow.

Joe called out some words to them that sounded to Johnny like Lakota. He had no idea what they were, but figured it was probably something like, *We won't hurt you.*

The boy began to run, but then looked back at the girl. She was down in the snow and was hanging onto a leg with one hand. She called out to the boy and made a moving away gesture with one hand. *Run!*

The boy turned and ran. The horses scrambled to their feet and charged off in a panic.

Joe started his horse forward at a walk, and Zack and Johnny followed suit. Johnny kept his rifle ready, in case the girl wasn't alone.

She was still on the ground, hanging onto one knee in both hands.

Joe swung out of the saddle but the girl pulled a knife. She looked at Joe with fury in her eyes, and she spat some words at him.

Joe held up his hands and said something back to her. Johnny didn't think either of them could understand each other. Joe was trying Lakota, but she was speaking something else.

Johnny stepped down into the snow and let Bravo's rein trail. He said, "She's not Lakota."

Joe shook his head. "Shoshone. I think."

"Make the hand sign for help."

Joe did, holding up his right hand in a fist but with the first two fingers pointing upright.

Johnny handed his rifle to Joe, then knelt down onto one knee in the snow, and with one hand he indicated her injured leg.

She waved the knife at him, like she wasn't sure.

Joe made a set of signs. "I'm sayin' white man help."

She gave Johnny a long look. Johnny nodded and thought about smiling, but then decided against the smile. It wouldn't be genuine. He thought people who prided themselves on honor should receive only genuine smiles.

She lowered the knife, but kept it in her hand.

Johnny found the knee was swelling. He gripped it lightly with one hand and she flinched. He lifted the knee, bending her leg.

"Don't think it's broken," he said.

"Prob'ly the same kind of injury I had when we first rode onto the Broken Spur."

"That seems like a lifetime ago, doesn't it?"

Joe snickered and nodded his head.

Zack was still in the saddle. He said, "What're we going to do?"

Johnny said, "We'll take her to her village. She can't make it on foot with a bad knee."

"Whatever we're gonna do," Joe said, "we better do it quick. That boy prob'ly ran straight to the village. We might find ourselves with a band of warriors ridin' down on us."

Johnny rose to his feet and held his hand out to her. She took the hand and let him pull her to her feet. She then let him assist as she made her way around to Bravo's left side.

She wasn't tall. She rose not quite to Johnny's shoulder, and he figured she weighed a hundred pounds at best. He placed his hands on her hips and lifted, and she swung a leg around to the other side of the saddle.

The girl's hem was cut at the knee, which was common for the Indian women Johnny had seen. Sitting astride the horse, the dress rose up a bit, and Johnny saw more leg than he had ever seen in public.

He climbed onto Bravo's back, sitting behind the girl. Joe remounted and they rode off toward the village, following the boy's tracks.

The village was a collection of teepees—Johnny counted twelve of them. Cookfires were burning and the smell of smoke and roasting venison was strong in the air.

The boy had arrived shortly ahead of them and had told them enough to get the entire village in an uproar. Men were running out of teepees with bows and arrows. One man had a rifle that Johnny thought at first glance might be an old Harper's Ferry model.

An older man emerged from a teepee. His hair was a steel grey and fell in two braids past his shoulders. He was in a buckskin shirt and leggings.

He looked at the riders. The girl said something to the man, and the man nodded. His eyes met Johnny's, and Johnny figured he was a man of authority.

Johnny knew enough about plains Indians to know authority wasn't assigned like in the white culture. It was earned, and was often tenuous.

The man nodded at Johnny, and Johnny slid out of the saddle. He then helped the girl down.

A warrior about Johnny's height approached. He was also in buckskins and had a knife sheathed at his belt. He looked at Johnny and put his hand on the knife hilt.

"Keep that where it is," Johnny said.

The girl spoke to the warrior quickly. He was listening to her but kept his gaze on Johnny. Finally he nodded.

The older man called out to them, and the warrior scooped the girl up and took her to the teepee the older one had just stepped out of.

Joe began talking with the older man while seven

warriors gathered around them. Some of the men held weapons. The one with the Harper's Ferry rifle was there. Johnny left his rifle in the saddle but kept his gun hand near his right-hand pistol.

Joe and the man were making hand signs back and forth. Johnny saw the sign Joe had made for *friend* a couple of times.

Joe looked at Johnny and Zack, and said, "He's a shaman and pretty much the chief of this little group. Near as I can tell, his name is Many Life. Or Many Lives."

"Quite right," a man said from behind them.

He was pushing through the crowd. He was a white man, clean shaven but with long, white hair. He was dressed as the others, except instead of a breechcloth and leggings, he wore full buckskin pants. An old Colt revolver was tucked into his belt.

"Neville Pierce, at your service," he said. He spoke like an Englishman. Though the accent was different than the woman they had rescued from the Lakota. Hers flowed gently, where his had a harsher sound.

Johnny said, "I'm Johnny McCabe. This is my brother Joe and our compadre Zack Johnson."

"Mighty odd to find three white men this far north, this time of year."

Johnny nodded. "You might say it's mighty odd to find a white man here in an Indian village, too."

Pierce gave a sort of nodding bow. "Touche. But you got the name right. Many Lives. Shaman, priest, and war chief of this little band of Shoshone."

The old Indian nodded at them. "I speak little English. Some, not much."

"I've been living among them for a time, now. Took a Shoshone woman as my wife. Then took another. They're quite accommodating that way."

Johnny decided to take the lead. And he decided to address Many Lives himself, as a show of respect.

Johnny said, "We mean no harm. Just looking for a place to spend the winter."

Many Lives looked at Johnny, squinting his eyes like some older men do when they have lived their lives outdoors, in the sun and wind. He said, "Ma-cabe?"

Johnny nodded.

Many Lives looked at Pierce. Pierce gave a coarse laugh, the kind of laugh that comes from too much whiskey over the years.

He said, "You must be that white man who killed the Lakota, Iron Hand."

Johnny was surprised. He glanced at Joe, who shrugged.

Johnny said, "You heard about that?"

Pierce nodded. "A Lakota hunting party came through this area before the most recent snow. Gathering meat to get 'em through the winter. They talked about a white man they call Ma-cabe. They spoke of you with such almighty reverence that I scarcely believed 'em."

Zack was grinning. He said to Johnny, "I never thought the word *reverence* would be used on you."

Many Lives said, "You our guest. Stay here."

He indicated a teepee toward the edge of their little village.

Pierce said, "No one's using that one right now. It's common among these blokes to have an extra teepee set up. Kind of like having a guest room in your home."

Johnny said, "I'd hate to impose."

Joe glanced skyward again. The clouds were heavy and a cold wind was starting blow.

He said, "Well, if we ain't gonna impose, we gotta get into the woods and get us a shelter built right quick."

"No," Many Lives said. "Stay. Be our guest."

Joe said, "I think it'll be all right."

Zack gave a wary glance at the teepee. "Will that thing keep out the cold? It doesn't look all that strong."

"You'd be surprised. See the way them edges are fastened down to the ground tight?"

Zack did. The teepees were made of buffalo skins

over a frame of wooden poles, and the bottom edges of the buffalo skins were tied down to stakes that were driven into the ground.

Joe said, "Not much wind will get through there. With a fire goin', we'll be toasty warm."

Johnny said to Joe, "How do we say thanks to these people?"

Joe shrugged. "Just say thanks, I suppose."

Johnny looked at Many Lives and nodded his head, and said, "We thank you."

Many Lives smiled and nodded back.

They stripped the gear from their horses and dropped it all in the teepee. Then Joe set to building a fire while Johnny and Zack took care of the horses.

The Shoshone kept their horses in a small corral beyond the village. Snow was coming down as Johnny and Zack led their horses to the corral.

At one side of the corral, a small three-sided stable had been built with a frame of pine poles and thatched with pine boughs.

Zack said, "Do you think the horses will be warm enough here? It's gonna get mighty cold tonight."

Johnny shrugged. "These Shoshone must know what they're doing."

Johnny pulled the hackamore free of Bravo, but then Bravo turned away and started running through the snow, off toward the ridge.

Johnny said, "He must not like the looks of that little shed, either."

"Now what're you gonna do? We can't catch him with this snow coming down."

"Don't need to catch him. If I whistle, he'll come."

# 31

THE WINTER WINDS HOWLED outside, but Johnny found Joe was right—inside the teepee they were warm.

Johnny had spread his bedroll on a buffalo robe, and once it was dark, he climbed into his blankets and pulled another buffalo robe over himself. He was mighty warm.

Johnny set his right-hand gun on the ground beside him.

He awoke to find the teepee walls shaking with an occasional wind. The fire was burning low, so he put some more wood on it.

He had no watch, but he tended to wake up a little before sunrise wherever he was, so he assumed it was probably about that time now.

He filled a coffee kettle with water. They had bought a few sacks of coffee at Bridger, so Johnny got out a sack of coffee and set some to boiling.

Once it was ready, he poured himself a cup. Then he shouldered into his coat and pulled his hat on. With his buckskin boots on over his feet and a pistol tucked in front of his belt, he grabbed his coffee and opened the tent flap.

The snow was still coming down hard, he found. It wasn't quite dark outside. More of a dim gray light. Probably about sunrise.

He stepped out and drank his coffee while he let his gaze travel about the village. He could see little beyond the teepees because the snow was falling so heavily.

He took a sip of coffee and stood while the snow pattered against the brim of his hat.

For the first time since Lura had left him, he felt calmness inside. A sort of peace. Not unlike the way he had felt in the little valley he, Joe and Matt had wintered in.

He wondered how Matt was. It had been nearly

two months since they had left California behind.

Johnny had no plans for the future, himself. None beyond the moment. Ever since he had emerged from the drunken spree he had gone on, he had felt it a triumph to just put one foot ahead of the other.

At the moment, though, he felt the darkness starting to pass. Like the snow and this impossibly clean mountain air was washing it all away.

As far as he was concerned, he might just remain in these mountains. Maybe run some cattle in the flat, grassy areas between ridges. Or maybe even just stay in the mountains themselves and live off the land. He could go back to the little valley they had stayed in the winter before or maybe remain in this valley.

Any thoughts of finding a good woman, like he had spoken of with Breaker Grant, were now gone. After Lura, he just wanted to be alone. A woman had never gotten hold of his heart like she had, and he had never known it could hurt so much when she pulled herself free.

Come spring, though, he thought he would send Joe and Zack back to California. Matt needed watching over.

Once his coffee was done, he went back inside. Joe and Zack were awake, and Joe was filling a cup from the kettle.

Neville Pierce came by with a chunk of deer meat, and they invited him to stay while they roasted it over the fire.

Pierce had also brought a jug of whiskey.

"Thanks," Johnny said, "but I'll pass. I think I've had enough of that for a while."

"You can pass," Zack said. "I'll just have to drink enough for the both of us."

They sat cross-legged on the ground in front of the fire while the meat roasted. Juices fell into the fire and sizzled, and smoke rose through a hole in the ceiling, leaving its scent behind. Johnny liked the smell of campfire smoke and sizzling venison.

Joe got out his long Indian pipe and filled the bowl with tobacco.

"Cheyenne," Pierce said.

Joe nodded. "Lived among 'em for a while."

"The Indian way is the better way, really."

Zack gave him a curious look. "Is that so?"

Pierce nodded.

"I've heard that, but I've seen some Indians who were little more than savages. Like that Iron Hand Johnny had to fight."

Pierce shrugged. Joe handed the pipe to him, and Pierce took a draw. He then handed it to Johnny, who held up a hand to say, *no thanks*.

"If you're of a mind to stay among the Indian for a time, you'd better get accustomed to smoking a pipe. Some do it just for the taste of smoke, but they have a lot of ceremonies that require a pipe."

So Johnny took the pipe. He allowed himself a draw and realized it wasn't bad. Somehow gentler tasting than a cigar. He handed it to Zack.

Zack said, "Are we gonna be staying here long enough for me to have to get used to an Indian pipe?"

Johnny grinned. "I don't see us going anywhere till this snow lets up."

"Especially since your horse ran off."

"He'll be all right."

Zack took a reluctant draw, then gave a nod of surprised approval. He handed it back to Joe.

Zack said, "Now, what I'd really like is for you to start handing that jug around."

Pierce chuckled. He pulled the cork, hooked his finger into the jug handle, resting the bulk of the jug against the crook of his arm, and lifted it for a drink.

He said to Johnny, "You sure you don't want any, mate?"

Johnny nodded. "I drank so much a little while ago that I think I lost the entire month of October."

Pierce chuckled again. "It's happened to me before."

He handed the jug to Zack and said, "In answer to your question, I've spent a lot of time among the Indian. I've found they're a lot like the white man, or the black man for that matter, in that some are grand, some are rotten to the core, but most are somewhere in between. Some are trustworthy and some are not. When I was younger, I sailed with the Queen's navy and found it about the same in every port we stopped. No particular race has any claim on virtue or crookedness."

Zack said, "How did a sailor in the Queen's navy find himself way out here in the middle of nowhere?"

Pierce gave a smile. "Got myself into a wee bit of trouble. Found I had to run. I was looking at probably a twenty-year stay in the stockade."

"Must have been a good bit of trouble," Johnny said.

Pierce smiled. His face was deeply lined, and he had a perpetual squint, just like Many Lives.

He said, "You could say that. Let's just say I was lucky not to get the noose. Anyway, I had a chance to run. One of the guards owed me a year's pay from some poker games he had lost. I told him to leave the cell door unlocked one night and we'd call it even. He did, and I left merry old England behind. Got myself here to the Americas. Went west and became a fur trapper. Been out here thirty years now."

Joe said, "Not much money in fur trappin', anymore."

Pierce shook his head. "That's a fact. The bottom fell out of the beaver market years ago. But I scrape by. Guided a few wagon trains that were bound for Oregon or California. Lived among the Indians more than once."

Zack handed the jug to Joe. Johnny knew Joe preferred beer, but Joe gave a shrug as if to say, *what the heck*, and he tipped the jug.

Pierce said, "I met Many Lives a few years ago. Struck up a friendship."

Joe handed the jug to him and said, "Ain't this a little far north to find a band of Shoshone?"

Pierce nodded. "Indeed. Blackfoot or Cheyenne, maybe, but usually not Shoshone. You see, Many Lives is a man of peace, and wants to distance himself from war. These mountains offer almost a barrier, in their remoteness."

Johnny said, "I thought war was the way of the Indian."

Pierce nodded. "To some degree. Indeed, they are a warrior culture. But war they conduct amongst themselves is almost a ceremonial thing. An Indian has to make accomplishments in war before he can be considered truly a man. But the war Many Lives wants to distance himself from is the war that is brought by the white man. It's a war brought on by opposing cultures that don't have enough common ground to be able to live together in peace. And a war like that is often fought until one culture is obliterated."

Pierce took a gulp from the jug and looked at Johnny. "You sure you don't want a taste?"

Johnny shrugged. *Why not?* he thought. After all, it wasn't the whiskey or tequila that had been the problem, but what he had done with them.

He took a mouthful from the jug and then handed it to Zack.

Pierce said to Johnny, "Is it true what they say about you, mate? That you killed Iron Hand?"

Johnny nodded. It was Zack who said, "You should have seen it. I thought I had seen hand-to-hand combat before, but that was unlike anything I had ever seen."

"They say Iron Hand was unbeatable. The Lakota believed him to have some sort of spirit essence about him. What Indians sometimes call *medicine*. A powerful, dark medicine that meant he couldn't be defeated by mortal man.

"He was a good scrapper," Johnny said. "I'll give him credit for that. The best I ever faced. But no man is unbeatable."

Pierce said, "That girl you brought in. She's the

daughter of Many Lives. Her name translates as Red Morning Sky. She's the intended of one of the warrior's here."

Johnny said, "Let me guess. The one who helped her off the horse and threw me a look like he wanted to skin me alive."

"Yeah. That one. He's been asking her to marry him for a while. She keeps saying no."

"Why does she say no?" Zack said.

"She said she saw in a dream that a great warrior would come along and win her heart. She's been waiting for that warrior."

Joe looked at Johnny with a grin. "You just walk into these situations, don't you?"

# 32

THE STORM CLEARED and the following morning the sky was a deep, winter blue. Johnny trudged through snow that was now knee-deep to stand beyond the teepee with his coffee in hand and look off at the far ridge.

He found Many Lives was already standing there.

Many Lives said, "Morning good time to think. To be one with world."

Johnny nodded. "My father used to do that. It's where I learned it from."

Many Lives nodded. "Father alive?"

Johnny shook his head. "Killed by a bad man two years ago."

"Did you catch the killer?"

"No. I wish we did."

"You look for him?"

Johnny nodded his head. "We looked for him. My brothers and me. But we couldn't find him. It eats me up sometimes."

Many Lives looked off to the far ridge. Johnny did the same.

After a few moments, Many Lives said, "You must forgive. Not for him, but for you. It eats you up, you let him win. Beat him by forgiving him."

Johnny had always found the broken English spoken by many Indians a little odd. He had known others who spoke limited English. Mexicans he had met in Texas and also Mr. Wong. None of them had the halting way of speaking as he had found with the Kiowa and the Comanche, and now also with the Shoshone.

That night, as more venison was roasting in their teepee, Johnny asked Joe about it.

Joe said, "I think it's because when most of them learn English, they're actually learning English words for sign language."

Pierce was sitting with them. He said, "It's easier

to learn sign than it is to learn their spoken language. Fewer words. No past or future tense. It's also better to learn it because the tribes from here to the Mexican border use almost the exact same hand signs. So when they're learning English from one of us, it's just easier to use sign as a frame of reference. If you see an Indian speaking a more complete form of English, you know he didn't learn it with sign language as his reference."

Johnny noticed Pierce spoke with a flair of education. He said as much.

Pierce said, "I was an Oxford scholar. I had finished my second year when I found myself press-ganged into the good Queen's navy."

"How does that work?" Joe said.

"Sailors go to waterfront taverns in London and elsewhere and if they find a patron drunk and passed out, and if he looks to be young and hardy, they drag him to their ship. If he's drunk but not quite passed out, they might help it along with a knock on the head. If he wakes up, then he's conscripted into two years of service."

Johnny was finding this man amusing. He said, "So, what was an Oxford scholar doing at a waterfront tavern?"

He shrugged. "I like my whiskey. Always have."

Pierce had brought his two wives with him. One was cooking, and the other was neatening up the teepee. She even took the blankets from the bedrolls outside and shook them in the fresh air.

Johnny said, "They don't have to do that. We don't want to be a burden."

"Ah, but they insisted. You see, in the Indian's world, work is clearly divided by the genders. The fairer sex finds it an insult for a man to do a woman's work. It's like we're saying they're not good enough at what they do."

Zack said, "Do the women ever hunt or go to war?"

Pierce shook his head. "It's been heard of, but it's

very seldom. I've never seen it myself."

When the food was ready, the men ate while the women held back. Johnny felt a little uncomfortable, but Pierce said, "A women would feel insulted if they were invited to eat with the men. It would be a man's way of saying she wasn't woman enough.

While Johnny ate, he let his thoughts drift back to what Many Lives had said earlier in the day about forgiveness. He wondered if he would ever truly be able to apply it toward the man who had killed Pa.

And he wondered if he would ever be able forgive Lura.

## 33

ON THEIR FIFTH DAY WITH THE SHOSHONE, the weather warmed. It felt like spring. The snow was melting fast, turning the earth to mud. Johnny saw that the location of every teepee had been selected so water would run away from it and not toward it. He gained even more respect for Shoshone wisdom.

Johnny and Joe were outside, looking at the ridge visible to the west. The sky was clear, and the horses had been turned loose to graze on patches of grass that were now visible.

Johnny was in his range shirt and had left the buckskin shirt in the teepee. He had a tin cup of coffee in one hand.

He said, "Is this normal? It's still early winter, but it feels like spring."

Joe nodded. "It's what they call a *chinook*. It can last a day, or as long as a week."

The following day, much of the snow on the valley floor was gone, though the ridges that surrounded the valley still had patches of white between the pine trees.

Johnny walked along with Many Lives. Johnny had his guns in place and was in his range shirt and vest.

He said, "How did you get your name?"

"As young man in battle, get hurt bad. Two times. Almost die."

Johnny nodded. "Many Lives. That's a good name for a fighting man."

Many Lives asked about the battle with Iron Hand, so Johnny gave him the details. Many Lives nodded a few times but said nothing as Johnny talked.

Then Many Lives said, "Indian way is to take prisoners. Many warriors take wives that way. White man thinks it cruel."

Johnny said, "Some prisoners have been treated

real bad."

"Warriors with honor treat their prisoners well."

They walked for a while, and Johnny said, "I've been thinking about what you said about forgiveness."

Many Lives nodded. "Forgive is a good thing. Don't forgive for the person who was bad to you. Forgive for your own sake."

Johnny realized Many Lives spoke better English than he realized. His speech was halting at times, but he had a good command of words.

Johnny said, "Neville Pierce is a friend of yours?"

Many Lives nodded. "Family. Married my daughter. Live with us a long time."

"He seems like a good man."

"He is. But he not warrior. You a warrior."

Johnny let those words settle on him. Coming from a man who was a warrior and apparently a good one, he thought those words were probably the greatest compliment he had ever received.

Many Lives said, "You stay with us? At least for the winter?"

Johnny nodded. "I think I'd like to. My spirit has a feeling of peace here."

Johnny saw a bird off in the distance. A hawk, he thought, drifting along in the wind above the ridge to the west. Being in this valley and among these people made him feel like how he thought that bird must feel.

Many Lives said, "Are you running from something bad?"

"Something hard."

Johnny told him about Lura.

Many Lives nodded. "Sometimes a woman can wound a man more than any weapon in battle."

Johnny grinned. "Ain't that the truth."

"Come spring, where will you go?"

"I don't really know. I haven't thought it through that far."

Many Lives grinned. "Warrior's horse ran off. You will need new one."

Johnny grinned back and shook his head. He put two fingers in his mouth and cut loose with a long, hard whistle. It echoed against the far ridge.

Many Lives was looking at him with a question in his eyes.

Johnny held up one finger, as it if to say, *wait a minute*. Then he cut loose with another whistle.

"Look there," Many Lives said.

Johnny followed his gaze to the southern corner of the valley floor. Bravo was approaching. Galloping along, his mane fluttering in the wind like a battle flag.

The horse slowed and trotted his way toward Johnny. Johnny then leaped onto Bravo's back. Bravo reared up, and Johnny held onto the mane with one hand and gripped Bravo's ribs with his knees. Bravo let out a sort of bellow, and Johnny gave out a Texas-style *yee-ha!*

Many Lives was laughing and clapping his hands and returned the yee-ha with a battle cry of his own.

Johnny rode into camp on Bravo, with no reins or saddle. He hopped down and the horse waited while he went into the teepee and fetched his Hawken.

He was in his buckskin boots. He hadn't put on his riding boots since they had arrived in the valley.

Pierce was walking along. He said, "I see you found your horse."

Johnny grinned. "He wasn't lost."

Johnny leaped onto Bravo's back, and with his rifle in hand, he started off toward the valley floor.

There were still small patches of snow, but for the most part the land was clear. Brown grass was still wet in some places from being trapped under snow, but much of it was drying in the sun. The wind was warm—what Joe called a chinook wind.

Ahead was a small river, and beyond it was a flat, grassy expanse. At one side of the expanse was a tangle of deep thicket. To the other side was a wooded ridge. Johnny thought there looked to be a small pass that would take a rider out of the valley.

Johnny took in a deep lungful of mountain air.

"This is paradise, Bravo."

The horse made a snorting, chuckling sound. Like he understood and was agreeing.

The grass beyond the stream was tall, and Johnny watched as a buck raised its head. Mule deer, he thought. A rack he estimated at ten points. The grass was so tall he hadn't seen the deer until it raised its head.

Johnny cocked the rifle. The wind was blowing from the deer toward Johnny, and the animal didn't react. Probably didn't hear it. Johnny brought the rifle to his shoulder and squeezed the rear trigger, bringing on the hair-trigger effect on the front trigger. He then sighted in on the deer, and gave a light tap to the front trigger. The rifle went off in a loud discharge, kicking back against Johnny's shoulder and sending out a cloud of black smoke.

Johnny nudged Bravo forward, and they crossed the small stream. Not so small, Johnny found. It was maybe fifteen feet across, but surprisingly deep. Bravo went down to his shoulders.

Once they were across, they rode up to where the deer was sprawled out in the grass. Johnny shifted his rifle to his left, so he could draw his right-hand gun for a finishing-off shot, but saw none was necessary.

He said to Bravo, "The folks back at the village have been providing us with meat. Time for us to return the favor."

Johnny drew a knife to gut the deer. Then, when he had the deer carcass draped across Bravo's back, he started out on foot to look for another. Bravo walked along behind him, stepping carefully so the deer would not slide off.

Johnny, Joe and Zack found themselves invited to Pierce's teepee for dinner. The mud in the little village had mostly dried and the night breeze was cool but not chilly. Pierce's wives had a fire going outside and were roasting some of the venison Johnny had brought in.

The men sat on buffalo robes on the ground.

Pierce said, "They're talking about it throughout the village. How you just whistled and that horse came galloping out of nowhere."

Johnny said, "He didn't come out of nowhere. He had hunkered down off in the ridges to wait out the storm. Maybe found a thick stand of pines. Many Lives says there's a small system of caves up on the southern ridge. Maybe Bravo found them. He always comes when I whistle."

"How'd you train him to do that?"

Johnny shrugged. "I've never trained him. I just whistled one day and he came to me."

"They're talking about how you rode the horse without even a hackamore. How the horse seems to know what you want and just does it. You rode out on that horse like a force of nature yourself, and came back with two deer carcasses for the village."

Joe said with a grin, "The stuff of legends."

Johnny shook his head. "Will you stop it?"

Zack said to Johnny, "She's watching you."

Johnny followed Zack's gaze down the open expanse between the grouping of teepees, which roughly formed a street. At the teepee of Many Lives, his daughter and another woman were working on a leg of deer meat Johnny had given them. She stopped and looked back at Johnny and smiled.

Pierce said, "Like I said, she had a dream or a vision that a great warrior would win her heart. And then here you are, riding in all larger than life, like something out of an old Indian legend. Beating a man they all believed had some sort of spirit medicine that rendered him unbeatable and commanding the beasts themselves."

Joe was laughing.

Johnny said, "That's not the way of it all. Like I said, no man is unbeatable."

"But it's the way they're seeing it. In my expcricncc, matc, it's not so important what happened, as what people think happened. It's not about facts. It's about perceptions."

Joe said, "And it looks like that little Shoshone gal is aimin' her perceptions at you."

# 34

"HOW MUCH LONGER WILL this chinook thing last?" Johnny said.

He and Joe were standing outside the teepee. It was morning and the sun was barely into the sky.

Joe shrugged. "I'm surprised it's lasted this long. Nigh onto five days, hasn't it been?"

Johnny nodded. "It's hard to keep track of the days, when every day is like the one before it."

"You can see how I don't take much stock in what day of the week it is. It's what the Indians call *white man date*. It don't mean much here. This is how it was when I was with the Cheyenne."

"I think we should take advantage of it while it lasts. Try to bring these people some more meat. Stock up on it. It won't go bad, because once the chinook passes, the meat will freeze solid if it's left outdoors."

Joe nodded. "Sounds good. I'll go saddle the horses. Unless you're thinking of riding Bravo bare-back again."

Johnny grinned. "No. I'll take a saddle. Let's bring Zack with us too."

Once the horses were saddled, Johnny told Many Lives and Neville Pierce what they were doing.

Many Lives said, "You have a good rifle."

Johnny nodded and held up the Hawken, and he said to Many Lives, "This rifle can shoot from a long distance away. And it shoots straight."

Pierce said, "No rifle was finer made than a Hawken."

"You want to come along?"

Pierce shook his head. "I'm afraid my time of spending all day in a saddle is behind me. Arthritis. I waded hip deep through freezing waters many a winter to tend my beaver traps, and it has caught up with me."

Johnny nodded. "We should be back before sundown."

They rode first to the little stream Johnny had crossed a couple of days earlier.

"Careful crossing," he said. "It's deeper than it looks."

Joe said, "You can tell by the banks it runs even deeper sometimes, like when during spring runoff."

They crossed. They had three packhorses with them, but they were Shoshone horses. Bred in the wild. The stream rising to their shoulders didn't frighten them any.

Once they were across, Johnny said, "This is where I shot the first of those two bucks."

Johnny stepped out of the saddle and let the rein trail. He walked up to a spot in the grass and turned to face the direction they had just come from. The tangle of thickets was a few yards to his right.

He said, "Can you imagine a cabin right here? In this very spot? A front porch right here, where you can stand in the morning with a cup of coffee and look off across the valley. See the morning sunlight shine against those ridges."

"You thinkin' on stayin'?" Joe said.

Johnny shrugged. "You never know. Maybe a barn right over there." He indicated with one hand a direction off toward his left. "And maybe a wooden bridge over that stream."

Zack said, "You've talked before of a good woman to build a life with. To bring children into the world with."

Johnny nodded. "I think those days are behind me now. After Lura, I think maybe I'd be better off just living here alone. A small cabin, big enough for one. Live my life in peace right here. On this very spot."

"I don't know." Zack stood beside him, and followed Johnny's gaze toward the far ridge on the south side. The ridge that helped form the pass they had ridden through. "That little filly back at camp. Red Sky Morning. She might make a good woman to spend your days with."

Johnny was silent a moment.

Joe was removing his canteen from his saddle. "A gal that purty, lookin' at me the way she looks at you, I'd think about it."

Johnny nodded. "I have to admit, the thought has crossed my mind. But I wouldn't want a woman to just be a replacement for Lura. Red Sky Morning deserves better than that."

Johnny looked at Bravo. The horse had been chewing at some grass, but was now looking at him.

Johnny said, "I think Bravo wants to run. And he's right. We're wasting daylight here. We have some hunting to do."

Joe took to the ridges. Johnny was going to cut across the valley floor and look for sign. Find a fresh deer trail and follow it. Zack said he would try the other side of the valley.

Johnny said, "We'll all rendez-vous at the village. Try to be there before sundown."

Johnny rode along with one pack horse.

He found some tracks, but they all looked a few hours old. A deer trail even half an hour old meant the deer could be miles away by now.

He remembered Many Lives saying there was a small lake toward the center of the valley, so he rode toward it.

He found the lake, not much bigger than a pond. He took a drink from it and found the water was cold and clear. He let Bravo have some. A body of water like this, he thought, with chinook winds that were soon to wear out, he figured the wild life would be coming here for water as much as possible.

Off toward the east, maybe two hundred yards, was a small stand of birch. Three white tree trunks, with branches that were bare because of the time of year. It might provide a good place where Johnny could watch the water.

He turned Bravo toward the trees and led the

packhorse along.

Once he was behind the trees, he slid the Hawken from his saddle. Then he loosened the girth and decided to let the horses graze. He picketed the pack horse, and looped Bravo's reins over the saddle horn. Bravo wouldn't wander far, and he would come when he was whistled for.

Johnny knelt by one birch trunk, and he waited.

A lot of success in deer hunting comes from being patient. Being silent and waiting.

It was warm. Johnny removed his hat and wiped some sweat from his brow. He had left his buckskin shirt and Pa's coat at the teepee. Hard to believe it had been winter just a few days before and would possibly be winter again tomorrow.

He kept his eyes on the small pond, but his mind was drifting to Lura. The good times that had been theirs. Lying on a picnic blanket and watching the night sky, talking of their love and the future they wanted.

And he thought of Red Sky Morning. Small in stature. She couldn't have been much more than five feet tall. Black hair that fell to her waist. She usually wore it in braids, but one time she had let it hang loose and it was impossibly thick. She had eyes that were a deep brown, and as she fixed them on Johnny, he found himself not wanting to look away.

She was so different than Lura. But he wondered, was it that her differences were part of the attraction? Was it that he needed someone different from Lura for a while, to help him get over her? Lura was civilized and a teacher, and Red Sky Morning was a child of the earth. Lura's father seemed rotten to the core of his being, where Red Sky Morning's father was a great man. Even physically—Lura had light hair and sky-blue eyes, where Red Sky Morning had black hair and eyes that were the color of coffee.

He felt he was right about what he had said earlier to Zack and Joe. Red Sky Morning deserved better than to just be part of Johnny's emotional healing. She deserved a man who could love her the way he had loved Lura.

Then, he noticed movement down by the water. Three deer. Two were does, and a buck was behind them. Mule deer.

He brought his rifle to his shoulder and cocked the hammer back.

Johnny had four deer carcasses strapped to the pack horse as he rode into the village. The sun was dipping low in the western sky, and cookfires were blazing.

Joe had already arrived, and some of the warriors were helping him pull carcasses from the back of the pack horse. Three mule deer and one elk.

"Where's Zack?" Johnny said.

Joe shook his head. "Haven't seen him."

Many Lives came over with Red Morning Sky and some warriors. Johnny noticed the warrior who had been asking her to marry him wasn't there. Pierce had said the man's name was Stands Tall.

Many Lives said, "We help you with this meat."

Red Sky Morning said, "You are a great hunter and a great warrior. You make a great gift to our people."

Johnny had to admit, he found himself not wanting to look away from her.

He said, "Your people are kind to us. It's only right that we give a gift."

When dinner was ready, Johnny and Joe were invited to the home of Many Lives. Pierce was there with them. They sat in the teepee in front of a small, smoldering fire, Many Lives got out a long wooden pipe. Similar to Joe's but with a design that was different. Johnny figured it was the difference between Shoshone and Cheyenne culture.

"This is a gathering of close friends," Pierce said. "Chief Many Lives is welcoming you into his circle."

Many Lives took a draw of smoke and then

released it from his mouth. Then he took another, and he released it in a direction that was forty-five degrees off from the first.

He did four as such, then handed it to Pierce.

Pierce said, "We give some smoke to each of the four directions. A way of honoring the Earth, which gives us life."

Johnny nodded. He liked this. When the pipe was handed to him, he did the same then handed it to Joe.

They talked for a while of hunting conditions. Many Lives didn't expect the chinook to last much longer and he was as surprised as Joe that it had lasted this long. Many Lives asked Johnny where he and Joe were from, and Johnny talked a little about Pennsylvania.

"It seems white man stays in one place and the Earth provides life," Many Lives said, "while the Indian roams about the Earth and the Earth still provides life."

Johnny gave a thoughtful nod. He said, "That does seem to be the way of it."

Many Lives made the observation that Joe had spent time among the Cheyenne.

"Good people," Many Lives said. "Have much honor. Sometimes enemies of ours, but sometimes friends."

When the pipe had been handed around a few times, they went out to eat.

Red Sky Morning handed Johnny a chunk of venison. She did so with a smile. Johnny noticed that Stands Tall had not been invited to dinner.

It grew dark, and they ate and talked. There was laughter.

Red Sky Morning openly gave smiles to Johnny. He felt she deserved better than he could offer, but she was pretty and he was lonely, and despite himself and what he believed was right, he found himself smiling back.

Then Johnny heard dogs barking.

"Rider coming," Many Lives said.

Johnny hoped it was Zack. Turned out it was.

Zack rode up to the teepee they shared, so Johnny said, "Excuse me," and got to his feet.

Many Lives said, "Go. See."

Zack was swinging out of the saddle. He had two deer across his packhorse.

He said to Johnny, "I hope you shot more than I did."

Johnny nodded. "We got a bunch. We were getting a little concerned about you."

Zack talked while he stripped the saddle from his horse.

"I took a ride outside the valley. Just to get a look at things. I thought maybe I'd find some game out there. What I found was some tracks made by unshod horses."

"Riders?"

He nodded. "Most likely Indian. They came within half a mile of the pass leading into the valley. They were about a day old. I followed 'em for a while, hoping to get a look at 'em. See what tribe they were. But I didn't catch up to 'em."

"That gives us something to think about. Remember what Pierce was saying about these people and the ceremonial war they conduct against each other."

"That's what we don't need. A group of Sioux or Cheyenne or Blackfoot attacking. This is a small village. Only eight fighting men here, not counting us."

"I think you should count us. If these people are attacked by anyone, white or red, I intend to stand with 'em."

Zack nodded. "Me too. And I think we can count on Joe."

Joe had come up behind Johnny. "You bet you can."

Zack joined them all at the teepee of Many Lives. Red Sky Morning handed Johnny a bowl of pemmican. She smiled widely, and Johnny returned the smile. One of Many Lives' wives scowled at Johnny and said, "No smile. No smile."

She then scurried Red Sky Morning away and into the teepee.

Many Lives and Pierce were laughing. Joe was, too. Johnny didn't see what was so funny. He thought the old lady seemed downright hateful.

Johnny told Many Lives what Zack had found.

Many Lives said, "How many riders?"

Zack said, "Ten. Maybe more. They rode over each other's tracks."

Many Lives looked weary. "Came to valley to get away from war."

Pierce said, "Many young warriors want war. It is the Shoshone way."

Many Lives nodded. "But things change. Our ways will have to change. The white man comes and his way of war is different. He fight to destroy. Indians will have to come together and learn to fight new way. If not, we may see end to our way of life."

Everyone became silent at the words of Many Lives, each with his own thoughts.

As Johnny, Joe and Zack headed back to their teepee, Johnny found Red Sky Morning scurrying to catch up with them.

She said, "I heard what you said. Riders outside of valley. You keep us safe?"

She leaned into him, and he found himself putting his arms around her. "I won't let anyone hurt you."

She nodded. "Much afraid."

"No need to be."

Then a woman called out from Many Lives' teepee. A bunch of syllables Johnny couldn't quite catch, but he thought the first were, *Ainga*. Or something like that.

He could catch the tone of voice, though. He thought it sounded like the hateful woman from earlier.

Red Sky Morning gave Johnny an apologetic smile, and then scurried off to the teepee.

Joe was laughing. Zack was grinning, too.

Johnny said, "I really don't see what's so funny."

Joe slapped Johnny's shoulder. "A courtship has just begun."

"What courtship?"

Now Zack was laughing. He said, "Sometimes the feller is the last one to know."

# 35

JOHNNY STRETCHED out on his blankets. It was a little chilly, so he pulled the buffalo robe over himself, and he kept his guns within reach.

Joe and Zack sounded like they were asleep, but Johnny found himself staring at the darkness overhead.

He found himself thinking about Red Sky Morning. He had liked the way it felt, having her in his arms.

And he thought about the possibility of enemy Indians outside the valley. He fully intended not to let any harm come to these people.

He decided he couldn't sleep, so he climbed out of bed and pulled back on his pants and then his buckskin boots. With a pistol in one hand, he stepped outside.

It was downright cold. Looked like the chinook was over. The sky was clear, though. Stars were bright overhead, like they often are in a winter sky.

Johnny listened to the night. All seemed quiet. He could hear the wind whistling in the distance, and it sounded cold. None of the dogs were out and about. The corral was nearby, and the horses seemed quiet.

Johnny thought for a moment about how he would approach this village if he was looking to attack. Since the pass was to the west, he would come in and turn either north or south and then circle around.

It was too dark, he figured, for riders to dare entering the valley tonight. There was no moon, any invading Lakota would have only starlight to ride by. Johnny could see only blackness where he knew Many Lives' teepee to be.

He went back inside and decided to put some more wood on the fire. Hold back the cold a little and maybe put some coffee on.

Joe propped himself up on one elbow while Johnny was setting the kettle on the fire.

Joe said, "Anything going on?"

"Nope. Quiet out there. Getting cold, too."

"Figured it would. You've been thinking about them tracks Zack saw."

Johnny nodded.

Joe said, "As long as the weather turns cold, I don't think there'll be any threat from any war parties. They'll be hunkered down, just like we're going to be."

"I suppose. But I can't sleep. I took a look around outside, then I figured coffee might help."

"If a gal had hugged me like she had hugged you, I wouldn't be able to sleep, either."

"I shouldn't be thinking about her."

"Why not?"

"What if all I'm doing is comparing her to Lura. What if I'm just looking for someone to replace her."

"You ain't gonna start bein' morose again, are you?"

Johnny shook his head and chuckled.

Zack was apparently awake. He said. "Morose? That's a word for it. You used to be downright fun. What happened to you?"

Johnny said, "I don't know what happened to me. A lot of things, I suppose. Riding home and finding myself feeling like a stranger. Seeing our father killed right in front of us. Not being able to find the killer."

Joe said, "That could do it."

"Maybe what you need is something you can't find here," Zack said. "Maybe we need to go back to those border towns. Find a cantina with some tequila and some senoritas who look lonely."

Johnny said, "I've had enough tequila. I don't know if I ever want to taste that stuff again."

"Well, if we're to stay here, you're going to have to decide what to do about Red Sky Morning."

"I don't know what I want." Johnny thought for a moment. "No, I do know what I want. But I want to make sure I want it for the right reasons."

The following morning the air was ice cold. Frost covered the ground and had turned the grass beyond the little village to silver.

Bravo had spent the night with the other horses, so Johnny went to the corral to fetch him. He brought the horse back to the teepee and then saddled up.

Joe was outside with a cup of coffee, and Pierce came wandering over.

Pierce said, "The ladies are preparing a nice breakfast. They wanted me to invite you all over."

"Mighty neighborly," Johnny said. "But I thought I might get an early start. I want to have a look around. I'll eat some jerky out on the trail."

Joe said, "Want some company?"

"Thanks, but no. Sometimes a man can make better time when he's riding alone."

Joe nodded. "If you need me, I'll be with Zack, down at the Pierce camp having breakfast."

Johnny had pulled on his buckskin shirt over his range shirt. A wide-brimmed hat also seemed to do a lot to keep him warm, and once the sun was fully in the sky, the day became warm enough that the frost melted away. It wouldn't be warm like during the week of the chinook, but it would be tolerable.

Johnny decided that with enemy raiders potentially outside the valley, he was going to play it safe. He didn't ride directly toward the pass, but instead toward the long ridge that led to the pass.

The snow on the ridge was about half as deep as it had been before the chinook, and it was easy going for Bravo. They stayed within the pine forest and avoided any open cliffs or barren slopes that still had a snow cover. Johnny didn't think the snow was deep enough for a slide, but he didn't want to take chances.

He started down toward the pass, then reined up on a ledge that was free of snow, and that gave him a view of the pass down below. It was still cold enough for him to see his breath. He didn't think it was going to get much warmer today.

He thought this might be a good spot for observation. He had a clear view of the pass. He could also see out beyond the valley, to the west. To the north there were more ridges, and from this view he could see a snow covered jagged peak.

He swung out of the saddle to give Bravo some rest, and he loosened the girth. Then he pulled out a strip of jerky and began chewing on it.

Very likely anyone riding into the valley would be using the pass. There was a much smaller pass to the south that he had seen earlier, when he shot a buck by the stream that was deceptively deep. Many Lives had said there were more such passes in various places around the valley. But the passes were wooded and mostly in deep shade. The snow would be too deep to easily ride through. The one below was the best bet, he thought.

Bravo began nosing at the ground. Mostly it was pine straw and bedrock, but there were a few clumps of grass.

The mountain winds were strong this high up in the ridges, and they were cold. Joe was right about how they seemed to wash your troubles away.

He got out another strip of jerky and began chewing.

After a time—he figured it might be nearly noon—he caught sight of movement off to the west.

Beyond the valley was a long, flat strip, mostly grass and rocks and gravel. Further out was a stretch of what looked like low gray bushes and more grass. Junipers and occasional trees. The land then rose to a long, low hill and then looked like it descended again. Beyond it was another wooded ridge.

To the north there were more ridges, and from this view he saw a snowy, jagged peak.

He saw something that might have been a dead tree. Or a rock. Or a horse. It was too far away, and even squinting, he couldn't quite see it. But if he looked away, his side vision could detect motion.

Might be an elk, he thought, or a stray buffalo. He, Joe and Zack had seen the tracks of a buffalo herd when they were still two days south of the valley. The critters must have numbered in the hundreds.

He waited. Not much different than hunting, he thought.

Bravo looked at him. Johnny thought the horse was getting bored.

The object out there was coming closer. It was moving like a horse but it was taller. Johnny figured it was a rider.

He waited. Bravo shifted his hooves and started nosing at the ground again. A crow called out from somewhere off in the valley.

Johnny was right. It was a rider and heading directly for the pass.

Johnny decided to go down for a closer look. He tightened the girth and swung back into the saddle, and he turned Bravo down the slope toward the pass.

They stopped behind a stand of pines at the edge of the pass, and that was where they waited. Johnny swung out of the saddle and then pulled his rifle free.

He could see the rider. Looked Indian he thought. Long dark hair and some sort of headpiece. Buckskin clothes.

The rider came directly into the pass, and Johnny stepped out from the trees, his rifle cocked and to his shoulder.

"Hold on, pardner," he said.

The Indian looked at Johnny wide-eyed, then pulled a rifle and brought it to his shoulder.

Foolish move, Johnny thought. Going for a gun when a man has the drop on you.

Johnny fired before the Indian could. The Hawken's lead ball caught the Indian in the chest, and he went over the side of the horse and landed hard on the ground. The horse reared up and burst into a gallop back in the direction it had come from.

Johnny dropped the rifle to the grass and pulled a pistol, and he advanced on the fallen Indian.

The Indian was face-down in the grass and not moving. Johnny rolled him over.

It had been a perfect shot. Johnny didn't think the Indian was still alive when he hit the ground.

*Lakota*, Johnny thought. He recognized the style of buckskin shirt and the beadwork on the man's sheath.

He didn't look much older than Johnny. There was no war paint, but Johnny didn't think Indians often hunted alone. At least the tribes he was familiar with didn't. Probably conducting reconnaissance, he thought. They were scouting the valley.

The man's horse hadn't run far, so Johnny mounted up and chased the horse down. He then tied the Indian to the saddle and sent the horse on its way. But he kept the man's rifle, powder horn and pouch of lead balls and patches.

Johnny turned Bravo back toward the village. It wasn't a matter of if Lakota raiders would be striking the village. It was just a matter of when.

# 36

ON THE WAY BACK TO THE VILLAGE, he found another rider drifting along between the village and the ridge. Keeping the horse to a casual walk and not seeming to be riding anywhere in particular.

It was Red Sky Morning.

Her hair was in its usual two braids, and she was in a buckskin dress and boots. She had a rabbit fur robe wrapped around her shoulders. The robe was long and fell to her knees.

She said, "I hoped to find you out here."

"Does your father know you're here?"

She nodded. "I go riding a lot."

"How is your leg?"

She smiled. "Much better."

The sun was working its way toward the western horizon. Johnny's stomach was reminding him that a few strips of jerky were all he had eaten today. And yet he found he could sit and just look into her eyes and time seemed to stand still.

He said, "What did that woman call you?"

She laughed. "That's my mother. She used my Indian name."

She rattled off the syllables again, just like the scowly Indian woman had. Johnny caught the first couple of syllables as *Ainga*.

He said, "Do you mind if I call you Ainga? We white men have trouble with long names."

She laughed again. "That would be fine."

He turned Bravo toward the village and she rode along. They kept their horses to a walk.

He said, "You speak English well."

She nodded. "Thank you. Neville has been with us for a long time. Most of my life."

They rode in silence for a while.

She said, "I have waited a long time for you."

Johnny knew Indians took serious stock of visions

and dreams. He had known white people who did, too. Aunt Sara back in Pennsylvania had always believed she was subject to premonitions. So he didn't want to dismiss this girl's ideas.

She was dang pretty, and there was a lot about her that he liked. A certain spirit in her smile. A certain energy about her. And she came from good stock. It would be all too easy to reach out to her.

"Ainga," he said, not really sure where to begin. "I had a woman. I was going to live my life with her."

"Was she killed by your enemies?"

He had to grin. Her question was asked in innocence, though, reflective of the only life she knew.

"No. She's still alive. But she decided she didn't want to build a life with me. I loved her more than I could ever say. When she left, it hurt more than..." How could he say it? "More than the mightiest blow from the mightiest warrior."

"Did she say why she left?"

He shook his head. "She left me a note to say goodbye, but never really said why."

She was looking at him with sorrow in her eyes. "Why would she do this? Why, when she could have the greatest warrior? The one who beat Iron Hand, when Iron Hand couldn't be beaten?"

He shrugged. "That was before I fought Iron Hand. But I don't think it would have mattered. You see, white women don't look at things like Shoshone women. I guess they don't value the same things."

"I value everything that you are. I would never hurt you. I would make you happy all of your days. I will bear you strong sons, and they will be great warriors too."

Dang, but she was making this difficult.

He said, "It wouldn't be fair to you. At least, not now. I would have to make sure I loved you for who you are, not just as a woman to replace the one who hurt me."

She nodded. It was making sense.

He said, "You're a great woman. You deserve a great warrior who will make you happy. A warrior you can give many strong sons to. Maybe that warrior is me, I don't know. But not yet."

"How long will it be before your heart is healed enough to be with a new woman?"

He shrugged. "I don't know. Maybe never."

They rode in silence for a while longer. The village was just ahead.

He said to her, "Could you tell your father that I need to see him? I need to see all of the men, including Stands Tall."

"Stands Tall won't want to see you. He very jealous."

"Tell him he can be jealous later. Right now, we all have to have a council of war."

She looked at him with fear in her eyes, then rode on to the teepee of Many Lives.

They met at the cookfire of Many Lives. The chief himself sat cross-legged on a buffalo robe. Pierce sat beside him, probably in deference to his age. Johnny had learned many tribes had respect for age and wisdom. The other men stood.

Johnny told them of the Lakota warrior he had seen earlier, and that he had shot.

Joe said, "Yeah, we heard your rifle shot."

"I wasn't really sure what to do. If I let him go, then he would have scouted the valley and then reported back to his chief."

Pierce was translating into Shoshone, for those who didn't understand Johnny's words.

Johnny said, "I decided to stop him. I got the jump on him, but then he tried to get off a rifle shot at me so I had to shoot him."

Many Lives nodded gravely.

That was when Ainga interrupted things by coming out of the teepee with a wooden plate and a knife.

"Daughter," Many Lives said. "You interrupt a council of war."

"Father," she said, not the least bit intimidated, "a great warrior has gone the day with little food."

She handed the plate to Johnny and smiled. But not the smile of before. No longer a young woman trying to attract the attention of a particular man. Now it was a smile of understanding and appreciation. He returned the smile.

Stands Tall was glaring at Johnny like he wanted to kill him.

Ainga went back into the teepee, and Johnny speared the venison steak with his own bowie knife and bit off a chunk.

"Forgive me for eating in front of you," he said, "but I'm starving."

Zack was standing there in his wide-brimmed hat and with twin Colts at his belt. He said, "So, what'd you do with the body?"

"Again, I wasn't sure what to do, so I strapped it onto the horse and sent it off. I figured the horse will take it back to the village."

Many Lives nodded. "You did all you could."

"We have to prepare for war."

Stands Tall said, "White man afraid. I see it in your eyes."

It was now Johnny's turn to fix him with a hard look. "I think you know better than that. But if it's going to be war, it's a war I want to win. I don't want anyone here hurt. The women. The children."

Joe said, "There's another storm comin'. Gonna be a good one."

It was now dark, and Johnny looked off toward the sky. One section of stars was blocked off, which meant there were clouds up there. And the wind away from the heat of the fire was bitter cold.

Many Lives said, "Cheyenne Joe is right. This storm could be worse than last one."

Pierce translated, then he said to Johnny, "I feel it

in my old joints."

Joe said, "I don't think anyone's gonna attack us with a storm comin' on. They'll all be hunkered down somewhere. It's afterward that we'll have to prepare for."

The council broke up, and Johnny finished his venison.

Ainga came out and said, "Is good?"

Johnny nodded. "I was real hungry, but even so, this is the best I've ever tasted."

"Special herbs I put on it. Picked them myself. Some are roots I dug."

"Well, you did a bang-up job. That's for sure."

"Bang-up is good?"

He nodded. "Bang-up is the best."

She smiled.

A gust of wind shot past them, wind so cold it almost hurt. She shivered and hunched down inside her rabbit fur robe as much as she could. It almost lifted Johnny's hat from his head.

He said, "Go inside and get warm. Stay warm. We'll have to wait out this storm."

She placed a hand alongside his face. "And while we wait out storm, let your heart heal. Then when it is healed, you can decide. Are we to be friends or more? Either way, I consider myself blessed."

He watched her go back inside the teepee. He realized what a great woman she was.

As he walked through the cold wind back to the teepee he and the boys were using, he asked himself a question he had asked before. *Am I a fool?* He had asked himself that over Becky Drummond, then again over Maria Carrera. He supposed three's a charm.

It was as he walked along toward the teepee, with only the cookfires for light, that Stands Tall attacked.

# 37

STANDS TALL MADE one mistake, which was to not know enough about your opponent before you strike.

He had waited for Johnny in the darkness between two teepees, and then he came running out in soft-soled buckskin boots that made almost no sound as they touched down on the ground. He had no weapon in his hands, as murder was not in his heart. He just wanted to show Red Sky Morning that the white man with the loud rifle was not invincible. The white man may have beaten Iron Hand, but Stands Tall was not one to believe in spiritual blessings that made you invincible. A man was just a man, and any man could be beaten.

His intention was to take the white man by surprise. His mistake was that he didn't realize how hard it was to get the jump on Johnny McCabe. Johnny was always on alert, always listening for a sound that seemed out of place. Always glancing through his side vision to the left and to the right as he walked along.

Zack had said it was some sort of battle fatigue. Sometimes a man could walk away from a battle, but sometimes the battle stayed with him and it did things to him.

Stands Tall learned of his mistake as he leaped at Johnny, but found Johnny already turning to face him.

Johnny grabbed him by one shoulder and turned, and Stands Tall's own momentum carried him past Johnny and he landed hard on the frozen ground.

He scrambled to his feet.

"Easy now," Johnny said. "I don't want to fight."

"You white men never want fight. Afraid."

"Where we're from, we're taught fighting is wrong."

Stands Tall charged at Johnny again, and he ran face-first into a hard left jab. It stunned him. He hadn't expected the fist and he staggered back a step.

Johnny stepped in and drove a right uppercut

into Stands Tall's midsection, then he twisted to his right and brought a left elbow strike into Stands Tall's face—a maneuver he had learned from Mr. Wong.

Stands Tall staggered back another step, and then Johnny let loose with a right cross. It made contact with Stands Tall's cheekbone, and the proud Shoshone warrior went down.

Johnny saw motion by the teepee and looked over to see Joe and Zack standing there. Joe had a cup of coffee in one hand.

Joe said, "Just enjoyin' a good fight."

Johnny was trying to shake the pain out of his right hand. When he had hit Stands Tall's face, there had been too much contact with the middle knuckles of his fingers and not the primary knuckles. Not the best punch, but Johnny's father had said, "A fight is often not a pretty thing. Chaotic and sometimes even sloppy. You practice your punches to get them as right as possible, but when a fight happens, things can get crazy fast."

Stands Tall got to his feet.

Johnny said, "I don't want to fight."

"You fight, White Man."

Stands Tall charged again.

Johnny tried to execute the same maneuver he had before, but this time he didn't get the turn going quite fast enough and Stands Tall brought him down.

They rolled in the cold mud. Stands Tall drove a knee into Johnny's ribs. Then they stopped rolling with Stands Tall on top, and he had his hands around Johnny's throat.

Pierce and his wives had come out of their teepee, and others were gathering around.

Johnny grabbed the man's thumbs and twisted. What Wong had called a thumb lock. He broke the grip but didn't let go of the thumbs. He twisted hard and made the man cry out.

Johnny kicked Stands Tall off of him, and then got to his feet.

Despite his injured thumbs, Stands Tall charged at Johnny again, but this time dropped and slid under him, and knocked Johnny's legs out from under him.

Johnny came to his knees in time to receive a buckskin boot in the face. Johnny went down and rolled over.

Johnny remained down, and Stands Tall raised his foot for one more kick into Johnny's face.

Johnny shot his own foot out and into Stands Tall's groin.

The Indian fell back and went down to his knees. Johnny got to his own knees, and he tried to shake the cobwebs out of his head. He had caught the kick on the eyebrow, and his eye was swelling shut.

Johnny didn't like resorting to kicking. When he was growing up, it would have been called dirty fighting. But the Indian didn't fight by the same rules and Mr. Wong had said the Chinese didn't, either.

After a few moments, Johnny got to his feet. Stands Tall was doing the same.

Johnny decided it was time to take control of the fight. So far he had been only reacting to attacks.

He came in for a right hook. Stands Tall weaved back and away, which Johnny was grateful for because his fist was still hurting.

But Johnny stepped in and turned his body and caught Stands Tall on the side of the face with a left hook.

Johnny then stepped in so his right foot was between Stands Talls' feet, and drove a right elbow strike into his face.

The Indian went down again.

Johnny stepped back. He hoped Stands Tall would stay down. But the warrior got to his feet again.

Many Lives stepped between them. He called out a word that sounded to Johnny like, "Pea!"

Probably meant *stop*, or *enough*.

Either way, Stands Tall stopped, which allowed Johnny to stop.

Many Lives said, "We need all men strong for war with Lakota."

Stands Tall said, "Prove this White Man just a man. Not great warrior."

Ainga was in the crowd that had gathered. She said to him, "Aiweape."

And she turned and walked away.

Pierce said, "She just called him a fool."

Stands Tall glared at Johnny one more time and turned to storm away. But his storming was a little slow, because he had taken some blows to the face and a solid uppercut to the ribs, and Johnny's kick had taken some of the life out of his walk.

The crowd was dispersing. Johnny snatched his hat from where it had fallen to the ground. He also snagged a revolver that had fallen from his left holster.

Many Lives was at his side. "Stands Tall tries to prove to Red Sky Morning that you can be beaten. Because you beat Iron Hand, many believe you can't be."

Johnny said, "I'll say one thing about Stands Tall. He's a much better fighter than Iron Hand was."

Joe said, "Or maybe it's just that he has more to fight for."

## 38

BY MORNING, the wind was blowing hard and the snow was coming down. Johnny stepped out for his morning ritual of greeting the day with a cup of coffee, and he found two feet of snow were covering the ground.

He pushed through the snow to the corral. Bravo had apparently decided to brave through this storm with the rest of the horses. Joe, Zack and some of the Indians had worked the day before to shore up the structure that served as a sort of barn. The Indian horses were mountain bred and accustomed to these winters, but Bravo had been running wild through the canyons of Mexico when he had been found. He wasn't accustomed to this kind of cold.

"Come on," Johnny said to Bravo and started walking away.

He looked and Bravo was standing with some of the other horses in the open end of the lean-to.

Johnny said it again. "Come on."

Then he clapped both hands together, and Bravo started walking toward Johnny.

Johnny opened the tent flap and stepped in. Then he held it open. The horse had to duck his head, and his shoulders caught the top of the doorway and stretched it upward a little and made the teepee shake.

Zack said, "What on Earth are you doing?"

"Bravo's not used to these winters. I've been through too much with him to see him freeze to death out there."

"He survived the last storm out there."

"He was off in the ridges and found himself some place to hunker down."

Once the horse was in the teepee, Johnny shut the flap.

Joe said, "Now it's gonna smell like horse dung in here."

"I'll clean it up. He's gotten me out of more than

one fix. I owe him."

The storm wore on.

"Gotta be ten below out there," Zack said.

The fire was blazing in the teepee. Even still, it was cold. Johnny sat on the ground near the fire with a buffalo robe wrapped around his shoulders.

He was flexing the fingers of his right hand. They were swollen and purple colored.

"One punch didn't land right," he said. "I hope nothing's broken. This is my shooting hand."

"Like Many Lives said," Joe said. "We need all our fighting men at full strength, not fighting each other."

"Didn't have much choice in it. He jumped me, out there in the darkness."

Bravo was lying down like a dog at the far end of the teepee. Johnny had already had to scoop a load of droppings and toss them out into the storm.

"I hope the wood lasts," Zack said. "After the storm we'll have to get some more. I just hope we don't run out before the storm ends."

Johnny stepped out one more time, just to see what was happening outside. The snow was still coming down and it stung his face like small, icy pellets. A drift stretched four feet up the side of the teepee.

It was getting dark. The day was almost done, but the wind was as strong as ever. Soon it would be growing even colder.

Johnny went back inside and he shook the snow off of the buffalo robe.

Before he could say anything, there was a knocking sound on the outside of the tent flap.

Johnny pulled it open and Pierce stepped inside. "Mind if we come in?" he said. "Our wood supply is gone."

Johnny stepped aside. Pierce's two wives came in. One was carrying a jug of whiskey, and the other had a stack of venison steaks on a plate.

"We come bearing gifts," Pierce said.

Pierce then saw Bravo in one corner. "You brought your horse inside?"

One of his wives was maybe forty, the other closer to Ainga's age. The older one looked at Bravo and nodded with approval, and she said, "Bravo has powerful spirit."

Joe nodded. "He's got powerful droppin's, too."

After dinner, the women curled up on buffalo robes and went to sleep. Pierce pulled the cork on his jug and took a swig.

"Here," he said, handing the jug to Johnny. "You look like you need one. That eye is nearly swollen shut."

"I'm more concerned about my hand. If we have a battle with Indian raiders, I'll need my gun hand."

Johnny took a pull from the jug.

They sat in silence a while, handing the jug around. Then Zack said, "So, how does it work, with two wives? How is it one isn't jealous of the other?"

Pierce said, "They're like sisters."

"I don't understand that."

"That's because you weren't raised in the practice. It's difficult to have an open mind to things you aren't accustomed to."

"It doesn't seem to hold you back any."

"Well, I was at sea a while. Saw some different lands. Sort of opened my eyes a bit. These Indians aren't so different from us as you might think."

Johnny took his third pull from the jug. He was starting to feel a little warmer, and his hand wasn't hurting as much.

He said, "I hope nothing's broken."

"Can you make a fist?" Pierce said.

Johnny balled up his fingers. Hurt like heck, but he held a fist.

Pierce said, "Nothing's broken. You'll be all right."

After a time, Zack said, "That little filly who's chasing you, I was amazed at how she walked right out into the council of war. Her father's the war chief, but she didn't seem to pay him any mind."

Pierce said, "The women actually run things around here. The men handle war and hunting, but it's the women that run the entire society. They build the teepees and decide where to place them. Many Lives' first and second wives picked the location. They oversee the distribution of food, too, after the men go hunting."

Joe nodded. "Same way with the Cheyenne. It's a better way. There's a word for that kind of society."

"Matriarchal."

"That's it. You sound just like our brother Matt."

"Oh? Is he an Englishman?"

"Nope. Just full of ten-dollar words."

Pierce laughed.

The following morning, the wind was still going strong.

Zack said, "Is it normal for a storm to last this long in these mountains?"

Joe was fixing coffee. "Last night, around midnight, the wind stopped and it was quiet for a while. I think this is a second storm that followed the first one in."

Johnny pulled on Pa's coat and said "I'm gonna go check on everyone."

With his hat on tight, he stepped out.

Zack said, "Tell me, how is it they decide on who's going to be the chief around here?"

"Respect," Joe said.

Pierce nodded. "That's how it works. Take your brother, for instance. Going around to check on everyone. And at our war council, he talked along with Many Lives, like an equal. He just seems to naturally take charge."

"Always been like that," Joe said.

"He's fast on his way to becoming a war chief, if he decides to remain with these people."

Zack looked at Joe. "Do you think he will?"

Joe shrugged. "It's a good way of life. I fell into it real easy."

Pierce said, "How long were you with the Cheyenne?"

"Nigh onto two years. Johnny seems to feel the same peace here that I felt. I wouldn't be surprised if he stays."

"But he's a white man," Zack said.

"One thing I've found, laddie," Pierce said, "there really is no white man. No black man. No Indian. Those are words we call ourselves but nothing more. We're all just people."

Joe nodded.

Zack sat a moment while he let those words settle in his mind. Pierce had given him something to think about.

The way the teepee was situated, the doorway was away from the wind, so the snow drifted away from it. Johnny figured it was no coincidence. The Shoshone women probably placed it this way intentionally. But once he was away from the doorway, he had to lift his legs to trudge through three feet of snow.

Johnny knocked on the teepee of Many Lives. The older woman who was the first wife of Many Lives opened the flap. Johnny was starting to think of her as *Scowly Woman*. She didn't look pleased to see him.

He said, "I come to see if everyone is all right."

She simply scowled at him. He didn't know if she understood English. He figured it probably didn't matter.

Many Lives called out, "Come on in, John-ee."

The woman stepped aside, but made it clear she was reluctant about it. Johnny ducked his head and stepped through the doorway.

Ainga was roasting some venison, and the smell was mouth-watering.

She nodded at Johnny and smiled. He returned both the nod and the smile.

Johnny said, "I am going around to make sure everyone is all right."

Many Lives was sitting cross-legged by the fire. He said, "We are warm and safe. You are a good young chief."

"We have enough firewood to last maybe the night and into tomorrow. Pierce's wood is gone, and he and his wives are with us."

Many Lives nodded. He looked at a stack of wood at one side of the teepee. "Once storm passes, we will gather more wood. Storm should be gone by tonight."

Johnny checked the other teepees, though he decided to avoid the one used by Stands Tall. No need to start more trouble.

When Johnny got back to his own teepee, Zack was saying, "So all of the squaws are really in charge?"

Pierce nodded. "But don't call them squaws. That's a word from an Indian tribe in the northeast. I don't know which one. The Shoshone word for woman is *hepi*."

Joe nodded. "In Cheyenne it's *he'e*."

Zack said, "Similar, in a way."

Johnny shouldered out of Pa's coat and shook off the snow in one corner, then sat down by the fire. He held his hands out to the flames to warm them.

He said, "One thing I've always wondered. Every tribe from the Kiowa all the way north to Canada has different languages, and yet they all seem to use the same sign language. Why do you suppose that is?"

Pierce shrugged. "I've never heard."

Joe said, "It's danged convenient, though."

Johnny stretched out on one buffalo robe and pulled the other one over him. He wasn't using his bedroll anymore, because the buffalo robes did the job so thoroughly.

As he stretched out, he heard the others breathing easily. He thought everyone was asleep. Bravo made a gruff sort of *harrumph* sound. Must be dreaming, he thought. When a dog made sounds in his sleep or twitched his feet, people often said the dog's chasing a rabbit in his dreams. Johnny wondered what horses chased.

He was thinking about Ainga. And he was thinking about Lura. He found he really liked Ainga. When she smiled at him tonight, he found himself smiling back. And yet he didn't want to do wrong by her.

Was he trying too hard? Was he becoming his own worst enemy? Was this why he was so morose much of the time?

He stared at the darkness overhead. He felt like sleep was evading him.

Then he realized he must have fallen asleep, because the night outside was now silent. No more wind, and the fire had burned down a lot.

He slid out from under the buffalo robes and put more wood on the fire.

Then he pulled on his buckskin boots and grabbed his hat, Pa's coat, and a pistol, and he stepped outside. He tucked the pistol into the front of his belt. His knuckles hurt when he made a fist, and he wondered if he would be able to pull the trigger if he had to.

It was so incredibly cold it felt like ice crystals were forming in his nose when he inhaled. But the air was still, and the sky overhead was clear. Stars twinkled brightly.

Snow drifted away from the teepee, and in places was five feet deep. Yet in front of the teepee, there were only a few inches of it

He looked up at the sky and said, "What do I do, Pa?"

As if Pa could hear him. Johnny remembered Ma saying those in heaven could hear you. He hoped so.

He began to pace a bit on the open area in front of the teepee. He sometimes thought better when he paced. Matt was like that. Pa had been, too.

He supposed what bothered him the most about the whole thing with Lura, the thing that nagged at him and refused to let him go, was that he couldn't imagine a girl who had looked at him with such love in her eyes could just change her mind and walk away.

He wanted to hear it from her. He wanted her to look him in the eye and say the words she had written in the letter.

Then it occurred to him, he actually wanted it. He wasn't being whimsical or rhetorical.

He had made his decision.

He went back into the teepee and found sleep took him easily.

In the morning, he was making coffee when the others began to awaken.

"The storm's passed," Johnny said. "And I've made my decision."

"What decision is that?" Zack said, sitting up in his buffalo blankets and stretching his arms out.

"I want to hear it from Lura. I want her to look me in the eye and tell me she doesn't really love me. That we don't have a future. When winter's passed, I'm going to go find her. And she's gonna have to tell me face-to-face."

Joe nodded. "Wouldn't hurt to check on Matt, too. Make sure his snake of a woman hasn't et him for supper."

Zack said, "But how will you find her? Where will you look?"

Johnny said, "I've been thinking about that. She has an aunt in San Francisco. She said this aunt was more of a mother to her than her own mother. I'd lay good odds that's where she went."

# 39

THE FOLLOWING DAY, the women built four travois with buffalo hides stretched along pine poles, and hitched them to horses. With snow shoes strapped to their feet, the women gathered the wood, taking branches from the ground or breaking off low-hanging pine branches that were dead and brittle. When there was enough wood loaded onto a travois, it would be brought back to camp and unloaded, and then taken back out for more.

The women were doing the work, Johnny noticed.

"Where I come from," Johnny said, "the men do the heavy, hard work. The women tend to cooking and raising the children. It's our way of showing respect to our women."

Many Lives nodded. "Respect can be shown in many ways. Among us, the women have their work. They are the backbone of our way of life. For a man to step in and do a woman's work would be insult to her. It would be saying the woman cannot do her sacred work."

They were on snowshoes, walking near the base of a ridge. Johnny had his Hawken in the crook of one arm, and Many Lives had an old, flintlock Harper's Ferry rifle.

There were women within sight, loading fallen pine branches onto a travois.

Many Lives said, "When I told my first wife we wanted to come along as guards, she said just don't get in the way."

Johnny noticed the old chief's use of English was improving. Pierce usually talked with him in Shoshone, so maybe it had been like Joe had said—Many Lives was pursuing English as a direct translation of sign language. But after talking with Johnny in recent weeks, he was learning more about the structure of English.

The sky was clear and the sun reflected against

the snow. A gust of wind picked up and lifted powdery snow into the air like a cloud.

Zack and Joe were with them. Zack pulled the collar of his buckskin shirt up to his neck and said, "Dang, but that wind is cold."

Joe was smiling and looking off at the sky. "I love the cold. It makes you feel alive. I'd forgotten how much I love these mountains in the winter."

Joe had his Enfield rifle with him. It didn't have quite the range of a Hawken, but it could still bring a rider down quite nicely. Zack had the rifle that had belonged to Iron Hand.

Zack said, "What are the chances that they'll attack today?"

"Not good," Many Lives said.

Joe nodded. "They're hunkered down somewhere, keepin' warm. Or gatherin' wood like we are. To get to these mountains, they have to ride over some open country, and it's gonna be mighty cold out there."

"It's good to be on alert, though," Johnny said.

A few days later, the weather warmed a little. Not like with a Chinook, but it was a above freezing. The snow was melting a bit. The men in the village took the opportunity to work with some wild horses they had caught before winter.

Johnny got to see the way a Shoshone broke a horse. Not by climbing on its back and hanging on while the horse tried frantically to buck you off.

He watched Stands Tall lead a horse about by a rope attached to a hackamore. After about an hour, the man laid a blanket across the horse's back and led him around.

The following day, he led the horse around again with a blanket across the back.

Many Lives said, "This how we get a horse used to a man."

Johnny said, "I've heard of this being done, but I've never seen it."

By the third day, Stands Tall was able to climb up onto the horse's back. The horse didn't buck. He didn't even look alarmed.

Zack stood beside Johnny, watching.

Zack said, "I've heard of that kind of thing, but I never thought it really worked."

"Apparently it does. I know if I ever have a ranch of my own, I'll be breaking horses this way."

After a few days, the weather turned cold again.

A few inches of snow dropped one night. In the morning, Many Lives took Johnny on a hike up one ridge. They had snowshoes strapped to buckskin boots. A gunbelt can be heavy, especially if it carries two guns, so Johnny left his at the teepee, and had a single pistol only tucked into the front of a belt that wrapped around his buckskin shirt. He also had his Hawken with him.

Many Lives took him to a rocky cliff that overlooked the southern third of the valley. To the left Johnny could see smoke rising from the village. To the right was the stream that was deceptively deep, and the grassy area where he had shot a deer. The place he thought that might be a good spot for a cabin.

"We winter here before," Many Lives said. "Four times, now. I come to this spot often."

Johnny drew in some mountain air. "It's in places like this that I feel closest to God."

Many Lives nodded. "God your name for Great Spirit."

Johnny's turn to nod. "I suppose so."

"I talk with Pierce much about white man religion. I think Great Spirit and God are the same. Different name, because different people."

On another day, they saddled up and went for a ride across the valley. Bravo loved high-stepping his way through snow drifts.

Johnny said, "Why do the Shoshone men have long hair? Most white men have short hair."

"Shoshone men and women all see hair as..." He

hesitated. "What is word? Part of our spirit."

"An extension of your spirit?"

Many Lives nodded with a smile. "Yes. We cut it when we mourn. When loved one passes onward. We cut it only then."

"You know, I could really embrace this way of life."

"You can join Shoshone tribe. You are welcome to become one of us."

Johnny nodded. "Part of me wants that more than anything."

"What part doesn't?"

Johnny chuckled. "The part of me that has to find some answers."

"What are the questions?"

"One question. A big one. A woman."

Many Lives nodded. "Ah. Woman is always biggest question."

Johnny told him about Lura.

He said, "I have to hear it from her. I have to have her tell me that she didn't really love me like I thought she did."

"So you leave in spring."

"Yes. I leave in the spring."

"Red Sky Morning wants you as husband. Stands Tall has been seeking her for years. I forget how many. But she always says no. She had dream that she would meet great warrior, and be his wife. She think that warrior is you."

"Yeah, I know. We've talked. Once I've found Lura and gotten my answer, I can see myself coming back here. Living here. Maybe joining the Shoshone. And if Red Sky Morning is still without a husband, I might marry her. But I have to have my answers, first. It wouldn't be fair to Red Sky Morning if I didn't."

"You think she have husband when you come back?"

Johnny shrugged. "She had her dream about a great warrior. Stands Tall is a great warrior. The best I ever fought. Far stronger than Iron Hand."

Many Lives looked at him with surprise.

Johnny nodded. "I say the truth. And Stands Tall loves her. I can see it in his eye."

Many Lives nodded. "She love him, too. But dreams and visions mean a lot to us. It how Great Spirit guides us."

"I think it's how the Great Spirit tries to guide the white man, too. It's just that white man often has too much pride to listen."

They rode in silence for a while. They were at the northern section of the valley. The land was more open and barren.

A ridge formed a wall at the northern side, and a wind lifted a flurry of snow from it, taking it like a small cloud up and into the air. Johnny and Many Lives sat in their saddles and watched.

Many Lives said, "Great Spirit graces us with beauty."

When they turned back toward the village, Many Lives said, "I would very pleased if you married Red Sky Morning. Be my son."

"I would be very pleased about that, too. But I have to have my answers if I'm ever going to give my heart to anyone."

Many Lives nodded. "I understand. Questions with no answers can eat away at a man."

"It wouldn't be fair to Red Sky Morning, either. And I really think that by the time I get back here, she'll have realized that Stands Tall is the man in her dreams."

A week later, Johnny stepped out of his teepee at sunrise with a cup of coffee and found it was warm. The wind was strong, but felt warm on his face. Snow was melting and a small stream had formed in front of the teepee. The smell of spring was in the air.

Many Lives was outside his own teepee. He saw Johnny and walked over.

"Chinook," Many Lives said.
Johnny nodded.
Many Lives said, "Now the raiders will come."

# 40

THEY ALL GATHERED for a council of war.

Many Lives said to Johnny, "You young war chief. What do you think?"

Johnny's idea was to split their forces.

He would position himself, Joe and Zack near the pass. With their rifles, and if they were positioned right, they could hold off a lot of riders. Pierce had a flintlock mountain rifle that was old and battered, but usable, and he was a capable shot, so he volunteered to join them.

The Shoshone warriors were to remain at the village and protect the women and the livestock and stop any raiders who got through the pass.

There were eight Shoshone warriors, including Many Lives. Some had rifles, but they were old flintlocks. These warriors could shoot well enough to hit a target, as long as the target wasn't too far away, but their primary weapons were the traditional ones. A tomahawk, a lance, or a bow and arrow. They would be much more effective at the village than in the pass.

Johnny said to Stands Tall, "I want you in charge of the village. Place the warriors where you think best."

Stands Tall looked at Johnny's right hand. "You can shoot gun?"

Johnny flexed his fingers and grinned. His hand still hurt but it was usable. He said, "I think I can."

Stands Tall returned the grin. "Shoot many."

At the pass, Johnny and Pierce took positions behind a grove of pines. The same pines where Johnny had shot the advance scout a few weeks earlier. They each had three rifles with them. The Shoshone had agreed to give up their rifles, because if any of the Lakota got through the pass and arrived at the village, fighting would be hand-to-hand.

Johnny said to Joe, "You and Zack should take

positions at the other side of the pass. Find some good trees to take cover behind. With enough powder in these rifles, we should be able to cover all of the ground between the two ridges."

Joe and Zack rode over to the other side of the pass and disappeared through a stand of pines.

"Now," Johnny said to Pierce, "we wait."

They took the horses back a ways. Pierce picketed his, but Johnny left Bravo to roam free.

Pierce said, "I know. He'll come if you whistle."

And so, they waited.

Pierce said, "There's another small pass, a mile or so south of here. Riders can get through, as long as they go single file."

Johnny nodded. "I thought about it. But it's not a plan I would use, if I was trying to take this valley. A couple of shooters could clean out ten men, if they caught them in that pass. If I was riding in to take the village, I would use this pass."

Pierce nodded. "You have a head for military strategy."

It was as warm as a spring day. Probably around sixty, Johnny figured. He had left his buckskin shirt at the teepee and was in a range shirt and a vest.

It was noon when Johnny saw motion out beyond the pass. A line of motion. It was a number of riders.

He stepped away from a tree so he still wouldn't be visible to any riders outside the pass, but so Joe could see him. Joe had already done the same, and Joe made a hand sign for *riders*. Johnny nodded.

They were coming in two lines, so getting their number was difficult. Many more than ten, Johnny thought.

He had considered posting a man at the small ledge further up the ridge. From there a man would have been able to count the number of riders, but if they were coming fast, he might not have been able to get down the mountain in time to join the battle.

The riders were keeping their horses to a

shambling trot as they approached the pass.

Pierce was squinting as he looked toward them. "Looks like they're wearing paint. They're not here on a hunting expedition."

"I was afraid of that."

Johnny raised the Hawken and sighted in. He picked the rider that he thought was probably their leader.

Johnny said, "Remember, shoot the man, not the horse. A dead horse is cover. A live horse is a great pile of panic."

"I would swear," Pierce said, "you were born for this kind of thing."

"I sure hope not."

Johnny waited, continuing to sight in on the leader. The riders were almost to the pass.

Pierce said, "When are you going to shoot?"

"I'm going to let them get fully into the pass. Then I'll take the leader. Then the rest of you'll open fire."

"Do Joe and Zack know to let you fire first?"

"They know."

"How? When did you tell them?"

"I didn't. But they know the way of things."

The riders came into the pass, keeping their horses to the same pace. Johnny could now easily see their number. Nineteen. They were shirtless and painted for war. One man's face was smeared red at the upper half, and with blue stripes running horizontally across his forehead and vertically down his cheeks and chin. Another had a white handprint across his jaw and mouth. The one Johnny thought to be the leader had painted the upper half of his face blue and the bottom half white. He had a wooden, ribbed breastplate across his chest. It wouldn't stop a bullet, but Johnny didn't figure it would matter. He was going to place his shot higher.

Johnny cocked the hammer and pulled the back trigger. Then he tapped the front trigger and the gun bucked and roared. The leader did a perfect backward somersault over the rump of the horse and landed in the dirt.

The riders were looking about quickly, trying to determine where the shot had come from. Then Pierce fired a rifle, and Joe and Zack fired.

Horses were spinning in panic. One rider fell to the ground.

Five riders kicked their horses into a gallop toward the center of the valley. Johnny had a Harper's Ferry flintlock to his shoulder and pulled the trigger. He had never used this rifle before and didn't know if the sight was right, so he pointed more than aimed and hoped his instinct was right. It was. One rider lurched, then fell from the horse.

Pierce fired his second rifle, and grabbed for the third one. There was no time for reloading.

Seven warriors were galloping directly toward them. Johnny had his third rifle in one hand, but then tossed it aside. It would do little good.

He stepped out into the open and drew his pistol. Time to do what he had done back in Texas. This situation wasn't much different.

But one rider reined up and called to the others. They did the same.

The rider called out, "Mac-cabe?"

Johnny squinted at him. It was hard to tell with the war paint, but Johnny thought it was one of the men who had been with Iron Hand.

"Mac-cabe!" the man called out. He rattled off some Lakota words to the men with him, and then said Johnny's name again.

One of the others said, "Mac-cabe."

Johnny stood, pistol in hand. He was holding it at his hip, ready to bring it up and begin firing if they charged.

But they didn't. They turned their horses and rode from the valley. Six more were lying dead in the pass.

Joe and Zack came running.

"What happened?" Zack said.

Pierce was smiling. "They realized who they were dealing with. The man who's medicine is strong enough to defeat Iron Hand."

Johnny said, "Grab your horses. Four of 'em went into the valley. We've got to get to the village."

They rode hard for the village. Johnny hadn't taken the time to reload his Hawken, but had just shoved it into the scabbard, and he had left the other rifles at the pass.

Bravo was a hard runner and was ahead of the other riders as they charged into the village.

They were too late. The four Lakota had arrived first.

Stands Tall had a bloody tomahawk in one hand, and three warriors were lying dead, scattered on the ground around him. He was bleeding from one shoulder.

Ainga came running for Johnny, and Many Lives was behind her.

Johnny said, "Where's the fourth one?"

"Dead," Many Lives said. Johnny then saw Many Lives had a bloody knife in his hand. "He learned not to challenge an old war chief."

Johnny looked at Ainga, and then turned his eyes toward Stands Tall, and he said, "Great warrior."

# 41

WINTER RETURNED, and Johnny and his men did what Joe called *hunkering down.* Spending much time in the teepee staying warm and drinking coffee.

Still, Bravo liked to run, so Johnny would saddle him up and take him across the valley floor. Often, Many Lives would join him.

One day, Many Lives said, "Red Sky Morning spending much time with Stands Tall, now. She see him different since attack of Lakota."

Johnny nodded. "I thought she might."

"You wise man, for one so young."

Johnny shrugged. "Some might say I'm a fool. Maybe they're right. A girl like Red Sky Morning doesn't come along often."

"When the time is right, you find the woman Great Spirt wants you to find."

"I hope so."

"You must trust, young one. Pierce says white man shamans call it *faith.*"

Johnny grinned. He wondered what the stodgy preacher back in Pennsylvania would have thought at being called a shaman.

One morning, Johnny woke suddenly. In his dreams, he had seen the faces of some of the men he had killed. The leader of the Lakota raiders. Iron Hand. Some of the men he had shot in a canyon in the Nations, when he was riding for Breaker Grant.

Sometimes he relived the gunfights in his sleep. Sometimes he just saw their faces looking at him with eyes that were sad or angry.

That day, he and Many Lives rode across the valley to the area Johnny thought would be good for a cabin.

It was there that Johnny told him of the dream. He said, "Indians believe in dreams and visions."

Many Lives nodded. "It's often how Great Spirit talks to us."

"What does my dream mean?"

"You have it before?"

Johnny nodded. "Many times. The men I have killed come back to me almost every night. Last night it was really bad. I was reliving the shootings. One after another. I woke up more tired than I was when I went to sleep."

Many Lives shrugged. "Sometimes a dream can mean one thing, sometimes another. What you think it means?"

"I don't know." Johnny paced a bit. The days were now a little warm and the snow would melt a bit, but then freeze again at night, so the snow was now hard and crusty. Johnny kicked a chunk of it and it sailed ten feet into the air as though he had kicked a ball.

He said, "Maybe I feel guilty for all of the killing."

"Maybe you just feel bad about it because you know life is sacred."

"If life is sacred, isn't it wrong to take it?"

Many Lives said, "All life is sacred. It given to us by Great Spirit. A gift. But if a man throws his away, it his choice. The Lakota would have killed the men at village. Maybe taken some of us back for torture and then death. They would take women back as slaves. That the Indian way. You killed the Lakota to save us. Killing was going to be done, but you chose not to let it happen to us."

Johnny thought he understood. "It's like the arrow of death was coming to the valley, and I changed its course."

Many Lives grinned. "Yes."

The weather grew warmer, but there was no strong, warm wind. The breeze was light and easy.

Joe said, "This ain't a chinook. This is spring."

They had been with the Shoshone nearly five months. Johnny's hair had grown, but he kept his face shaved so the Shoshone wouldn't call him *dog face*.

The women went to the lake for a bath. The water was cold and they had no soap, but the water was high in minerals and did a tolerable job. Then it was time for the men.

Joe stood with his rifle while Johnny and Zack took a swim. The water was so cold Johnny felt his toes going numb after just a few minutes, but when he came out, he felt clean. Then he stood watch while it was Joe's turn.

Within a week, the snow was fully melted, and wild flowers were starting to show their heads.

Johnny rode out to his little spot. The place he wanted to one day build a cabin. Many Lives came with him.

The stream was now flowing hard and strong with spring runoff. Johnny wasn't even going to attempt to get Bravo across, so he and Many Lives sat in the saddle and looked at the area that Johnny had taken such a liking to.

Johnny said, "I wanted to come back here one more time to say goodbye."

Many Lives nodded. "You leave soon?"

"I'm thinking so."

"We leave soon, too. Maybe in one more moon. Join with larger village to the south."

"Will you be back here next winter?"

Many Lives shrugged. "Not know. Things change. Old Indian ways are going away. We might have to winter with larger village. Strength in numbers."

"Because of the white man."

Many Lives nodded. "Because of the white man."

They were silent a moment. Johnny took a deep inhale of the mountain air. It was now tinged with the scent of wildflowers and of a land opening up and coming alive after a cold winter's sleep.

Many Lives said, "You be back?"

Johnny nodded. "I would like to. I hope you know, here or wherever I am, you are always welcome. You and your family."

Red Sky Morning was going to marry Stands Tall. She wanted to tell Johnny herself.

It was evening and even though the day had been warm, the nights could still be chilly. Johnny was in his father's coat and standing at the edge of the little village, watching the evening sunset rays paint a long flat cloud the color of a campfire.

Red Sky Morning walked to him, and she told him.

Johnny couldn't help but smile. "Stands Tall is a good man. I wasn't sure at first, but I've seen he is. A good warrior."

She returned the smile. "I know him for years. He was always there, trying to win my heart. And I did love him, but I never give myself to him. I didn't know the great warrior of my dreams was Stands Tall all along."

"In your dreams, did you see the face of the great warrior?"

She shook her head. "His face always hidden."

"You're a good woman, Ainga. The kind a man could be happy with for the rest of his life. I hope Stands Tall finds that happiness with you, and you with him."

"And you go back to white man's world, to find the girl Lura."

He nodded.

She said, "To hear her tell you why she go away."

"We leave tomorrow. We have a long ride ahead of us."

"I was hoping you could be here for wedding. We have before we all leave the valley to go further south."

"I would like that. But we need to get moving. Our supplies are running low."

"Will you come back to this valley?"

"One day, I might. I think I'll be leaving a piece of my heart here."

Johnny watched as she walked back to the teepee

of her father, and he thought he was going to be leaving a piece of his heart with her too.

The sun was barely in the sky as Johnny tightened the girth on Bravo's saddle. Joe was tying his bedroll to the back of his own saddle. Zack had made a rifle scabbard out of buckskin and tied it to his saddle, and he was pushing the rifle into it.

Pierce was there, and his wives. Many Lives came over, with his wives and Ainga. Stands Tall was walking with her.

Many Lives said to Johnny, "Be safe. Always remember, you are like a son to me."

"And you are like a father to me."

Johnny had found the Shoshone shook hands much like white men, so he extended his hand. Many Lives took it but then pulled Johnny in for an embrace.

Ainga then stepped forward. She said, "Things are not simple with us."

Johnny shook his head with a smile. He said, "Be safe. And be well."

"And you." She gave him a light embrace, and then a kiss on the cheek.

She said, "Find this Lura. Get the answers you need."

Then Stands Tall stepped forward. He extended his hand, and Johnny took it.

Johnny said, "You are the greatest warrior I ever fought."

Stands Tall's English was not good, but he nodded and said, "Mac-cabe fight good."

"Take care of her, Stands Tall. Treat her right."
He nodded.

Then the first wife of Many Lives stepped forward. The woman Johnny thought of as Scowly Woman.

He said, "Take care of them."

She nodded, and then surprised Johnny by wrapping her arms around him for a hug.

Pierce had shaken hands with Zack and Joe, and

now he extended his hand to Johnny.

Pierce said, "You three be safe in your journeys."

"You also. I want to thank you for all you've done for us. I hope to see you again."

Pierce nodded. "Even if you don't, I have a feeling we'll be hearing about you. Men like you tend to cut a wide swath through history."

Joe was grinning. "Brings it on himself."

Johnny had to smile.

Piece said, "He does indeed."

They mounted up.

"We've got a lot of miles to cover," Johnny said. "Let's ride."

They turned their horses toward the pass.

When they arrived there, the site of their skirmish with Lakota raiders, they reined up. Johnny turned for a look over his shoulder at the valley.

Zack said, "I like this place. Do you think you'll ever be back?"

Johnny said, "I'd like to say yes, but you never know what the future holds."

"That you don't," Joe said. "It's like the twisting and turning of a fast moving river."

Johnny gave him a curious glance. "Getting poetic, are you?"

Joe shrugged. "Matt ain't here. I figure someone's gotta do it."

Johnny laughed.

# PART FIVE

## *The Circle M*

### 42

Montana
April, 1882

BREE SAID, "This is the lookout where you and Many Lives stood."

Johnny nodded. "And the little place where I wanted to build a cabin, that's where the house now stands."

"I never knew you had a gunfight right out there in the pass."

"Seems so long ago. And yet, it seems like just yesterday. It's hard to believe it's been, what?" He did the quick math in his head, "Twenty-three years."

"Did you ever see them again? Many Lives and Ainga? And Stands Tall?"

Johnny shook his head. "I heard talk that the great war chief Many Lives had died at Bear River, back in sixty-three. I tried to get confirmation. I rode to an Army fort and asked questions, but they weren't sure. They had never heard the names Many Lives or Stands Tall. One Army sergeant called me a dirty Indian lover, and that cost him his front teeth."

She shook her head. "That's so wrong. Why can't people live in peace?"

"I asked Many Lives that once, on one of our rides through the valley that winter. He said it's the way of things, when two cultures that are so different come together. There's bound to be misunderstandings and fear, which lead to conflict. Eventually war. The stronger of the two cultures survives. He said there were people in this land when the Shoshone first arrived, and those people were driven back or killed. And there were probably people here when those people first arrived."

"Still, it seems wrong."

Johnny nodded. "Much of the world seems wrong, but all we can do is take care of our own little part of it. Treat people right. It doesn't matter what part of the world their ancestors come from, what the color of their skin is, or their religion. We're all children of the Great Spirit, or God. Many people disagree with me on that and probably always will. But it's the way your Aunt Ginny and I taught you and the boys. And the way Jessica and I are teaching Cora."

"And when Charles and I have kids, it's the way we'll teach them."

"Then you'll be leaving the world a better place."

Bree had a cup of coffee in one hand, and she took a sip.

"So, when you and Zack and Uncle Joe left the valley, did you head directly to San Francisco?"

Johnny nodded. "As direct as we could, back then. There was no railroad. Many parts of the west didn't even have stage coaches. We rode overland, just like we had come. We stopped at Fort Bridger for supplies, and I think Joe was hoping he would see Kate Waddell there, but he wouldn't admit it. I asked about the wagon train, but they had headed out a month earlier."

"And then you got to San Francisco and met Aunt Ginny for the first time."

Johnny nodded. "And I think the Earth shook and lighting struck."

Bree laughed. "I bet it did."

# 43

Sun Francisco
July, 1859

JOHNNY THOUGHT San Francisco might be even bigger than St. Louis. Buildings seemed to cover the hills, and then worked their way down to the harbor. And the harbor was filled with ships, their masts standing tall.

Johnny still had some money left over, so he bought a room in a hotel. It wasn't the best hotel in the city, but it was far removed from some of the flea-ridden establishments toward the edge of town.

He bought baths for all three of them. They sat in tubs while their clothes were taken care of at a Chinese laundry.

Zack had a professional shave and haircut.

As he rose out of the barber chair, in clean clothes, he rubbed one hand against this smooth jaw and said, "I feel human again."

They had been on the trail for months, so Johnny sat in the chair and the barber gave him a shave.

The barber was a man about the age Pa had been, with a waxed, curly mustache and hair that was slicked down and parted in the middle.

He got out a pair of scissors, but Johnny said, "No, just the shave only."

The man was puzzled. "No haircut?"

Johnny hadn't had a haircut since Greenville, a few weeks before he was given Lura's note. About ten months ago. His hair was about five inches long in back and touching the base of his neck, and his ears were covered.

He said, "No. No haircut."

Zack said, "If it gets much longer, you'll be able to tie it back in a tail."

"Maybe I will."

Then it dawned on Zack. "Like Many Lives."

"The Shoshone wear their hair long for a reason. I think it's a good reason. So, just the shave."

When the barber was done with the shave, Joe stepped in. His hair was now well past his shoulders, and Johnny thought maybe he now understood why. The Cheyenne probably had similar beliefs.

Joe had kept his face clean-shaven when he was with the Cheyenne, to look pleasing to the girl he loved, but he had stopped shaving when she left him. Now his beard fell almost to his chest.

Joe said, "Been doin' some of what you call reconnaissance. She's here, all right. Livin' with her aunt in a big house in a high-falutin' part of town. Near the water but back a ways. The house ain't what Breaker Grant lived in, but it's every bit as nice as the McCarty ranch house."

Johnny thought for a moment. "I don't remember her mentioning that her aunt was rich."

Joe shrugged. "Well, looks like it. The aunt's name is Virginia Brackston. Sole owner of Brackston Shipping, and part owner of a number of other businesses. She's up to her eyeballs in cash."

"Don't matter any. I'm planning to knock on that door and have Lura say it to me. Look me in the eyes and tell me she never loved me like I thought she did."

"So what do you do after she tells you?" Zack said. "Go back to the McCarty Ranch and see if you can have your old job back? Or go back to Nebraska Territory and find Many Lives and his band of Shoshone?"

"Don't know. I'll cross that bridge when I get to it, I guess."

"When you gonna go ask her?" Joe said.

"Right now."

Johnny went alone. Joe and Zack volunteered to go along but he felt this was something he needed to do alone.

He could have bought a Sunday-go-to-meeting

suit, and ridden up to the house in a carriage, all proper-like. But he felt he needed to do this as himself, not putting on airs. So in his range shirt and vest, with his guns buckled on and his wide-brimmed hat pulled down over his temples, he rode up to the Brackston house on Bravo.

The horse was brushed down and in fresh, iron shoes, and his hooves clapped along loudly on the cobblestone street. Bravo seemed to be holding his head extra high, and Johnny wondered if he felt proud, all clean and with new shoes on.

Johnny found the house. It was three floors high, with a widow's walk on the roof, and a porch that wrapped around the front. There was also another, smaller porch at the second floor. A black, wrought iron fence lined the property, and there was a gate.

Johnny didn't know proper protocol for a house like this. If he was supposed to somehow let them inside the house know he was here, then some butler-type of fellow would come out and open the gate. So he said the heck with it. He was a cowboy and wasn't going to be anything but. He reached down from the saddle and opened the gate himself and rode through.

There was no hitching rail here. He didn't expect there would be.

A flagstone walkway led to the wrap-around porch. He rode Bravo up to it and then swung out of the saddle. He left Bravo's rein trailing.

He walked up the steps to the porch. There was a large double door, and long narrow windows that ran vertically at either side of the door. The windows had white, lacy curtains. One of them moved suddenly, so Johnny figured the folks inside knew he was here.

He had to admit, he was a little nervous. This would be the first time he had seen Lura in almost a year.

What would happen when she said she didn't want him in her life? That she hadn't loved him the way he had loved her? How would he feel?

He walked across the porch to the big double doors. He reached up to a brass door knocker and gave it a couple tries.

The door opened. A woman stood there. Johnny would put her age at about forty. She rose a little past his shoulders and had brown hair pulled back in a bun. Spectacles were perched on her nose.

"You must be *him*," she said. She said it firmly, like she figured her voice was law.

He pulled off his hat. "If by *him* you mean Johnny McCabe, then you're right. I'm here to see Lura. I know she's here."

"You took long enough to get here."

That caught him by surprise. "You've been expecting me?"

"If you're even half the young man Lura seems to think you are, then yes. We've been expecting you."

She was standing firm, though. Not stepping aside to let him in. She was fixing him with a glare, like she expected to cut through him just by looking at him. He gave the glare right back to her. He had never backed down from anyone and didn't plan to start now.

He heard Lura's voice from inside. "Aunt Ginny?"

Without taking her gaze from Johnny, the woman called back to her, "You have a guest."

Only then did the woman step aside.

Johnny went in.

The entryway was large enough to picket a couple of horses, and beyond it was a stairway with a mahogany bannister. Partway down the stairs was Lura.

She looked as beautiful as he remembered her, and he found for a moment he was no longer angry. Her hair was pulled back in a bun, and he found it would still be easy to get lost in her hauntingly blue eyes.

It was a moment before he realized she had a bundle in her arms. A baby.

Johnny blinked with surprise. First the old woman said they had been expecting him, and now Lura had a baby?

"Hello, Johnny," Lura said.

Johnny nodded. He didn't know what to say.

Lura descended to the first floor. She then pulled back the blanket a little so Johnny could have a full look at the baby's face.

Lura said, "Meet your son. Joshua McCabe."

# 44

"MY SON?" JOHNNY LOOKED at the little sleeping face, then back at Lura. "I have a son?"

She nodded.

"How?" he said.

The woman shut the door and said, "If we have to explain that, then you're in worse shape than I thought."

Johnny gave her a look and said, "I know how."

Then he looked back at Lura and said, "But, how?"

Lura said, "Why didn't you come here when my parents told you? I've been waiting so long. I thought what we had was real. I never thought a baby would frighten you away."

He blinked with surprise again. "When your parents told me? They never told me about this."

"Then, what did they tell you?"

Johnny told her, telling it all quickly. He had never been one to talk much, but the words spilled out of him.

It was Lura's turn to blink with surprise. A tear ran down to a cheekbone.

She said, "How could you think I would ever write you a letter like that?"

He shrugged. "Because I had the letter. It looked like your handwriting."

The woman who had opened the door said, "I suspect there is treachery afoot."

Johnny looked at her. He had forgotten she was there.

"Johnny," Lura said. "Meet my aunt, Ginny."

Ginny was fixing him with an iron gaze again.

Johnny said, "Yeah. We met at the door."

Lura said to her, "What do you mean, treachery?"

Ginny said, "I mean, your father, dear."

Johnny was caught a little by surprise. He

wouldn't have said anything bad about Doc Buzzard in front of Lura. But Lura didn't even flinch.

Ginny softened her gaze a little—but not much—toward Johnny and said, "Do you have the letter on you?"

Johnny shook his head. "I threw it in the fire."

"That's not very helpful."

"Put yourself in my place."

Ginny reared herself up. Somehow the little woman seemed a whole foot taller. "In your place, I think I would have believed in Lura and questioned the letter."

Johnny didn't know what to say. He wanted to stand strong in front of this woman. He didn't back down from anyone. And yet, Pa had said more than once, don't try to defend an argument you know is wrong.

Ginny said to Lura, "I'll take the baby. You two have a lot to talk over."

The house had two parlors, and they took one.

Lura said, "Would you like a scotch? Brandy? A glass of wine?"

Johnny shook his head.

They sat on a sofa that faced a hearth.

"I'm so sorry," Johnny said. "If she's right...if I didn't believe in you or in us enough...I don't know what to say."

"Start from the beginning. The letter."

Johnny told her about it in more detail. How he had come back from the extended roundup. The herd had been scattered by a tornado, and he found her gone.

"Your mother said you had gone away and didn't want her telling me where you were, and she gave me your letter."

"Do you remember what it said?"

"I can almost quote it word-for-word."

He did. She looked at him wide-eyed.

She said, "It really looked like my handwriting?"

He nodded. "I've only seen it a couple of times, but I was convinced."

"How could you believe I would have written such a thing?"

"I'm so sorry. But you have to understand, the whole thing was such a shock. I suppose I wasn't thinking clearly. And your mother was so convincing. She looked like she felt sorry for me."

Lura laid a hand gently to the side of his face. "I really shouldn't blame you. I might have felt the same way."

"But how could this happen?"

She shrugged. "You don't know my father."

"I don't feel right saying something bad about your father in front of you. And really, I don't know him all that well. People say unkind things about him, but I should know better than to take stock in someone based on what's said about him."

Lura shook her head. "In this case, it's all true. Even worse, I'm afraid."

She told him how she had found she was pregnant, not long after he had left for the roundup. And her father had threatened to kill her if she didn't leave town. She also told him that her father admitted to hiring the man who had tried to kill them.

He said, "So, it's your father's money I've been spending all this time."

He told her about the money Joe had taken from the killer's pocket.

"I'm so sorry," she said. Another tear ran down her face. "Maybe I should have tried to find some way to contact you. I was just so afraid he'd have you killed."

"Better men than him have tried to kill me. So far, they haven't been successful."

She had to grin. "So I've seen."

He returned the grin. "And maybe I shouldn't have let myself sink so much into sorrow. Maybe if I had been more clear-headed, I would have figured where you had went and come here in the first place."

"Maybe we're both sorry."

"Maybe we're the ones who shouldn't be. After all, none of this is your fault, and it's not really mine, either."

"We'll deal with him later."

He took her in his arms and they kissed long. And then they held each other even longer.

Then he said, "We have a son?"

She nodded.

He said, "There's only one thing we need that we don't have."

"What's that?"

He looked her in the eye. "Lura Marker, you need to make an honest man out of me."

She laughed. And so did he. Long and hard.

## 45

JOHNNY MCCABE AND LURA MARKER WERE married in the garden behind the main house. The sky overhead was a deep, California blue, and they stood beneath a wooden archway that was covered with vines. Hedges were trimmed and formed a little row. The wedding was small, and wooden folding chairs had been brought out for the small number of guests.

Joe stood up with Johnny. He had said he would shave his beard and cut his hair if Johnny asked him to.

Johnny said, "No, I've had enough of people trying to appear to be something they're not. What's Matt call it? Pretense? I want you to be yourself."

Aunt Ginny stood up with Lura. Ginny was going to have the maid, Julia, tend to Joshua, but Lura wanted the baby up with her too, so Ginny held him.

Johnny had wanted to contact Matt, but Lura was afraid her father would find out.

She said, "I don't want anything to happen to spoil our day. And I'm afraid he'll try to kill me. Or even worse, the baby."

Johnny understood. He figured Matt would, too. Johnny wasn't afraid of Doc Buzzard, but he knew he couldn't be with Lura and the baby every moment. And he didn't like the idea of Lura having to hide in Ginny's house, fearing for her life.

The minister was from a local Methodist church. He recited the vows, which Johnny and Lura repeated, and Johnny slipped the ring on her finger.

He said, "With this ring, I thee wed."

He kissed her, and the small crowd of neighbors and friends from Ginny's church clapped their hands. Joe and Zack let out loud whoops and cheers. Johnny smiled and Lura laughed, and Johnny kissed his bride again.

Ginny's gift to them was a two-day cruise up and down the coast in a small two-mast schooner. It had belonged to Ginny's father, and he used it when he needed to travel. He had taken the ship to China twice, and at one time was a part owner of a shipping outfit in Shanghai. After he died, she kept the ship, even though she seldom used it.

There was a captain, a man about fifty with a white beard and wearing a black Greek sailor's cap. A man was at the wheel, and there was a deck hand. All that was necessary for a two-day cruise along the coast. The crew was available if Lura or Johnny needed anything, but otherwise the newlyweds had their privacy. Johnny and Lura had the main cabin, and the captain and crew slept below decks.

On their first night, the sails had been drawn and the captain laid anchor about a thousand feet off the shore.

The night was warm, and Johnny was in his range shirt and canvas cowhand pants. He had left his vest and hat in the cabin, though his guns were still in place.

Lura was in a nightgown and robe, and her hair was falling freely down her back.

Johnny leaned his elbows on a gunwale, looking off toward the shore. He had a goblet of white wine in one hand. Lura was beside him, holding her glass with two hands. Johnny's free hand was around her shoulders, pulling her in close.

The sea was calm and carried a reflection of the moon that shimmied and danced.

The shore was dark. They could hear an occasional night bird.

"It's so beautiful out here," she said.

Johnny nodded. He looked at her and said, "But what I'm looking at is the most beautiful of all."

She smiled. "Are you always going to say things like that?"

He nodded. "Most likely. You'd best get used to it."

"I don't know if I ever will."

She took a sip of wine. She didn't dare drink too much of it because she didn't want it to get into her mother's milk.

She said, "I hope Joshua's all right."

Johnny grinned and gave her shoulder a little squeeze. "I'm sure he's fine. I'm sure your aunt and Julia can handle things."

"It's just that I've never been away from him for this long."

"How long have you been away from him?"

She had to think for a moment. "An hour, once."

Johnny laughed. He said, "Your aunt strikes me as capable. She doesn't have much use for me, though."

"Oh, on the contrary. She thinks quite highly of you."

He gave her a look that said, *are you serious?*

He said, "The way the woman glares at me, you'd think I was the last person on Earth she wanted in her home."

Lura shook her head. "Aunt Ginny is a creature of subtleties. It takes a while to get used to her. But she's full of love and generosity. She cares more than anyone I've ever met."

She told Johnny about the night before their wedding. Ginny had made a veil for Lura to wear, and Ginny said, "He's a good one, Lura."

Lura nodded. "I know. He is."

"He's a solid, upright young man. Most men wither when I fix them with the Gaze. Until now, only one other man has been able to withstand it. I've mentioned Addison to you."

Lura nodded. The young man who was the love of Aunt Ginny's life, and who had been lost at sea.

Ginny said, "Johnny not only can withstand it, but he can give it back."

Lura told Johnny about it, and he nodded. He said, "I think I'm starting to understand her. She's a warrior."

Lura grinned. "I've never thought about her that way, but I think you're right."

## 46

GINNY SAID, "Now that you're back, I'd like to give you a second wedding gift."

They were at the dinner table. Joe and Zack were there, too. They were staying in guest rooms upstairs.

Lura said, "Aunt Ginny, you've already been more than generous."

"Hush, child. I can't very well give a gift that lasts only two days and call it done. You two are going to be building a life together."

She looked at Johnny. "Have you given any thoughts to what vocation you're going to pursue?"

He shrugged. "The only thing I'm good at that could earn any sort of money around here would be cattle."

"And I take it you've decided against returning to the McCarty Ranch."

"Well, I need to ride out there for a visit. I need to see my brother Matt, and square things with Mister McCarty. But no, living anywhere near Greenville would probably be out of the question."

"Then, allow me to present the second portion of my wedding gift."

She looked at Julia, who brought over an envelope.

She said, "In this envelope is the deed to two thousand acres of grassland a day's ride southeast of the city. Father had intended on expanding into cattle, but then his untimely death prevented it. I still have the land. Two thousand acres won't be enough to run a sizable herd of longhorns, of course, but the land beyond is open range. It is within riding distance of Greenville, but I daren't think it's close enough to be of any concern to parties we need to be concerned about."

"That's okay," Johnny said. "I've told Joe and Zack all about it."

"Regardless, I am concerned the mention of the

man's name might make the wine go bad."

Joe let out a guffaw. Johnny grinned, and Ginny gave him a little hint of a grin. Johnny was finding he liked this woman.

Johnny said to Lura, "Are you all right?"

She was grinning, too. "Yes, I'm fine. I lived with him a lot of years. Nothing that can be said about him would hurt my feelings."

Ginny said, "This land is undeveloped. You would have to do any building yourself."

Johnny nodded. "That can be done."

Lura said to him, "We would need cattle."

"I can see if Mister McCarty would sell me some stock on credit. There's also wild stock running through the canyons of southern New Mexico Territory."

He looked across the table to Joe and Zack. "We'll be needing some hands. Not that we'd be able to pay anything at first. Meals and a bunk would be all we could provide, until we sell some stock."

Zack said, "Well, I think that's the best offer I've had in a long time. I'll take it."

Joe grinned. "Count me in."

# 47

LURA AND LITTLE JOSHUA STAYED with Ginny while Johnny and the boys rode out to the McCarty Ranch.

As they rode into the ranch yard, Evans was leaning his back against the bunkhouse wall, rolling a cigarette. He looked up at the riders and let out a whoop.

Johnny rode over to him. "Hey, don't you have anything better to do than lounge around?"

"Sorry, Boss," he said with a grin.

Johnny reached down from the saddle to shake his hand.

Johnny said, "How've you been?"

"Fine, Boss. Are you all right?"

Johnny nodded. "It's been a rough year, but things are panning out nicely."

Evans banged one fist on the bunkhouse door and called out, "Hey! The Boss is here!"

Quint came out, and Valdez

Quint gave a squinting smile, and said, "Well, I'll be. Welcome home."

Johnny reached down for more handshakes.

"Where can I find my brother?"

Evan said, "At the main house. Some things have changed while you were gone. Matt and Miss Verna are married, and they have a young'un. Mister McCarty has retired, and Matt runs the family businesses. And Quint's the boss, now."

Quint nodded. "That's a fact. Matt made me the ramrod."

Johnny said, "I can't think of a better man to be the ramrod of this place."

"Are you back for good, now? If so, I'll step down because I've never met anyone who can lead men like you."

Johnny shook his head. "I'm just here for a visit, that's all. I think you're the man for the job, Quint. I think it's long overdue."

Johnny looked from him to the other two. "Of course, if this old scoundrel doesn't treat you fair, you ride on down to my place. I'm gonna be setting up a ranch of my own south of here."

Valdez was grinning. "We'll keep that in mind."

Johnny, Joe and Zack rode on to the stable. Moses Timmons was there, in a leather apron and working with a hammer on an anvil, trying to shape a piece of iron into a horse shoe.

He looked up and broke into a wide grin. "Johnny McCabe! Joe! Zack!"

He left the horse shoe and the tongs holding it on the anvil, and there were handshakes all around.

He rubbed Bravo's nose. "Hello, Bravo. This here galoot treating you right?"

Johnny said, "Oh, he's been all over the country. All the way to the mountains, in northern Nebraska Territory. Wintered with a band of Shoshone."

Moses looked at him like he thought Johnny was joshing him. "You serious?"

Johnny nodded. "Now I'm back in California. I'm married to Lura and life just can't be better."

Moses nodded with a big smile. "You deserve it. Give her my best."

They left their horses with Moses and walked to the main house. Johnny put his knuckles to the door.

They waited a moment, and then Moses's son greeted them. He was now in a black tie and tails.

He looked at them passively. For all they knew, he didn't recognize them. But then, that had been the same expression on his face when he shot Ern Cabot out of the saddle.

Johnny said, "I was wondering if Matt was in."

"Do you have an appointment?"

Johnny grinned. "I don't have the patience, boy. And I won't be as easy to deal with as Ern Cabot was."

Timmons stepped aside. Johnny walked past him, followed by Joe and Zack.

Zack said to Timmons, "I like the way he makes an appointment."

Johnny figured he knew where to find Matt. He pulled open the double doors that opened into Mr. McCarty's study. Matt was there, behind the door.

"Well, bless me," Matt said with a wide smile, rising to his feet.

Matt was in a tie and jacket, and Johnny saw Matt now had a mustache.

Johnny strode across the floor and Matt came out from behind his desk. A handshake was followed by a hug, then the same for Joe. Zack got a handshake and a slap on the shoulder.

"Where have you been?" Matt said. "I got the letter you mailed from Fort Bridger. What were you doing way out there?"

"It's been a busy year," Johnny said. "Hey, what's that growing on your upper lip? You been forgetting to shave?"

"Looks like a caterpillar," Joe said with a grin.

Matt said, "*You* should talk, with that beard you look like a grizzly."

They laughed, and Matt said, "I'm running the whole thing, now. All of the McCarty properties. I thought I should look a little distinguished. Besides," he gave the mustache a rub with one finger, "Verna likes it."

As if on cue, Verna said from the door, "Why, Johnny. Joe."

Johnny turned to face her. She looked about as she had, but now she was wearing a dress that was more gown than dress. Her hair was in some sort of fashion that created little ringlets that fell down along her neck in back.

"Verna," he said.

"I didn't know you were in town. Are you staying long?"

She was smiling, but with a smile that wasn't really a smile.

"Not long. We'll be out of your hair soon."

She laughed. "Oh, Matthew. Your brother always makes me laugh."

"That's Johnny," Joe said. "A barrel full of jokes."

Verna said to Zack, "And have I had the pleasure?"

He pulled off his hat. "Zack Johnson, ma'am. I rode with Johnny with the Rangers down in Texas for a while. I also worked for him here, for a short time."

She held out her hand, and to Zack's credit, he didn't grab it and give it a manly shake. He grasped her hand gently. Johnny didn't know Zack was that cultured. But, he supposed, he really didn't know much about Zack.

Verna said, "I'm sure you're about to break out cigars, and I don't much care for the smell, so I'll leave you men. Nice to meet you," she said to Zack, and to Joe and Johnny, "And it's great to see you both again."

Once she was gone from the room, Matt said, "I like the way she thinks."

There was a cigar box on his desk, so he flipped the lid open and handed them out.

By the fireplace were a sofa and two Queen Anne chairs, so they all sat and lit their cigars.

They talked about the past year. Johnny told of the ride north and spending the winter with the Shoshone. And of his wedding to Lura.

Matt said, "I wonder who wrote that letter?"

Johnny figured Matt would relay everything he said to Verna—Johnny had no secrets from Lura and doubted Matt did from Verna. But Johnny didn't want Verna to know anything that he didn't want Doc Buzzard knowing. He wouldn't put it past Verna and the doctor to team up, as they both probably considered Johnny a mutual enemy.

Johnny shrugged and said, "I doubt we'll ever know."

Zack and Joe both looked at Johnny. They followed his lead and said nothing.

Matt told of the past year at the ranch. He and Verna had been married only two months after Johnny left.

He said, "We found she was in the family way. A lot of that going around, lately."

Johnny grinned and nodded.

"So we moved the wedding up."

Joe said, "So, we hear you're runnin' this whole shindig now."

Matt nodded. "Frank decided to retire. He had me shadow him for a couple of months, learning the various details of running things, and then he retired. I know he would love to see you, but he and Lorraine are down in Mexico, right now. An old friend and business partner of his has a hacienda on the ocean. He invited Frank down for a few months."

Johnny said, "And you made Quint the ramrod. Good choice."

"Yeah, he's working out fine. Frank wasn't sure he had the leadership skills for it, but he's earned a lot of respect among the men and they fall in line."

Eventually, the talk got around to Ginny's gift of range land.

Johnny said, "I'd like to start up a herd. There's wild stock in New Mexico territory, but it would be easier if we could start by buying some local stock."

"How much do you need?" Matt said. "Just say the word."

"Well, the thing is, I don't have any money."

"Johnny, your credit is as good as gold around here. Not only because we're brothers, but because of all you did for this ranch. We've followed up on your idea of expanding the horse business. We're supplying horses to stage companies and the Army. We're making real cash from it. Corry's still the primary bronc buster, and he has two men who work for him now. Frank is so happy about the business, he'd probably straight-out give you some stock."

Johnny didn't want any gifts. He wanted to feel

like he was earning it. In the end, he allowed Matt to sell him five hundred head on credit at twenty percent of the value.

Matt said, "I'll loan you Evans and Valdez to get the stock down to your range. You can pay me back whenever you can. I'll never mention it again."

Johnny said, "Matt, I don't know what to say."

Matt shrugged. "You'd do the same for me."

Matt invited all three of them to stay for dinner, but Joe said, "Thanks, but I got me some business I gotta take care of in town."

Joe, forever the mysterious one.

Matt looked at Johnny with a shrug and said, "I hope you three will all stay the night. I won't take no for an answer."

Joe rode into town as the sun was drifting toward the western horizon. *Greenville hasn't changed much*, he thought.

He rode up to the doctor's office. A sign was nailed in place above the door, and it read, J. MARKER, M.D.

He swung out of the saddle and tried the door. It was unlocked.

He found Doc Buzzard behind his desk.

The doctor rose to his feet. "Can I help you with something?"

Joe said, "You don't recognize me, do you?"

But then, the doctor did. He reached into his desk and grabbed a revolver. He had it out and was about to aim it at Joe, but Joe had crossed the floor and grabbed the man by the wrist. Joe just squeezed, and Marker yelped and let go of the gun. It fell to the desk.

"You know who I am and why I'm here," Joe said.

He grabbed the doctor by his vest and yanked him upward until the doctor was standing on his toes.

"We know what you done," Joe said. "You threatened to kill your daughter, and you somehow got that letter writ. My brother would never kill a man, except in self-defense. You'll be safe from him as long as you leave him alone. But I ain't my brother. Leave me and mine alone, or I'll stick a knife in your gut and watch you die slow. And I just might lift your scalp while I wait. You understand?"

The doctor tried to say *yes*, but all that came out was a stammer, "y-y-y."

Joe let go of Marker, and Marker fell backward and bounced off of his chair and landed on the floor.

Joe picked up the revolver. "Nice lookin' gun. Colt thirty-six, it looks like."

He tucked it into his belt, along with the revolver that was already there.

Marker said, "I'll send for the marshal."

"You do and I'll stick a knife in your gut. Weren't you listenin'?"

Marker said nothing.

Joe said, "Good day to you, then."

He walked out the door. He swung into the saddle and rode on out of town.

Now all they had to worry about, Joe thought, was surviving a night under the same roof with Verna.

## 48

IT TOOK a day to get the cattle to the new range. Johnny thanked Evans and Valdez for their help. Evans and Valdez spent the night by the campfire on Johnny's range and headed back in the morning.

Matt also threw in six horses of Johnny's choice, because he said a ranch needs a remuda. Matt said to consider them a wedding present.

Johnny said to Zack and Joe, "Three men ought to be able to handle five hundred head."

Zack nodded. "As long as we're not moving 'em anywhere."

They set up camp in a gravelly area where the grass wasn't good. Off to the south, a high hill overlooked the camp. In the other three directions, the land was made up of low, gentle hills. Mostly grass with occasional scrub oaks, except one stand of alders that grew about fifty feet away. There were also a couple of apple trees, one that grew nearby.

"I'm gonna head back to the city tomorrow and bring Lura out," Johnny said that night, with a campfire crackling away and a tin cup of coffee in one hand. "Will you two be all right till I get back?"

Zack said, "I think we can handle things, Boss."

"I'm going to come back with a wagon full of supplies. Maybe see if I can find an old Army tent. I have a little money left, and if I have to, I'll see if Miss Ginny will float me a loan."

Joe dug out a can of beans and dumped them into the skillet. He said, "Wouldn't hurt for one of us to do a little huntin' tomorrow. Bring in some deer. We ate a lot better'n this on the trail to Nebraska and back."

Zack nodded his head. "That we did."

Johnny said, "We've got to think of a brand. All those cows have the Bar M brand."

Zack said, "You know, Matt's in a pretty good situation. He and his wife will likely inherit that ranch.

He won't have to change the brand."

"I been thinkin' about a brand," Joe said.

He took a stick and drew a capital letter M in the dirt, and drew a line under it.

He said, "That's about how the brand looks now."

Zack nodded. "That's it."

"How about this?" Joe extended the line up and around the M, in a sort of almost circle.

"The Circle M," Johnny said.

Joe nodded.

Zack said, "Has a nice sound to it."

At sunrise, Johnny mounted up and rode Bravo back to San Francisco.

He talked to Ginny about a loan, and she said, "Nonsense. You're family. The money's yours."

"With all due respect, I don't want charity."

"It's not charity. Your wife is my sole heir. The Brackston estate is sizable. Consider it an advance on your inheritance."

Johnny filled an open-backed wagon with supplies, and a team of two good horses were hitched to it.

Ginny was going along, too. She had never actually seen the land. She was in a two-seated carriage. The man who handled her horses and served as her chauffeur, an old vaquero by the name of Martinez, handled the reins. Ginny sat in back, alongside Lura and the baby.

Johnny had insisted Lura and Josh ride in the carriage. With its springs, it would be a much softer ride.

With Bravo tied to the back of the supply wagon, they started out. Where Johnny had made it in four hours riding Bravo, the wagons moved much more slowly. They left the house at seven in the morning, and the shadows were stretching long when they arrived at the camp.

Johnny helped Lura down from the wagon, and

then Ginny.

Ginny was holding the baby. She looked about and said, "It doesn't look like much. It's all open. I don't know what I was expecting."

"It's rangeland," Johnny said. "It's exactly right."

Lura took Johnny's hand. "It's ours. I think it's beautiful."

"I was thinking we could build the house right here."

"Right where we're standing?"

He nodded. Then he aimed one hand toward the south. "We can put a barn right there, near that hill. And a small bunkhouse for Joe and Zack."

"What'll we do for water?"

"We'll dig us a well. See those alders? There's bushes growing around 'em. Junipers and such. They wouldn't be growing there if there wasn't water. We'll dig right near there, and then run a pipe to the house. Maybe a hand pump in the kitchen."

Ginny was dubious. "Are you sure this is what you want, Lura? It all seems so rustic."

"Oh, yes, Aunt Ginny." She spun around with her arms held out into the air. "It's all just so perfect."

Ginny had an old circus tent. It had been left behind from a circus that had passed through San Francisco years ago. She generally kept it folded up in a shed, but she had told Johnny he should take it.

Johnny and Zack set it up not far from the campfire site.

"Where's Joe?" Lura said.

Zack said, "Off with the herd."

Lura didn't know much about cattle, so Johnny said, "Sometimes it's good to ride about when a herd is on new range, while they get used to it."

"And we don't need fences? I've always wondered about that."

Johnny shook his head. "A longhorn needs a lot of range to graze on, and there must be two million acres of open range to the east. We'll keep an eye on the herd, and make sure they don't roam too far."

"So, a lot of it is just watching them."

He nodded. "And making sure no trouble starts."

"Poachers," Ginny said.

Johnny nodded again. "We call 'em rustlers, but essentially, yeah. And every so often we might need to move the herd to fresh grass."

"We've gotta brand 'em," Zack said. "It won't be fun branding full-grown critters."

Johnny got a stick and drew the Bar M brand in the dirt, and showed Lura and Ginny Joe's idea.

"The Circle M," Lura said. "I never thought I'd be a rancher."

"What do you think of the idea?"

"I just love it."

As it grew dark, they settled in for the night. Ginny had brought food with her and insisted on cooking them a meal of something more than beans from a can.

Once they had eaten, Ginny had Martinez fetch a rocking chair from the wagon. Johnny spread out a blanket on the ground for Lura and himself to sit on. A cradle had been brought, and Joshua was asleep.

Johnny said, "We're going to have to get some lumber out here for the house. And we'll build a corral. We're going to go to the mountains and bring back some mustangs."

Ginny said, "Are you skilled in bronc busting?"

Martinez was standing by the fire with a tin cup filled with coffee. He was in black pants with silver conchos running down each leg and a range shirt.

He said, "Breaking a horse can be dangerous work."

Johnny nodded. "We're not going to do it the traditional way. We're going to do it the Shoshone way."

"How's that?" Lura said.

Johnny described the process.

While he was talking, Lura reached up to the back

of his head and ran her fingers through his hair, pulling it gently back and down.

She said, "Your hair's getting long."

He told her what Many Lives had told him about hair.

Ginny said, "They sound like a spiritual people."

Johnny nodded. "Their religion is about respecting life. When they kill an animal for food, they say a little prayer song to thank the animal for its sacrifice."

Joe came riding in. "Hope I didn't miss supper."

Ginny said, "We're keeping some warm for you."

"Any trouble?" Johnny said.

"Nope. All's well. There's a stream about a mile east of here. The herd could smell the water and all headed over there."

"A mile is kind of far," Johnny said.

Zack said, "Maybe I'll ride on out. Ride a little night herd."

Johnny nodded.

Joe said, "I'll go along, too, after I eat. You," he looked at Johnny, "stay here with the women. Zack and I'll handle it."

Lura was a little concerned, but Johnny said, "It's just part of tending the herd. Everything will be all right."

The following morning, Johnny talked with Lura about living arrangements. He wanted her and Josh to stay with Ginny in the city. Johnny would be there to visit all that he could.

"Living out of a tent wouldn't be right for a woman and a baby," he said.

"I don't like the idea," Lura said. "I don't want to be away from you that much."

They were standing near the morning fire. Coffee was boiling away in the kettle and Ginny was in her rocker with the baby.

Joe and Zack had ridden back to camp a little

after midnight and were still rolled in their blankets.

Johnny said, "I don't want to be away from you either. As soon as we can build a house, you and Josh will move in."

"How long will that be?"

He shrugged. "We have to sell some beeves. And we have to build a herd. It could be a while."

Ginny said, "Oh, for goodness sakes, John. I'll have some lumber brought out and you can start building next week."

Johnny sighed with impatience. "Look, Miss Ginny, I know you mean well, but like I said before, I don't want charity."

It was Ginny's turn to sigh with impatience. She got out of the rocker and handed the baby to Lura.

She said to Johnny, "Two things. One—it's not charity. No one can start from absolutely nothing. Everyone has to have a helping hand originally, one way or another. My father did. Your father probably did."

Johnny nodded. He had to admit, she was right. Pa and Uncle Jake were given their farmlands by their father.

Ginny said, "You're a true, stand-up sort of man, John. I can count on one hand the number of stand-up men I've met over the years. I can't imagine my niece finding a man any better. I want the best for you both. The Brackston estate is going to go to Lura when God finally plucks me from his green Earth. You might as well use some of the money now. Someday Joshua will be grown, and you'll be helping him start out. And he will help out his children, and so on. That's the way of things. Lura doesn't have a mother who can help her. Let me do it. It would be my pleasure."

He looked at her and found himself smiling despite himself.

"And two," she said, "don't call me *Miss* Ginny. It's *Aunt* Ginny, or even just Ginny. But no more of this *Miss* nonsense."

"All right. *Aunt* Ginny."

She smiled. "That's more like it."

Lura took the baby to a spot about fifteen feet from the nearest apple tree.

She said, "Johnny, can we build the house so the back door is right here? I want to be able to step out the back door and pick an apple. And I so love apple blossoms in the spring."

Johnny walked over and wrapped his arms around her, and in doing so, wrapped them around the baby, too. "Anything you want."

Little Joshua gave a gurgling, chirping laugh.

Johnny said, "And you'll grow up right here, Josh. With your mother eating apples and me teaching you about cattle and horses."

Lura laughed. "*Josh*, is it? Not Joshua?"

"Sure. Josh is a man's name."

"But he's not a man, yet."

"Sure he is. A boy is always a man, at heart."

She leaned her head back, against his shoulder.

She said, "I never thought it would be possible to be this happy."

# 49

LUMBER ARRIVED by the wagon load the following week. Ginny also had some granite slabs transported, to serve as a foundation for the house.

"Granite slabs?" Zack said.

Johnny shrugged. "She didn't say anything about them."

"Apparently she wants this house to have a good foundation."

Johnny and Joe had learned carpentry skills from their father. Zack demonstrated that he knew something about it too. When they weren't watching the herd, they were working on the house. The tent was set up and Ginny stayed with them to help Lura with the baby.

Within two weeks, a house was built. Johnny had wanted a Cape Cod style, like the old farmhouse he had grown up in. A peaked roof, three bedrooms on the second floor. A small, narrow stairway at the center of the house that led up to them.

He and the boys hauled in stones, and they built a chimney and hearth of them. Ginny had an iron stove brought out for the kitchen.

They dug a well. They found water eight feet down, and a pipe was set up and an iron pump installed in the kitchen.

In the evening, Johnny and Lura would sit by the fire in their parlor. Sometimes Joe and Zack would join them, and other times it would be just the two of them.

Josh had been nearly bald when he was born, but soon he had a thick head of hair, and it was the color of his mother's.

Lura had him in a high chair one morning and was trying to teach him to eat. He would take a mouthful of food but then let it dribble down his chin to his bib.

Johnny was in from the range and covered with dust. He leaned close to the high chair and said, "Can you say Daddy?"

Josh said, "Da-da-da."

"That's my boy." Johnny had a wide grin.

Josh laughed and kicked his feet.

They went in to Aunt Ginny's for Christmas. She had a tree that reached all the way to the high ceiling in the main parlor.

A year later another boy was born. Jackson, named for Johnny's grandfather. His hair was darker. Where Josh was impatient, Jackson was calm. Contemplative.

Johnny's hair grew ever longer, and he began tying it back in a tail. Aunt Ginny would tease him about it, calling it *Shoshone hair.* But he liked the sound of it. Unlike the Shoshone, he did cut a couple inches off every so often, but no more.

For the first two roundups, Matt sent some men to help. Hardy and Corry one year. Evan and Valdez another. By their third year, Johnny had sold some cattle to two different buyers and could hire extra hands of his own.

Twice, he and Zack headed into the mountains for a week of mustanging. Lura and the boys went to San Francisco for a week with Aunt Ginny. Both times, horses were brought back, and Johnny broke the horses Shoshone style.

When Josh was three, a third child joined the family. A little girl with a shock of dark hair.

Lura said to Aunt Ginny, "We're naming her Virginia Sabrina."

Ginny's eyes twinkled. "I am so honored."

There had been an attempt to call her Little Ginny. But somehow the name didn't stick. By the time she was a year old, the name had been forgotten and she was called Bree.

Ginny now joined them for Christmas. She believed children should have Christmas in their own home.

She said, "To come out of your bedroom on

Christmas morning and see the tree in all of its glory, and Santa's presents beneath it, is one of the wonders of childhood."

One night, when the children were in bed, Johnny stood with Lura on the front porch of their little ranch house.

He was behind her and had wrapped his arms around her. She leaned her head back against him.

"Is that peach I smell?" he said.

She smiled. "Aunt Ginny gave me a new bottle."

"I've always liked it." He gave a little kiss beneath one ear and began working down her neck.

"Johnny," she said, "we're out here on the porch. Joe and Zack might see."

"Well, we can always go inside."

She giggled. Then she looked off at the dark horizon, and the stars overhead.

"Are you happy here?"

"Absolutely," he said.

"I know you loved that valley you talk about, up in Nebraska Territory. I guess they're calling it Idaho Territory now."

He nodded. "I did love that valley. But it wouldn't be right to take you so far from Ginny. She's the only family you have, really, on your side. And without us, she'd be alone."

"Maybe someday you can go back. Maybe you can take me there, when the children are older."

"Maybe. But I don't need to be there to be home. Anywhere you and the children are, is home to me."

*   *   *

Montana
April, 1882

Johnny said, "I had thought my childhood years on the farm were the happiest of my life. That was until I saw the three of you. Watching you take your first steps. Seeing your mother teach you to take a spoonful of food. Seeing you learn to talk."

He and Bree were sitting by their campfire. He had a cup of coffee in one hand.

Bree said, "And then Ma died."

He nodded.

She said, "You don't have to talk about it if you don't want to."

He drew a deep breath and let it out slowly. "No, it's all right. There was a time when I couldn't, but I've made peace with it all. At least for the most part. But one bullet changed everything, for all of us."

## 50

## California
## 1863

WAR WAS raging back east, and Johnny didn't know if the country would survive. Or if it did, if it would ever be the same.

He would welcome some changes, he thought. Slavery was an abomination. His mother and father had always been abolitionists, and she had said once that we were all God's children and one shouldn't enslave another. She said another time that she couldn't understand how a country founded on the principal of freedom could endorse slavery.

And yet, out on his ranch in California, it was like the war didn't exist at all. He would read about it in newspapers, but it didn't seem real. He said as much to Ginny once, and she nodded and said, "It seems surrealistic."

Ginny was spending about half of her time at the ranch, helping Lura. There were three children now, two of them still in diapers.

The herd now numbered over six hundred head. It would have been more, but Johnny had made sales to a few buyers. Ships bound for the Orient needed beef for their crew. The Army had a stronger presence in California, now that the War was on, and they needed beef.

Johnny still couldn't pay Joe and Zack a regular wage, but when he made a sale he was able to put some cash in their hands.

One morning, Johnny had been out with the herd. Joe and Zack were, too. They were in the middle of a small drought, and the stream was running low. If they didn't get rain soon, the herd would have to be pushed a couple of miles out into open range, where there was a water hole that was filled by a spring.

It was late morning when Johnny rode back to the house. Lura stepped out the front door and waved at him. He turned Bravo toward the door and swung out of the saddle.

"I thought I heard you riding in," she said. "I can always tell when it's you. Especially when you're on Bravo, but even when you're not."

"Oh?" he said. "And how is that?"

"When you ride, it's like you and the horse are one. And the horse seems to step a little livelier, a little freer."

She had many smiles, but at the moment she was giving a smile that she reserved only for him.

She said, "Where are Joe and Zack?"

"Back with the herd. They'll be along in a little while."

She raised a brow. "The children are down for a nap. That means we might actually have an entire moment alone."

"And what do you want to do with that moment?"

Her smile took on an extra pinch of daring, and then he took her in his arms and pressed his mouth to hers.

She pulled back after a time.

She said, "Why, Mister McCabe. You are such a flirt."

He chuckled. "I've been called many a thing before. But never a flirt."

She was grinning playfully. "And what are some of these things you've been called?"

Then there was a gunshot. It was muffled a little with distance, but then Lura lurched backward a couple of steps.

A hole had been torn into her dress two inches below her collar bone, and blood was already beginning to soak the fabric.

Johnny stared, wide-eyed, his mouth hanging open. He had seen many people shot. More than he could ever count. But not now. Not Lura.

She staggered another step, and her eyes met his. She wasn't in pain or afraid. She was just looking at him with surprise.

Then her knees buckled and she fell backward.

Johnny caught her but she went limp and began sliding out of his arms. He went down with her, landing on his knees in the dust. He cradled her head. Blood was soaking the front of her blouse.

She was going into shock from the rapid blood loss. Her eyes were open but she was no longer seeing.

"Lura, no," he said. "Hang on, Sweetie. Hang on."

She gave a shuddering breath, then another. And then she stopped breathing.

Tears streamed down, cutting rivulets in the trail dust that covered his face. He looked upward to the sky overhead, still blue in the late afternoon, and screamed out her name. Long and hard.

His gaze landed on a rider sitting at the top of the hill just to the south of the ranch yard. Johnny couldn't make out his face from this distance, but he could see a dark, wide-brimmed hat. And in his hands was a rifle.

The man sat in the saddle a moment, then turned his horse and was gone.

Bravo still stood where he had been ground hitched. He had shifted a little to one side at the gunshot but hadn't bolted. Johnny thought for a moment about leaping into the saddle and going after the shooter, but for only a moment. He couldn't leave Lura lying in the dust.

Zack and Joe came riding up.

Joe said, "We heard a gunshot. Didn't sound like your rifle."

Then they saw what had happened. Zack left his saddle on the fly and was at Johnny's side.

"Who done this?" Zack said.

Johnny couldn't get the words out. He just looked off toward the hill.

Joe was still on his horse. He said, "I'll get the sum'bitch."

He turned his horse and charged toward the hill. But his horse was tired. It had logged a lot of miles chasing strays. By the time Joe was at the top of the hill, his horse was spent. To push it any further would probably kill it.

Zack rode hard to San Francisco. He brought two horses with him so he could change saddles and keep riding.

Ginny came back to the ranch just as fast, with Martinez pushing the team of horses to the limit. A doctor was with them, and the county sheriff.

Johnny had brought Lura's body to the front porch and wrapped it in a sheet. He didn't want to bring it inside and let the children see.

In the house, Josh said, "Where's Mommy?"

Johnny had to choke back sobs. He didn't want to upset the kids.

"Mommy's gone for a bit," he said. He kept his voice calm, and he was wiping away tears. "But Aunt Ginny's coming out."

When they got there, the doctor took one look at the body and shook his head.

Johnny stood with Ginny. There was nothing the doctor could do. Lura had been gone for hours at this point. But the doctor had to write up a certificate of death, he supposed.

Lura was buried out behind the house, under her apple tree. The tree had grown a lot, and it seemed fitting that she would lie forever in its shade.

Johnny stood with Jack sitting in the crook of one arm, and Josh standing beside him and holding his hand. Ginny was holding Bree.

Matt and Verna had come out. Quint and Hardy were there. Valdez and Evan and Corry. Moses Timmons stood and stared in disbelief at the wooden casket on the ground beside the grave.

Martinez was there, and Julia. She had worked for Ginny a lot of years and had become a family friend, and had seen Lura grow up.

Ginny's minister said the usual things. Johnny wasn't really listening. He felt numb all over, like he had at Pa's burial, six years earlier.

He would have to write to Ma and Luke about this, he thought. How would he ever be able to find the words?

*I wish you were here now, Pa. I could use your strength to lean on.*

He could almost hear his father's words in his mind. *You have my strength, son, inside of you. I gave you that.*

That night, Jack and Bree had fallen asleep in the parlor, so Johnny carried them upstairs to bed.

As he was tucking Josh in, the boy said, "Pa, where's Ma? What's going on?"

Johnny paused for a moment, trying to find the words and not wanting to choke up in front of his son.

He said, "Ma's gone to heaven, son."

Josh's head was on his pillow and he looked at his father with big eyes.

Johnny said, "Remember when we've talked about God?"

Josh nodded.

"And how He's always watching over us?"

Josh nodded again.

"Well, He's in this bright and beautiful place called heaven. And that's where Ma is now, too."

"When will she be comin' back?"

Johnny drew a breath on that one. He said, "She can't come back, son. Once you're there, you can't come back. But you know what? Her spirit is here now. Watching over you. Watching over all of us."

"Over Jack and Bree, too?"

Johnny nodded. "Over all of us."

"Why'd she have to go? Didn't she like it here?"

Johnny nodded. "Sure she did. But she didn't have a choice. I knew a wise man once. An Indian by the name of Many Lives."

"A real, honest-to-gosh Injun?"

Johnny nodded. "And he was a very wise man. You know what he said?"

Josh shook his head.

"He said we all go when it's our time. It's already written in the clouds. And on the wind. It was Ma's time, that's all. But like I said, her spirit is still with us. Do you understand?"

Josh shook his head.

Johnny couldn't help but smile, even though he felt tears coming. He hoped it was dark enough in the room so Josh wouldn't notice. "Neither do I. Not really. But I do believe Ma's in a better place. And somehow, she's still with us, in our heart."

Johnny sat on the edge of the bed until Josh fell off to sleep. At one point Johnny thought he heard the clattering of hoofbeats outside, but he was scarcely listening. Joe and Zack were here. They would take care of any trouble that came about.

When Josh was asleep, Johnny planted a light kiss on his forehead then headed downstairs.

The county sheriff had come back. A man by the name of Huston, with a fat stomach and a thick mustache.

Johnny said, "Kind of late for you to be out, isn't it sheriff?"

It was well after dark.

Huston nodded. "I had to see you. I wanted to talk to you. I wanted to get here in time for the burial, but I got held up by other business."

"It's all right, sheriff," Ginny said. "We understand."

Johnny had nothing to talk to the sheriff about. He didn't mean to be rude, but he was so tired even his bones ached. But he knew it would be a long time before he got any rest.

He said, "Ginny, I need a favor. I need you to stay here a few days with the children."

She nodded. "I was planning to."

"In the morning, Joe and Zack and I are riding out. We're going to find the man who did this."

Huston said, "Now, hold on. That's why I came out here to talk to you."

"We've got nothing to talk about. My brothers and I sat around doing nothing while we waited for the law to find the man who killed our father. By the time we started taking matters into our own hands, it was too late. The killer got away. It's not gonna happen this time."

"You let the law take care of this, son."

Johnny shook his head no. "There's no law going to be involved in this. I'm going to find him. And I'm not bringing him back."

"Don't do this, son."

Johnny said, his voice low and almost hissing, "I'll say this once. Don't get in my way."

Huston took a step back. Then he looked at Ginny. "Could you talk some sense into him?"

"I could try, but I find I agree with him."

He looked at her with surprise.

She said, "Sheriff, we've had a long, trying day and you have a long ride back in the dark. Good night."

Huston turned and went out the door.

Johnny looked at Ginny and she looked back at him. No words were spoken. None needed to be. She turned and went to the guest room Johnny had built onto the house. Johnny pulled a chair up in front of the hearth. A low fire was burning, and he stared into it.

After a time, he got to his feet and went to the kitchen, and to a specific drawer where Lura kept her sewing things. He took a pair of scissors and went out onto the porch.

The Shoshone didn't cut their hair, except when they grieved.

Johnny loosened the strip of rawhide he used to tie his hair back, and then he began to snip away.

## 51

IN THE MORNING, Johnny saddled Bravo. His hair was now only an inch long all around, and his hat fit a little looser.

When he led Bravo back to the house, Ginny must have noticed his Shoshone tail was gone but didn't mention it.

"I don't know how long I'll be gone," he said.

She was standing on the porch. "Do what has to be done. I'll take care of the children. Martinez and Julia are here, too. We'll be all right."

Then she said, "Find him, John. Put a bullet in him. But don't get yourself killed. These children don't need to lose both parents."

He nodded.

Joe and Zack were in the saddle, waiting for him. Matt was there, too. He had sent Verna to the hotel in Coulterville, but he had stayed and slept in the bunkhouse. He wanted to be part of the manhunt.

The four riders climbed the hill to begin following the killer's trail. The herd was unattended, but Johnny thought finding the killer was the first order of business.

As they rode, Johnny said, "That bullet has to have been meant for me."

"You don't know that," Joe said. "Could have been her father sending a man to kill her."

Johnny shook his head. "Why would he wait all this time? Four years. In all that time, neither Lura or me set foot in Greenville. We stayed away from him. We never bothered him. Why would he do this?"

"I had me a talk with him, when we first rode back to the Bar M to see Matt. You and Zack had supper at the ranch. I rode into town to see the old buzzard."

"You saw him in town?"

Joe nodded. "That's why I rode into town. I told him what I would do to him if he ever bothered you or

Lura again. I think I made him pee his pants. If it turns out he's involved, I'll do to him what I said I would. I'll stick a knife in his stomach and then scalp him and watch him die slow."

Johnny shook his head. "If he was involved, I'll take care of it."

They followed the tracks for three days.

At night, they would heat beans in a skillet and boil coffee. Matt handled most of the cooking duties. Johnny often just sat and stared.

By day, they followed the trail. It seemed to be heading straight east.

Toward the end of the third day, they were in the foothills, and they saw clouds forming to the northwest.

"Gonna rain," Joe said.

Matt said, "What'll rain do to the tracks?"

Joe shrugged. "Nothin', if it don't rain too hard."

Johnny rode along in silence.

That night, the rain came down. They were now high enough in the mountains that they were surrounded by pine trees, and they slept under one, using it as an umbrella.

Johnny didn't lie down, though. He sat with his back against the pine. At times he would doze, but he never really slept.

He was caught in a sort of nowhere land between sorrow and rage. Like he wasn't really alive but not quite dead.

Come morning, the sky was clear and birds were singing, announcing that the storm had fully passed. But the tracks were now gone.

"There's no way we can follow him now," Joe said. "I doubt even a bloodhound would be able to pick up the trail after that rain."

Then his gaze landed on something in the pine straw. Small and brass. He knew what it was. He put a foot over it so Johnny wouldn't see it.

Johnny said, "I'll find him. Somehow, I'll find him."

Zack shook his head. "No. It's time to call this off."

Johnny looked at him like he couldn't believe he was hearing these words from Zack Johnson.

Matt said, "He's right, Johnny. Those children back there need you. They need their father. You persist in trying to find this man long enough, you might succeed. What do you intend to do when you find him?"

"Shoot him down and watch him die."

"And then you'll either be rotting in prison the rest of your life or swinging from a rope. The best thing you could do to honor your love for Lura is to be there for your children. Go home to them. They need you."

Johnny looked at him long and hard. He wanted to tell Matt he was wrong. He wanted to yell at his brother and tell him to mind his own affairs. And the same for Zack. But he found he couldn't.

Joe said nothing. He seldom said much. But he looked at Johnny and nodded his head.

"Come on," Zack said. "Let's go home."

Johnny turned, lifted his saddle and carried it over to Bravo.

No one was looking, so Joe knelt down as casually as he could, and he took the brass object in one hand. A button. On one side was a French symbol Matt had called a *fleur des lis*. Matt had said *fleur* is French for flower, but Joe never saw how the symbol looked like a flower. It always looked to him more like swords.

Joe had seen only one man ever who wore something with those buttons.

No need to let Johnny know. Johnny would want to kill the man, and Joe thought Matt and Zack were right. Johnny's young'uns needed him alive, not swinging from a rope.

He tucked the button into his pants pocket.

## 52

MATT STOOD on the front porch and said, "Are you sure you're all right?"

Johnny nodded. "I have to be. For the children."

"If you need me to stay, I will."

Johnny laid a hand on Matt's shoulder. "You're needed at your ranch. You have a lot more money on the table, and a lot more irons in the fire. They need you there. And you have a son. Thomas needs you home with him."

Matt nodded. "If you need me, just send and I'll come running."

"I know that."

They shook hands, then gave each other a quick hug, slapping each other on the back like men do when they hug.

Matt stepped down from the porch. Joe was waiting for him with a horse.

Matt said, "Take care of him, will you?"

Joe nodded.

Matt said, "And take care of yourself."

"You too."

They shook hands, then there was another back-slapping hug, and Matt stepped into the saddle.

Johnny stood on the porch and watched Matt ride along the trail, which took him up a long, low hill that was mostly grassy. The trail went over a long, rounded summit and then turned right, and Matt was lost from sight.

Joe climbed the steps to the porch.

He said, "Matt's come a long way. From a farm boy to a first mate on a ship, to runnin' one of the biggest ranches in California."

Johnny nodded. He said nothing.

Joe said, "Well, we got us a ranch to run."

Johnny nodded. "That we do."

Ginny moved in to help with the children. She and Johnny had a small discussion one night about the children moving in with her in the city, because Johnny hated to impose on her.

They were sitting by the little hearth in the parlor. Johnny was on the sofa, and Ginny was in the same rocker she had used when they had camped on this spot, before the house was built.

She said, "It's not imposing. I'm helping my family. The children are going to have a difficult period of adjustment, and I think the fewer changes in their life, the better. They belong in their own home."

One day worked its way gradually into another. One week blended into another, and Johnny lost himself in his work.

He and Zack brought fifty head to an Army post outside of Sacramento.

The drought broke with a rip-roaring thunderstorm, and it brought hail that damaged the barn roof. Some shingles had to be replaced.

Johnny rode night herd a lot. There was no floating outfit, no line cabin, so he and the boys would take turns riding out to the far reaches of the range they used. Make sure no one was doing any rustling. Make sure the cows didn't wander too far.

There were times when Johnny would sit in the saddle out on the range and just stare at the horizon.

At night, he would tuck the children in. He would lead them in their nightly prayers, and when they asked for blessings on the family, Josh would add, "And please bless Ma and let her know we love her."

The children were growing. Josh turned five and Jack turned four.

Christmas came. Johnny and Joe rode out to the mountains and came back with a blue spruce. Ginny led the decorating, with the boys helping. Little Bree was learning to walk and put a couple of glass balls on the bottom branches. Johnny could see it coming—she dropped one and it shattered on the floor.

She looked up at Aunt Ginny and was about to cry, but Ginny scooped her up and said, "That's all right, honey. Accidents happen."

And yet, somehow, none of it felt real. When Bree dropped the glass decoration and it shattered, Johnny's heart went out to her, and when Ginny scooped her up it brought a smile to his face. And yet, somehow it all felt dreamlike.

When he realized it had been six months since Lura's death, he was a little startled. It seemed like it had been just a few days.

One evening in January, he was standing on the porch with a cup of coffee and watching the rays of sunset light up some distant clouds. Joe walked up.

Joe had cut his hair so it barely touched his collar, and his beard was now only a few inches long. You got covered with trail dust when you spent a day on the range, and it was miserable with longer hair and a fuller beard.

Johnny was in the waist-length jacket he had acquired when he worked for Breaker Grant, all those years ago. Seemed like a lifetime ago. The hair he had hacked off was growing back, and in a few months it would be long enough to tie back again.

Joe said, "I see you standin' and starin' a lot. I see you sittin' in the saddle, starin' off at the distance. I knew what you were goin' through the first time. When you thought Lura had left you, and we rode all the way north to that valley. I had gone through the same kind of thing. But not now."

Johnny said, "I really couldn't say how it feels. I guess I just feel sort of numb. Or like I'm walking through a fog."

Joe followed Johnny's gaze to the distant cloud. It had been a fiery orange but now was a softer crimson.

Joe said, "Do you ever think about our time with the Shoshone?"

Johnny nodded. "Just about every day. I think about how I'd like to talk with Many Lives about this.

Get his ideas. His wisdom. And there was just a sort of feeling of peace about those mountains and that valley. Almost a feeling of healing. I was so heartbroken over that letter I thought Lura wrote, but I would stand on a particular cliff on that southern ridge and it felt like the mountain winds were washing my troubles away."

They were silent for a while. They could hear a squealing giggle from Bree, inside the house. And they could smell dinner. Aunt Ginny was fixing roast beef.

Joe said, "Maybe that's what you need. To go to that valley again. Breathe that air, again."

Johnny shook his head. "I couldn't bear to be gone from the children that long. When you and Zack and I rode north, I had no ties here. Nothing to bring me back, until I decided I needed to hear Lura say in person what the letter said."

"Best decision you ever made, too."

"Worst, if you think about it. That bullet was probably meant for me. If I hadn't come back, she would still be alive. And she would have Josh, raising him with Ginny in San Francisco."

"But Jack and Bree wouldn't be here. And you wouldn't have had the years you did with her."

Johnny looked back at the sky. The crimson was fading to gray.

Joe said, "Didn't Many Lives say once that we all go when it's our time?"

Johnny nodded.

Joe said, "So, if you're gonna follow that line of belief, and I do, then even if you hadn't come back, and Lura was raising little Josh at Aunt Ginny's, she would've died some other way. And then Josh wouldn't have any parents in his life."

Johnny was silent a moment. He took a sip of his coffee and found it had gone cold, and tossed the contents of the cup to the front yard.

He said, "I want to believe, Joe. I really do."

"Sometimes believin' comes all at once. That's how it did with me. I was sittin' by a campfire in front of my teepee in a Cheyenne village, and all of a sudden it just sort of hit me. I believed. But sometimes it takes a while. A step-by-step sort of thing."

Johnny shrugged.

Joe said, "I think you do believe, in your heart. It's just you're having' trouble gettin' your head to accept it."

"Maybe when the kids are grown, I'll take a ride north to that valley."

Joe said, "Why wait? Why don't we all go?"

Johnny looked at Joe like he wasn't sure if Joe was serious or not. "Who would look after the ranch?"

Joe shrugged. He was saying it all as it occurred to him. "Close up the ranch. We can sell off part of the herd and take part of it with us. We can load up a couple of wagons. Bring the kids and even Aunt Ginny, if she wants to come along."

"So we go and what? Spend the summer and then come all the way back? That's a lot of miles overland."

"Who said anything about coming back? That little spot you said would be good for building a cabin? Why not build it? You'll have me along to help you, and I'd be surprised if Zack didn't come along too. Whatever cattle we bring with us, they're sure gonna like the grass that grows in that valley."

"You mean, build ourselves a ranch right there?"

Joe shrugged again. "Why not?"

Johnny began to think on it, and he started to pace. "The valley isn't big enough for a large herd. But there's good grass out beyond there, to the east, in the foothills."

"And that little stream can provide good, clean, cold drinkin' water until we can get a proper well dug. And I don't think we'll have to go too deep to find water."

Johnny looked at Joe. "Do you really think we could do this?"

Joe nodded. "Wouldn't have said it otherwise. I ain't one for empty words."

"No, that you're not."

Johnny began pacing again. "It's still January. If we start out in a few weeks, we can be settled in by July. Have a cabin up by October."

Joe nodded. "Sounds reasonable."

"The thing is, there's been Indian trouble since then. Settlers have been attacked."

"The Indians we'll see on the way are tribes we're familiar with. Shoshone, Cheyenne, Lakota, maybe even Arapaho. And remember, you're the famous Mac-cabe. You killed Iron Hand, the man who couldn't be beat."

Johnny gave him a look. "They're not gonna remember that. It was five years ago."

"Trust me, they're gonna remember."

That night, after the children were in bed, and Joe and Zack had gone back to the bunkhouse for a game of cards before climbing into their bunks, Johnny and Ginny sat by the hearth. Johnny had built a small fire and it was throwing off some warmth.

Johnny had a cup of coffee in one hand, and Ginny had a glass of wine.

Johnny said, "I want to talk to you about an idea Joe and I started tossing around tonight. A crazy idea, sure, but I'd like you to hear it out before you give your opinion."

"All right."

"Did I ever tell you about that valley up in Idaho Territory? Where we wintered with a band of Shoshone?"

# PART SIX

## *Shoshone Valley*

### 53

Montana
April, 1882

BREE SAID, "So that's how you decided to bring us all here."

Johnny nodded.

"What did Aunt Ginny say? She must have thought you were out of your mind."

"One thing about your Aunt Ginny, she always seems willing to consider the outrageous. It took a few days, but the more she started thinking about it, the more I think the idea sort of intrigued her.

"By mid-February, we started out. I sold the old ranch to Matt. He said he would probably use the range for extra grazing. Then he eventually sold it. We sold all but two hundred head, and kept a couple of bulls for breeding. We loaded up two wagons as full as they could be, and we started out. And we had a string of twenty horses."

"I was too young to remember it. I wasn't even two, yet."

Johnny shook his head. "You turned two here in the valley."

"Tell me all about it. The trail. What it was like."

"Well, I hadn't been through that country in five years. The land can change, and I wasn't in the same place in my life anymore. And yet when I saw those mountains as we approached Fort Bridger, I felt like I wasn't quite home yet, but almost.

"Often you would ride in one wagon with Aunt Ginny. Josh would sometimes handle one team. Even at five he was already a take-charge kind of kid."

She smiled. "That's easy to imagine."

"Often Aunt Ginny would have the reins of one team and either Joe or Zack would have the other. Much of the time the boys would walk along beside one of the wagons, sometimes bouncing a ball against it. I was usually on Bravo, scouting ahead and such."

"What about the man who drove Aunt Ginny's buggy back in California. What did you say his name was? Martinez? Why didn't he come along, and the maid."

"They stayed behind. Their lives were in San Francisco. Their families were there. Their job was to take care of the house. Aunt Ginny wanted it ready should she ever return. She also left her attorney in charge of her financial affairs and overseeing the various businesses she owned. I think her original plan was to go back, once you kids were grown."

"But then she found Addison. Or, he found her."

Johnny nodded. "I doubt she had any notion she'd be living out her days running a small restaurant and saloon in Montana Territory."

"So, what was it like, traveling all the way here from California with two wagons, three kids and two hundred head of cattle?"

"Let me tell you all about it."

## 54

Idaho Territory
June, 1864

THEY CAMPED in a flat area that was grassy, with some scattered brush. A wooded ridge stood off to the west, and another to the east.

When it got dark, Ginny could see nothing beyond the circle of firelight. The wind was a little cool, even though the day had been warm.

She stood at the edge of the firelight and looked off into the darkness. Joe and Zack were just beyond her, rubbing down the horses and picketing them.

Johnny walked up to her, a cup of coffee in one hand.

She said, "Oh, John, it's so wonderfully remote here. I went to sea with my father more than once, and this is how it felt out there. Nature, wild and untamed."

A coyote howled from somewhere out in the darkness.

"Wild and untamed is the word for it," he said. "This is the kind of place I feel drawn to. This, and the mountains."

"I can see why. How much further until we reach your valley?"

"At the pace we're going, I would say maybe four days."

She could hear the bawling of a cow from somewhere out in the darkness.

He said, "We've done quite well. Lost only eight head. This is a long drive, and we've had to go slow to make sure they can graze along the way. They've lost some weight, but not much."

"John, how are you doing? Are you all right?"

He nodded. "I think I will be. Or, at least, as well as I can be. It's like I've had a part of me ripped away. But I have to be strong for the kids."

"What would you have done if not for the children?"

He made a sort of shrugging motion with his brows. "Probably kept on looking for the killer. I doubt I would have found him, and I would have figured that out after a while. I never got a look at him, and the rain washed the trail away. Eventually, I would have drifted. Probably headed up to the valley."

"And that's where you're going, anyway."

He nodded. "To raise the kids there. Someday I'll return to California, to visit her grave. But not anytime soon. Now's the time to focus on the children."

From behind them, they could hear Jack call out. "Josh! Stop pushin'! Pa, Josh is pushin'!"

Josh called out, "Am not!"

Ginny grinned. "Sounds like they need to be focused on right now."

Ginny's tent was pitched, and she and the children went to bed. Ginny was on a cot, and the children were in blankets.

Johnny went to the fire, and with a bandana, he grabbed the hot kettle and filled his cup with coffee.

Zack and Joe were there, each with a cup.

Johnny said, "I was thinkin'."

With a nod of his head, Zack indicated the tent. Johnny looked over to see Josh standing outside.

Johnny walked over. "Josh, what're you doin' out here?"

He shrugged.

Johnny said, "You should get in and get to sleep."

"Can't sleep."

"You were only in there two minutes."

He shrugged.

Johnny said, "Tell you what. You come out here and sit with the men a while. How's that sound?"

Josh nodded.

Johnny took his hand and led him over to the fire.

A wooden folding chair was there, so Johnny took it and then perched Josh on his knee.

Joe said, "We're travelin' real high class, this time. Wagons filled with supplies, and chairs to set in."

Johnny nodded.

Josh said, "How'd you do it last time, Pa?"

"With just what we could carry on our horses. We sat on the ground around the fire. We slept on the ground, out in the open."

"Wow."

Johnny grinned. "That's right. Wow. It was quite an adventure."

Josh said, "Pa, can Ma see us out here?"

"Why sure she can."

"I'm afraid she's gonna look down from heaven at our house and find us gone, and she won't know where to look for us."

Johnny set his coffee down and gave Josh a little hug. "She'll know, son."

"How?"

"Because I talk to her every night. And a few times during the day."

"You talk to her?"

Johnny nodded. "Sure do."

"Does she talk to you?"

"In a way. I can in hear in my heart what I think she might be sayin'."

"Do you think if I talk to her, she'll hear me too?"

"I'd bet on it."

Then Johnny said to Joe and Zack, "I've been thinking. I know it's gonna be hard, but I figure we're about four days out of the Crazies, if we push and travel long days. I'd like to do that. We can get caught up on our rest once we're there."

Johnny wanted to talk to Joe and Zack about an idea he had. So far, they had been taking things slowly. Traveling a few miles a day, and one day a week taking an entire day off from traveling for rest. The reason was Joe, Zack and Johnny were riding night herd every night, working in shifts of two, and weren't getting much sleep. This wasn't like the range back in California. The cattle couldn't be left alone at night. There were wolves and coyotes out here, and even Indians.

Among the plains tribes Johnny knew of, stealing horses or even cattle wasn't considered a lowly thing, like it was among the white culture. It was considered one of the methods of a young warrior proving his worth to himself and the village. Johnny understood the concept, but he didn't want to donate any horses or cattle to the cause.

Joe said, "We been lucky so far. No contact with Indians at all."

"We got four more days," Zack said. "Let's hope our luck holds out."

"They stampede the herd, and we'll be a lot longer'n four days gettin' there."

Johnny nodded. "Let's hope it won't come to that."

Joe finished his coffee and said, "I'm gonna go saddle up. You comin'?"

Johnny nodded.

Zack said, "I'm the odd man out, tonight. Just keep the coffee hot."

The usual rotation was they would each have an alternating pattern of four-hour and two-hour shifts, so that two of them were with the herd at all times. Zack was the odd man out tonight because he would be getting two four-hour shifts. Johnny had been the odd man out the night before.

This was arranged to not only allow them to get some sleep throughout the night, but so one of them was always here at the camp with Ginny and the children.

Come morning, Johnny had managed four hours of sleep between his four-hour shift and his two-hour one, but he didn't feel very tired.

When the sun was rising in the sky, the wagons were loaded and moving.

Johnny was driving the lead wagon, and Bravo

was saddled and tied to the back. The children were taking turns sitting with him. Whenever they stopped to rest the horses, they would switch. Ginny was driving the second wagon.

Joe and Zack were bringing the herd up behind them. Johnny kept the wagons either ahead of the herd or to the side, so they wouldn't be eating dust.

Johnny watched their back trail and off to either side, looking for any indication of riders. It was a little after noon that he saw one to the far left. A lone rider, coming toward the herd.

He pulled the wagon to a stop. Jack was with him, so he said to Jack, "Run back to your Aunt Ginny."

"How come, Pa?"

"Because I told you. Now get to it."

Jack climbed down and ran back to Aunt Ginny. Johnny untied Bravo and swung into the saddle.

Ginny said, "What is it?"

"Nothing, I hope."

He rode toward Joe, who had already seen the rider.

"Indian," Joe said. "What you gotta watch for is one rider getting your attention, and then more approaching from up ahead."

Zack rode over. Johnny said, "We're gonna ignore that rider, and keep our eyes up front."

Zack nodded.

The cows were moving on their own, so Johnny rode ahead of them. Joe and Zack were at his side.

Then Johnny saw them. About thirty riders coming out of what must have been a small canyon toward the front of a ridge, off to their right. The canyon wasn't visible from where Johnny sat.

He said to Joe and Zack, go get your rifles and stay with the wagons. We'll let 'em have the herd, if we have to. Keep Ginny and the kids safe."

Joe and Zack turned their horses toward the wagons. The rifles were in Johnny's wagon. Joe's old Enfield was there, and Johnny's Hawken. But there were also two of the new, lever-action Henry rifles that each took sixteen cartridges.

Joe sat in the seat of Johnny's wagon with his Enfield in his hands and one Henry beside him. He would use the Enfield first, because it was more accurate. Then he would switch to the Henry and use it as the riders got closer.

He said to Zack, "As far as I'm concerned, they ain't getting' the family or the herd."

Zack took the other Henry. He had long ago gotten rid of the old rifle the Lakota had given him. He rode back to Ginny's wagon and climbed up into the seat beside her. He told the children to get into the wagon behind the seat, and to lay low.

Ginny said, "Is there going to be trouble?"

Zack nodded. "Most likely."

"And Johnny's riding right into it."

Zack nodded again. "Seems to be what he does best."

Johnny reined up two hundred feet ahead of the wagons. The herd was starting to lose its sense of momentum at the sight of riders approaching.

Johnny loosened both pistols in their holsters.

The Indians reined up about fifty feet from him. They were Lakota, and painted for war.

"We take your herd," one of them said. Apparently the leader.

"You take nothing," Johnny said. "You go back the way you come or I'll shoot you out of your saddle."

He laughed. "You only three men. And a woman and children. We thirty."

"You'll be the first one I shoot."

"You don't have gun in hand."

Johnny pulled his pistol and before the man could say another word, the gun was cocked and aimed at him.

"First shot," Johnny said, "takes you out. My men and I will cut the rest of you down. We have more than thirty shots, and we don't tend to miss."

The man had stopped laughing, and he now looked at Johnny with wide-eyed awe.

He said, "Mac-cabe."

Johnny nodded.

The Lakota said, "Only Mac-cabe can move so fast. Beat Iron Hand's medicine. Man who has guns fast as lightning."

"What's it gonna be?" Johnny said. "Ride away, or die."

The man said, "It honor to meet the great Mac-cabe."

The men were muttering the word *Mac-cabe* to each other.

They began to move their horses forward and partially surround him. Not trying to threaten him, but to get a look at the man called Mac-cabe. The man who had beaten Iron Hand and whose guns were as fast as lightning.

Johnny kept his gun aimed at their leader and called back to Zack.

Zack got back into the saddle and rode up.

Johnny said, "I want you to cut out six steers for these men. As a gift."

The leader nodded his head as a sort of bow. "A gift from the great Mac-cabe."

Zack still had his rifle in one hand, but his horse was a good cutting horse and was able to cut out six steers regardless. Three of the warriors took the steers.

Johnny said to the leader, "Now, go."

"We go." He bowed his head in honor again. "Lakota friend of Mac-cabe."

Johnny said, "And McCabe is friend of the Lakota."

The man nodded his head again. Johnny returned the nod, and the Lakota warriors took their gift of six steers and rode away.

Johnny eased off the hammer and holstered his gun.

Johnny said, "You know, I might stop complaining

so much about this talk of being a legend."

## 55

JOHNNY SAT on the wagon seat in the pass between the two ridges. Joe was in the saddle, beside the wagon. They were gazing off toward the grassy valley floor.

"There it is," Johnny said.

Joe nodded. "Yep. Right where we left it."

Johnny grinned.

Josh was sitting beside Johnny. "Is that it, Pa? Is that where we're gonna live?"

Johnny nodded. "That it is, son."

Ginny pulled the other wagon up beside Johnny's. From the pass, the valley floor appeared to be flat. A line of trees danced across about a quarter of a mile away. Beyond was the sort of hazy green effect trees seemed to have from a distance, and then another ridge began rising.

"Why, John," Ginny said. "It's beautiful."

Johnny nodded.

Joe said, "Why don't you folks start on in? I'm gonna go back with Zack and bring in the herd."

Johnny said, "We're going to head for the center of the valley. I don't expect to find them there, but we're going to see, just in case."

"The Shoshone," Ginny said.

Johnny nodded. "And then we'll head for that little spot I picked out for a cabin."

Joe nodded. "See you there."

Johnny started his wagon forward.

He found, as he had suspected, the valley floor was deserted.

Land can change over five years. A stand of alders they rode past was taller than he had remembered, and there were saplings where before there had been none.

The land that Bravo had crossed over easily was a little rough going for the wagons, and they took it slow and careful.

After about an hour, Johnny reined up. "This is

the spot."

He hopped down from the wagon. Bree was sitting beside Aunt Ginny, but she reached for her father, so he walked over and lifted her down.

Josh and Jack began climbing down.

"Boys," Ginny said. "Stay with your father."

Johnny walked over to a certain section of grass, holding Bree's hand.

He looked back at Ginny and said, "This is the spot where we had our teepee."

The grass was growing tall. There had been nothing here to flatten it down in a while. He looked at where their cookfire had been. It had been surrounded by small rocks, and most of the rocks were still there, but the grass was growing tall and some of the rocks had been rolled aside a few inches.

He said, "I don't think anyone has been here in a while. Maybe a couple of years or more."

He looked around. It felt so familiar, and yet different. In his mind he could see the teepee that had belonged to Many Lives. He could see Ainga coming out of it and tossing him a smile. The curve of the land from here to where the teepee of Many Lives once stood was still as it had been. But the center of the little village, which had been worn down to dirt, was now covered with tall grass.

"All right," he said to the children. "Let's climb back into the wagons. I'm gonna show you where we're gonna build the cabin."

It took more than an hour to get the wagons to the little stream. He was sure a trail would one day form and taking a wagon across the valley would be easier.

One thing he hadn't thought about was how deceptively deep the stream was. Any spring runoff had long since passed and the stream was no more than fifteen feet across. But when he took Bravo into it, the water rose almost to Bravo's shoulders.

Johnny turned Bravo back. He said to Ginny,

"We're not gonna be able to get the wagons across. The bottom of that stream isn't flat. It's U shaped."

"Would they get stuck?"

Johnny shrugged. "I don't want to take the chance. We'll set up camp on this side. Then Joe, Zack and I'll build a bridge. Haul some logs down from the ridge."

By late afternoon, the herd was grazing on the lush grass of the valley floor, and Ginny had a campfire blazing. The boys had butchered a steer, and she had some beef roasting.

"Mmm-boy, don't that smell good," Joe said.

Johnny had pitched the tent, and the children were running through the camp, laughing and playing tag.

Ginny called out to them, "Now, you boys play nicely with Bree. She's little and can't keep up with you."

Johnny said, "Give her time."

That night, Zack had crawled into his bedroll and was out cold. Ginny and the children were in the tent.

The fire was burning gently, and Johnny stood off at the edge of the firelight with a cup of coffee. The sky was filled with stars.

Joe walked over beside Johnny and they stood in silence for a time, breathing the mountain air.

Then Johnny said, "I'm home, Joe. I'm home."

# 56

THEY TOOK a week to let the horses rest. The men needed rest, too.

Joe cut a fishing pole and dug some worms at the edge of the stream. He showed the boys how to fish. Bree wanted to try it too, and she ended up sitting on Joe's lap helping him hold the pole.

Johnny said to Ginny, "Whatever the boys do, she has to do, too."

Ginny said, "She'll outgrow that."

"I don't know. Something about her makes me think she might not."

When the week was done, the men took the two teams of horses to the southern ridge, which was a quarter mile away. They had brought axes and saws with them, so they dropped two tall pines and limbed them, then cut the tree trunks into two half-lengths. Attaching chains to them, they used the horses to pull them back to the stream. Then they went back to the ridge to cut more logs.

When they went to the ridge, they did so in pairs, with one man always remaining with Ginny and the children.

They cut logs at ten foot lengths, but left two at a length of twenty feet each. The ten foot lengths were lashed crosswise to the two longer ones with ropes, and then with the horses pulling the structure, they managed to drag it to the stream, dropping across at the narrowest point.

"It's crude," Johnny said.

Joe nodded. "I've seen worse."

"It'll be rough getting the wagons across. But it should hold under their weight."

"Maybe as time allows, we can carve some wooden pegs and drive them in, because those ropes aren't going to last forever."

Once they were satisfied the bridge was sturdy

enough, they hitched the teams to the wagons and brought them across.

Johnny stood at the spot he had found five years earlier.

He said to Ginny, "This is where the front porch will be. Eventually. First we build a cabin to get us through the winter. And then next year, when we have more time, we'll work on building the house itself."

"This is a good spot to build a home."

"It doesn't bother you, a place as remote as this valley is?"

"It won't be as remote as it was when you were first here, apparently, if those men we saw back on the trail are successful."

The day before, they had happened upon three men platting a town that was going to be called *Bozeman*. The men introduced themselves as John Bozeman, William Beall and Daniel Rousse.

Bozeman said, "If you folks want to buy a plot to build a house on, you should grab one now, while they're going cheap."

"Thanks," Johnny said, "but we're heading north. A little valley up in the Crazies."

"I know that valley. It's a long haul from here. Why would you pick a spot like that?"

"I didn't. It picked me."

A trail that was starting to be called the Bozeman would lead settlers to the town of Alder Gulch. There was also now a small mining town called Last Chance Gulch, one that was called Virginia City, and a boom town by the name of Bannack.

As Johnny stood where he hoped to one day build a front porch, he said, "When we wintered here, there were no settlements at all between here and Fort Bridger. But now there are already four settlements within no more than a day's ride, and if John Bozeman has his way, there'll be a fifth one. I hope it doesn't become a trend."

Ginny grinned. "Well, this valley will still be a lot

more remote than your ranch was in California. And with a town within riding distance, it'll be easier for us to buy supplies."

Camp was set up, and the following day, the men began hauling logs from the ridge. They worked in pairs, as they had before.

According to Bozeman, there was a quarry starting up at Last Chance Gulch, and Johnny thought they might buy some stone slabs to serve as foundation for the house. But for the cabin, they used short cross sections of pine logs at the four corners and hauled a few stones in to place at the center.

The work went slowly. They still rode night herd, because nearly two hundred head of cattle at the center of the valley might seem tempting for a wild cat, or Indians.

By late August, the roof was up. They had made wooden shingles by splitting oak wood into thin slabs, and then once they were in place, they began smearing pine tar over them to make them water resistant.

Ginny stood by the partially completed structure, late one afternoon. The doorway was still open, as were the windows.

She said, "I have to say, I'm impressed. To build a structure like this out here in the wilderness, with no materials purchased. Everything made by hand."

Johnny had a cup of coffee. "It's the way my great-grandfather, John McCabe, built his first home in the Pennsylvania wilderness. There's an old stone chimney out in those woods, all that's left of the cabin. We chinked the logs, just like was done with those old log cabins. Made the shingles the same way."

"Well, it's all quite impressive."

"We do have to buy one thing, though. We're going to need a stove. It's already late August, and winter comes early in these mountains. And it won't be like any winter you've see in California. I wanted to build a stone chimney and hearth, like we had at the ranch. Maybe next year. I'll start working on it early in the season, because it can be slow going, hauling all of the rocks that will be necessary."

"Where do you plan to get a stove?"

"Tomorrow I'm going to take one of the wagons to Last Chance Gulch and see if I can buy one. Maybe there are some buildings set up in Bozeman's town, and I won't have to go so far. But I'm going to leave early, in case I have to go all the way to Last Chance."

Joe heard the plan, and once it was dark and they sat around their campfire eating supper, he said, "I don't want you goin' tomorrow. You should be here. If any Indians come, it would help if the man they know as Mac-cabe was here. I should be the one goin'."

"Why you?" Zack said. "Why not me?"

"I'm more familiar with the Indians in this part of the country. But I'll take my Enfield and a Henry, in case my bein' familiar with them ain't enough."

Johnny didn't like the idea of another man going in his place, but he knew Joe was right.

Come sunrise, the horses were hitched to a wagon. Joe had a Henry and his Enfield on the wagon seat. He also had a horse saddled and tied to the back of the wagon.

Ginny said, "Why do you need a saddle horse?"

"In case I have to make a run for it."

Johnny gave Joe a wad of cash. Money from the sale of the ranch.

"Josiah," Ginny said. "I don't know what kind of facilities they'll have in this Last Chance place. But if they have tea, I could sure use some."

"Ye'sm. How much?"

"Five pounds, if you can buy that much. And, dare I say it, if they have any wine..."

He grinned. "I'll get you a few bottles."

She reached into her apron for some money, but Johnny said, "No, this'll be on me. You've done so much for us, already."

Joe started out, the wagon wheels clanking across the crude wooden bridge.

Much of the work on the cabin would require more lumber. They needed to build a door. Since there was no glass for windows, they would be building shutters that could lock tight. But they would wait for Joe to return before there were any more forays to the ridges.

The floorboards had been crudely cut by splitting pine logs. They were rough and Johnny didn't want anyone to get splinters if they were walking in their socks, so he spent some time with his bowie knife smoothing the floor down.

Zack rode out to the herd for a look around.

He came back around noon. He said, "I went to the pass and saw some tracks of unshod horses. Looked like two. Someone was scouting the pass."

Johnny nodded. "It's no secret we're here. I hope Joe is careful out there."

As the afternoon wore on, Johnny saddled Bravo and took a ride out to the pass, himself. He left the Henry with Zack, and had his Hawken tucked into his saddle.

He rode up a slope of what he was starting to call McCabe Ridge because, well, why not? He found the spot he had found five years earlier, the small clearing at the side of the ridge that gave him a view of the pass down below and the range out beyond the valley.

He saw a lone rider out there. The rider seemed to be coming from the north, in a direction that would take him past the mountain pass. Johnny figured the rider might be a mile or more away.

Johnny rode Bravo down the ridge toward the pass. The pines grew tall and were far enough apart for easy riding.

Johnny came out into the pass, and as the rider approached, Johnny rode out to meet him.

The rider pulled up. He looked Indian. Long, black hair. He wore a broadcloth shirt, but it looked like it had seen better days. Whether he had acquired it at a trading post or by taking it in a raid, Johnny had no way of knowing.

Johnny held up a hand in greeting, and the man returned it.

Johnny knew enough of sign language to have a little conversation with him.

Johnny thought the man might be Cheyenne.

He gave his name. Little Buffalo. Johnny gave his, just saying, "Mac-cabe."

The man's eyes widened. "Mac-cabe?"

Johnny nodded.

The man was silent a moment, then made the sign *you kill Iron Hand.*

Johnny nodded.

The sentence structure in the sign language of the plains Indians was a little limited. Johnny had learned much from Joe, and some from Many Lives.

Little Buffalo held his right hand up, fingers open and pointing upward, and he turned the hand at the wrist a couple of times. It meant he was asking a question. Then he gave the signs for *you* and *here.*

You had to do a little assuming when using Indian sign language. The question was *why are you here?*

Johnny answered that he is living here now. He pointed to the valley.

Little Buffalo nodded.

Johnny gave the signs for *all stay away.*

Little Buffalo nodded again.

To give Little Buffalo a small gift, following the Indian way, Johnny pulled a strip of jerky from a shirt pocket and handed it to him. To Johnny's surprise, Little Buffalo pulled a knife and handed it to Johnny.

The knife had a steel blade, but a bone handle. The bone looked to have been hand-carved. Probably from buffalo bone.

Quite a gift, Johnny thought. He nodded and Little Buffalo nodded.

Then Little Buffalo continued on his way. Johnny sat in the saddle and watched until Little Buffalo was gone from sight.

Once he was back at camp, he showed the knife to Zack and Ginny.

Ginny said, "Let's hope the respect they seem to have for you will be enough to keep them away."

"Just to be safe," Johnny said, "We're building the cabin so it can be easy to defend. Rifle holes in the shutters to shoot through, and a door that will be heavy and that can be barred shut with a heavy timber. And it's near enough to a heavy thicket that would be nearly impossible to climb through. That means they have to come from either the west or the north."

"That old mountain man Neville Pierce said once to Joe and me that you think like a military tactician," Zack said. "I think he's right."

They waited for Joe. It began to grow dark, and Ginny put dinner on. A beef stew she had made. She had a pot suspended from a tripod.

Johnny had left his vest and hat with his bedroll, and stood in his range shirt looking off toward the pass. Hoping he would see a wagon coming.

That night, he sat up with Zack for a while. Ginny and the children were asleep in the tent.

Johnny said, "I hope nothing happened to him. Things haven't been good between the Army and some of the tribes."

"Things weren't good that winter we spent here. They're worse now."

They had heard of the Bear River massacre. It was a two or three day ride from here. Some Shoshones had been butchered by the Army. Johnny sure hoped Many Lives and his band was not among them.

"It's their last stand," Zack said. "All of these people. Their way of life is ending, and they know it."

"I wonder if I was a fool to bring Ginny and the kids out here."

Zack shook his head. "Doc Buzzard tried to have you killed outside of Greenville. Violence can happen anywhere. I don't see why we can't all build a home here, as long as we're careful."

Johnny and Zack slept outside that night, by the fire. The remuda was behind them. The valley at this end formed an almost natural barrier, with about two hundred acres of grass for the horses to graze on and frolic in, so Johnny hadn't yet built a fence to close them in. He thought he might not.

Come morning, the fire was burning low, so Johnny added some more wood. He and Zack went to the stream with a couple of buckets so they could have water at camp. Then Johnny started some coffee boiling.

Ginny was awake. She said, "I don't see how you men can drink the coffee that you do. It's so strong and rough. I'd swear it could take the rust off a nail."

Zack laughed. Johnny said, "We call it *trail coffee*."

"I suppose you have to call it something."

Ginny whipped up a breakfast of steak and eggs. It was as Johnny was eating that he saw motion from out on the valley floor.

He stood up and watched.

"It's the wagon," he said. "And there's another man with Joe."

# 57

HE WAS the biggest man Johnny had ever seen. He had a beard as bushy and wild-looking as Joe's, and he wore a floppy, wide-brimmed hat, and a revolver was mounted at his side.

When he climbed down, the wagon actually shifted a little because of his weight. But he wasn't fat. He was just big boned and loaded with solid muscle.

"This here is Hunter," Joe said. "He helped me out of a scrape in Last Chance."

"Hunter?" Johnny said.

The man nodded. "Just Hunter."

"Johnny McCabe." They shook hands. Hunter's hand almost swallowed Johnny's.

Introductions were made all around.

Joe said, "I told him all about what we're doin' out here. He's lookin' for a job. I told him to talk to you."

"Well," Johnny scratched his head. He didn't know quite what to say. "You know anything about cattle? Horses? Or building cabins?"

Hunter nodded. "Done a lot of work with cattle and horses. Growed up in a log cabin. I helped the man who raised me work on it many a time."

"Can't pay you. At least not yet. Maybe not for a year or two. All we can offer is room and meals. And right now, the room is actually sleeping out in the open by the fire."

Hunter nodded. "Good enough for me."

Johnny was silent a moment, thinking it over. Then he said, "It's not usually my way to ask questions of a man. Your business is your own. If Joe vouches for you, then that would normally be good enough for me. But I have children here, and their safety comes first, so I have to ask. Are you running from something?"

He nodded. "That I am. Trouble I got into in Oregon Territory. Had to kill a man in self-defense. Except they don't believe it's self-defense. If you don't want me here, I understand."

Ginny had walked over, and she said, "Mister Hunter, I fancy myself a good judge of character. I think you'll do. What about you, John?"

"I fancy myself a good judge of character, too. Mister Hunter, you're hired."

"Thank you. And thank you, *Miss* Brackston."

"Mister Hunter, to anyone working on this ranch, I'm Aunt Ginny. I won't have any of that Miss Brackston nonsense."

"Yes'm."

Hunter joined them for breakfast. Joe was hungry too.

He and Hunter had camped the night before halfway between Bozeman and the valley, and had eaten jerky only.

Johnny asked, "What kind of trouble did you get into in Last Chance?"

"A couple men decided to relieve me of that roll of cash you gave me. They got the drop on me. I knocked the gun out of the hand of one of 'em and stuck a knife in him."

Ginny said, "Oh, goodness."

"Then Hunter came up behind the other one and caught him in a bear hug, and squeezed him till he was unconscious."

Hunter said, "I hate thievery."

Johnny said to him, "I really appreciate what you did."

"Not at all. You gave me a job, and a place to lay low for a while."

"As long as you like."

Ginny said, "Mister Hunter, do you have any long term plans? Having your own ranch, maybe?"

Hunter shook his head. "For as long as I can remember, I wanted to have my own saloon. A place where men can come in after a hard day's work and laugh and drink some beer or whiskey."

Joe had a cast iron stove in the back of the

wagon. He had also grabbed some sacks of flour and coffee. He had two pounds of tea for Aunt Ginny, and four bottles of chardonnay.

When Ginny saw the bottles, she smiled and said, "Josiah, you're precious."

He grinned. "Don't think I've ever been called that before."

"Well, you are."

Joe said, "I had quite a bit of money left over. I bought us one more Henry rifle, and some boxes of ammunition."

It turned out Hunter did the work of two men. He also hadn't exaggerated about knowing how to build with logs. By the start of September, not only was the cabin finished, but there was a bunkhouse for Joe, Zack and Hunter, and a barn.

The cabin was little more than a large kitchen and a bunkhouse for the family. The stove was on one wall, and the stove pipe was inserted through a small hole. Johnny made certain the pipe didn't actually touch the logs, and he fashioned home-made mortar from mud and applied it around the edge of the hole to hold the stove pipe in place.

There was a table and chairs, all made from pine logs, and against the far wall were two sets of bunks, and a small separate bed for Bree.

Johnny and Hunter made a small smokehouse. Ginny smoked all the beef she could, in preparation for the long winter.

Johnny said to her, "How is it a woman of finery and prosperity knows how to smoke meat?"

She said, "Ah, but I am a woman of mystery."

The mountain winds grew colder and the leaves on the maples in the valley began turning red and the birch were turning yellow. Johnny and Joe did a lot of hunting, and by the time of the first snow, they had smoked beef and venison stockpiled.

Johnny had noticed a small blue spruce growing at the edge of the field used for the remuda, and it became the family's Christmas Tree.

With the winter winds howling outside, they had a Christmas morning. It turned out Santa did arrive. Aunt Ginny saw to that, with a few boxes of items she had hidden away in a wagon on their journey from California.

Snow covered the valley floor and drifted high against the cabin. Johnny and Joe had made snowshoes, which were now necessary if you wanted to walk far outdoors.

A chinook struck in early January, and the snow began melting. The little stream ran deep and fast, and almost washed away the makeshift bridge.

It was during this chinook that Johnny rode to the rocky cliff that overlooked the valley. The one where he and Many Lives had stood and talked of life and the Great Spirit.

From there, Johnny could see the smoke from the stove of their little cabin.

It was good, the life they were building here. And yet, there was an empty spot in his heart. There always would be, he figured.

As he stood looking off at the valley, feeling good about the life he and his family were building here and yet missing Lura, he thought he caught a scent of peach on the wind.

Peach trees don't grow out here, he knew. And yet, the scent was there. And then it was gone.

He found he felt warm. Like, just for a moment, Lura had been there with him.

He couldn't explain it. He thought it made no sense at all. But for a moment, the pain of her loss was gone.

# 58

THE TALLY BOOK AT SPRING ROUNDUP SHOWED the herd had grown a fair amount. Of their nearly two hundred head, almost half were cows and they had all delivered calves. The valley floor wouldn't have enough grass for a herd this size for more than a couple of months, so they were moved to the grassy foothills east of the valley.

Bozeman had grown into a fully functioning small town, and Johnny and Zack took a wagon there for supplies. While they were at the town, they hired three men to help with the roundup. One of them, Dan Bodine, decided to stay on afterward, willing to work for a bunk and meals only.

Dan was a Cherokee, from the Nations. He had been educated in schools and spoke English like it was his first language. He dressed like a cowhand, and rode as well as any man Johnny had ever seen.

They built a small cabin outside the valley to serve as a line shack. Two men would be stationed there. Dan didn't mind being a permanent floater. Zack and Hunter took turns being the second. Johnny rode out twice a week to check on them and help with any rounding up that was necessary.

Each man at the line cabin had plenty of ammunition, and they were on the lookout for Indians or rustlers at all times.

With Hunter's help, when he wasn't at the line cabin, construction on the main house began in June. Logs were hauled down from the ridges, chinked and put into place. Johnny bought some granite slabs from the quarry in Last Chance Gulch. He hauled stones, many from the stream bed but some from rocky areas on the valley floor, and built a chimney and hearth that was similar to the one at the small ranch house in California. Except this hearth was much larger, because winters here could be so much colder. He used a roughhewn piece of pine timber for the mantel.

He decided to keep the original cabin to function as the kitchen, and a doorway connected the kitchen to the rest of the new house. The stove pipe now plugged into the chimney from the back side.

A second floor was built, with a roughhewn pine staircase attached to one wall. The bedrooms would be on the second floor, except for Aunt Ginny's. Hers was in a small, single-floor addition off of the parlor.

And Johnny built the front porch where he had wanted to. From the porch, he could look off at the barn and the bunkhouse, and beyond them to the stream and the makeshift bridge. He planned by the next summer to replace the bridge with a more permanent one. Maybe a covered bridge.

He would stand on the porch in the morning and watch the rays of sunrise hit the ridges that lined the valley, and a couple peaks that were visible beyond. In the evening, he would stand there again and watch night descend on the valley.

Every so often, he would return to the rocky cliff and look over the valley. Look at the house from a distance, and know his children were safe there.

It was late August when Joe said to him, "I think it's time I was moving on."

They were in front of the hearth. It was night, and the children were upstairs in bed. Though it was still summer, nights could be a little cool in these mountains, so a small fire was burning.

Johnny had built himself a chair out of pine poles and cowhide, and Ginny was in a rocker she had brought with her from California.

"What do you mean, moving on?" she said.

"Well, ma'am, it's just that sometimes I get feelin' sort of like I just gotta be movin' on. The term I heard once was *itchy feet*."

Johnny nodded his head. "You've mentioned before that you just get the urge to wander, sometimes."

He nodded his head. "I didn't want to leave you in a bind. But now you got Hunter and Bodine. And you still got Zack."

Johnny said, "I sure appreciate you staying as long as you did."

Joe nodded.

Johnny said, "Where do you think you might be going?"

He shrugged. "Might just wander the mountains for a while. Live off the land. Maybe head south and try to stay ahead of winter. Or maybe go west and check on Matt."

Johnny grinned. "Make sure that snake of a wife hasn't et him for supper."

Joe grinned back. "Something like that."

Then Johnny grew serious. "Do you think you'll be back?"

"Here? Oh, sure. I ain't gonna stay away forever. I just need to wander for a while."

Come morning, Joe was up before anyone else was. He had his horse saddled, and was about to mount up when he saw Johnny walking toward him.

Joe said, "I should'a figured you'd be awake."

"I just wanted to say goodbye. Words can't express how much it means to me, all you've done for me. These have been some tough years, and you were right there at my side for all of it."

"That's what family's for."

Johnny held out his hand and Joe shook it, then they pulled each other in for a back-slapping hug.

Then Joe swung into the saddle. He looked much like he had when Johnny first found him on the trail, all those years ago when they were both heading east to visit the farm. Joe's hair was touching his shoulders again and his beard was so long it fully covered his neck. He was in a buckskin shirt with a belt strapped around his middle, and a revolver was tucked into the belt. A knife was sheathed in one boot, and his Enfield was in his saddle.

"Take care of yourself," Johnny said. "Be safe."

Joe nodded. "I will. And you take care of that family."

"I will."

"You got three great kids there."

"Sure do. And they love their Uncle Joe."

"And their Uncle Joe loves them."

With that, Joe turned his horse away, toward the mountain pass.

Johnny walked up to the front porch. He stood and watched as Joe crossed the makeshift bridge and rode off toward the pass that led out of the valley.

Joe rode along easy in the saddle. He was in no hurry to leave this valley. In fact, he actually hadn't been struck with the wandering spirit at all. But there was a place he had to go, and that place was south. He had a lot of miles to cover.

Would he ever be back? He didn't know, but he doubted it. Once he did what he would have to do, he was sure there would be reward posters with his name on them from the Canadian border to the Rio Grande. From San Francisco to St. Louis.

But it had to be done. Eventually, Johnny would figure out who had most likely killed Lura. Johnny seemed to be much more stable now than he had been in those first few months after she was murdered, but if Johnny figured out who had done it, he might be hit with a fury that would be beyond his control. And once Johnny found the killer and did what had to be done, he would either be hanged or thrown in prison. And those children would be growing up without a mother or a father.

Joe reached into a pocket and pulled out a hollow, brass button. The one he had found when they had been trying to track the killer. It had a fleur de lis on it. Joe still thought they looked something like swords. There was only one man he had ever seen who had buttons like this, and that man was in Texas.

Joe stuffed the button back into his pocket, and rode out through the pass and was gone.

## 59

Texas
Early November, 1864

THE BROKEN SPUR WAS the fanciest dang ranch house Joe had ever seen. Some of the mansions in St. Louis and San Francisco had nothing on this place. When he rode away from the Broken Spur seven years earlier, he never thought he would be back. Not until he picked up the brass button from the ground, back in California.

He wasn't even sure Coleman Grant still owned the ranch, but he had asked some questions at a saloon a couple of days earlier. Coleman was still here, but the ranch was falling onto hard times. Most of the men had left after Breaker died. And Coleman wasn't as skilled at handling business as he had thought.

It was midnight as Joe rode into the ranch yard. The bunkhouse and the barn were dark. In fact, the place felt empty.

One window was lighted in the house, though. On the second floor. Joe knew the house well enough to know which room it was.

Joe swung out of the saddle and gave the rein of his horse a couple of loops around the hitching rail.

He didn't bother to knock. He tried the front door to see if it was unlocked. It was. In the bigger cities, Joe had heard people sometimes kept their doors locked at night, but he didn't expect anyone would out here.

A lamp was burning in the entryway. Looked about the way he remembered. Queen Anne chairs at either side and a huge crystalline chandelier overhead.

He didn't wait. He strode across the entryway and up the stairs. He was going to find Coleman Grant and do what had to be done.

The lighted window Joe had seen from outside belonged to Breaker Grant's old study. Joe opened the door and walked in.

Coleman Grant was sitting at the desk, a glass of whiskey in one hand.

Coleman looked up and said, "Who let you in?"

Joe said, "Don't recognize me, do you? It's been seven years."

Then Coleman's mouth fell open a little.

Joe said, "Yep. You remember."

Joe walked up to the desk and tossed the button down in front of Coleman.

Joe said, "You should be careful what you leave behind when you go shoot someone."

Coleman stared at the button a moment, then looked up at Joe. He said nothing, but the color drained from his face.

Joe said, "You ain't gonna leave this room alive. But I'm gonna let you go get a gun. I ain't never shot an unarmed man."

Coleman didn't move. He stared but said nothing.

Joe said, "You're all brave when you're shootin' at someone from a distance, but it's different when you're up close, ain't it?"

Coleman still said nothing.

"You took the life of a mighty good woman. I want to tell you that. And now her three kids have to grow up without their mother."

"That was never the intention. I never meant to hurt her. The bullet was meant for him."

"Why'd you do it? Why'd you go all the way there just to shoot him?"

"Emotional closure, I suppose."

Joe squinted a little at him. Sounded like the kind of words Matt would use.

Coleman said, "Maria preferred him over me. Breaker preferred him as a son, over me. The men preferred him. They all quit when he left, and I haven't been able to retain a decent crew. The ranch is failing. All of the other businesses are failing."

"And how is any of that Johnny's fault?"

"I just can't stand a man who will always think he is better than me. I had to do something about it."

"He *is* better'n you. *Every* man is better'n you."

Coleman went back to saying nothing. Joe figured there was nothing for him to say.

Joe said, "Now the time has come to pay for what you done. Grab a gun."

Coleman shook his head. "I won't. And if you don't leave, I'll send for the county sheriff."

Joe had never shot a man who didn't need it. And now would be no different. Except the man wouldn't be shooting back. He reminded himself that if he didn't do what had to be done, Johnny would eventually be doing it.

Joe drew his gun, cocked it, and put a bullet in Coleman's head.

Joe turned and walked out of the room. He tucked the gun into his belt as he descended the stairs. He then was out the front door, shutting it behind him.

His horse was waiting for him. He swung into the saddle and rode away into the night.

Carlotta was in the parlor when she heard the gun shot. She had stayed with the house because she believed she should, out of loyalty to the memory of Mr. Grant. But Coleman was miserable to work for. A man with no spine and no honor. She didn't think he deserved the name Grant.

She should have been long asleep, but she had stayed awake while she decided what to do. She sat in the parlor because there was still a low fire burning, from when Coleman had been in the parlor, earlier in the evening.

She finally made up her mind. Miss Maria was now running her father's ranch, and had just a week ago offered Carlotta a job. One of many Miss Maria had offered over the years. Now Carlotta decided to accept it.

That was when she heard the gun go off.

She went to the doorway that opened onto the

entryway, and she saw a man coming down the stairs.

She knew him immediately. The man she had called Mr. Joe, when he worked here. The brother of Johnny McCabe.

Joe hadn't seen her, and just strode out of the house.

She knew what must have happened, but she had to see it for herself.

She went upstairs to Mr. Grant's study. There, behind the desk, was Coleman. He was leaning back in his chair, his eyes were open, and there was a bullet hole in his forehead.

About time someone took care of him, she thought. What surprised her was it hadn't been done sooner.

She was not going to let Mr. Joe go to jail for this. She had always believed Coleman was somehow responsible for Mr. Grant's death. Now things were squared.

She cleaned this room a couple of times a week, and she knew where things were. Coleman had a revolver in his front desk.

It was one of those new kinds of gun that took metallic cartridges. A Smith and Wesson.

She knew guns. Her father had been a vaquero and a hunter, and made sure she knew how to shoot. The window was open, so she gripped the gun with both hands, hauled back the hammer until it clicked into place, and then she fired the gun off into the darkness. Then she put the gun in Coleman's hand.

Poor man, took his own life in the middle of the night. In the morning, the county sheriff would check the gun and find one shot had been fired from it. Carlotta would look the sheriff in the eye and say she was sound asleep downstairs and didn't hear any shot at all.

Two shots had actually been fired, of course, but there was no one else within hearing distance to give any statements to the sheriff. No one else in the house.

The bunkhouse outside was empty, too. No one wanted to work for Coleman Grant.

She went back down to the first floor, feeling that justice had been served. She went to her bedroom and found sleep no longer eluded her.

## 60

Montana Territory
September, 1865

BY THEIR SECOND SPRING ROUND UP, the herd had increased by a full third. Johnny was selling beef to the miners in Virginia City and Bannack, and to the Army. He was also building up their herd of horses and selling some to the Army. But he insisted on breaking them Indian style, the way he had learned from the Shoshone.

The ranch was making a little money, and he was now able to offer regular monthly pay. He had hired two new men, and they became the regular floaters. Bodine now lived full time in the bunkhouse, with Zack and Hunter.

The summer had been good, the ranch was growing, and they were now getting ready for another winter.

The sun was trailing low in the western sky as Johnny stood on the cliff overlooking the southern end of the valley. He could see the roof of the house, and smoke drifting from the chimney. Ginny was fixing dinner.

Bravo stood behind him and shifted a hoof. Johnny let go of Bravo's rein, because he knew the horse wouldn't wander far.

He knew it wouldn't be long before this valley was knee-deep in snow. Just as it had been that winter with the Shoshone.

It seemed so long ago, that first winter. Almost like it was from the distant past. So much had happened since then. He had married the love of his life and now had three children. Children he loved more than he thought possible.

Once, when Johnny was twelve, his Pa said, "Do you know how much your mother and I love you?"

Johnny shook his head.

"And you won't know it either. Not until you become a father yourself."

Now Johnny knew what Pa had been talking about.

And then the love of his life had been taken from him. He had wondered more than once if he would be able to carry on, but Ginny was right. He had to carry on for the children. Matt had said it, too.

His mother and Luke were running the little farm back in Pennsylvania. Johnny wrote letters to them, and they wrote back. Luke was now married, and a father.

Ginny and the children were down at the house. Johnny knew he had the love of all of them, and yet, as he stood here on the cliff overlooking the valley, he felt alone.

"I'm going to be all right, Lura," he said. "I'm surviving. I'm taking it one day at a time, but I'm surviving. And the children will have a good life. I'm going to see to that. And Ginny's here. Like she always was for you."

He felt a tear run down his face, and he reached up to wipe it away.

"Oh, it's hard." His voice shook a little. "It's so very hard. But I'm going to make it" He gave a chuckle. "I suppose I'm too stubborn to do anything less. But know this, Lura McCabe. I love you and always will."

He could almost hear her voice. *And I love you. And always will.*

The early autumn breeze was cool as it touched his face. He thought tonight would be chilly. But as he was about to turn away from the cliff and climb into the saddle, he noticed a hint of peach blossom on the breeze.

Odd this time of year, he thought. And yet it reminded him of Lura. So he stood and enjoyed the scent as it lingered for a moment.

And he stood on the cliff now, all these years later. Bree was standing beside him and was almost twenty. Grown into a fine woman and due to be married in a few days.

Johnny's hair was still tied back in a Shoshone tail, but it had grown gray over the years. The two pistols he had worn had been replaced with Remingtons, and eventually by a single Colt Peacemaker. His joints creaked a little on cold nights, and his ribcage where he took a couple of bullets a few years ago still bothered him from time to time.

His fine horse Bravo was now gone. Johnny had a horse nearly as fine by the name of Thunder.

The sun was trailing low in the sky.

Johnny said to Bree, "Do you realize we've been up here all day?"

She nodded. "I'm glad. I've come up here a lot over the years and thought of you and Ma, and thought of those early days when in this valley. I've thought of the love you had for her, and the love you now have for Jessica."

"Your Uncle Matt told me once that we're lucky to find that kind of love just once in our lifetime, but I've been blessed by the love of two good women."

She smiled. "That's how it is with Charles and me."

He returned the smile. "I know, Punkin. I see how you two look at each other. You have to have felt that kind of love to recognize the look when you see it."

The fire they had built had gone out, and the coffee kettle was empty.

"We should be heading back," Johnny said. "I'm sure Temperence has dinner cooking."

Bree stuffed the kettle back into her saddle bags. Johnny walked over to where Thunder and Midnight were grazing.

He saddled both horses. Johnny and Bree mounted up, and Johnny looked over at her and said, "You know, I was feeling a little reluctant about the upcoming wedding. Like I wasn't quite ready to let go of my little girl. But now I realize I'm not letting go of you.

Life changes and we change with it, but some things never change. One of those things is that you'll always be my punkin."

"Always," she said.

"And I'm ready to walk you down the aisle now."

She smiled. "Let's get riding. We don't want Temperence mad at us."

As Johnny touched his spurs to Thunder and the horse started moving into the woods, Johnny thought he caught a scent of peach blossom on the wind. He smiled.

# 61

BREE WAS in her wedding dress. White and lacey, with sleeves that came down to a lacey cuff. Johnny thought Ginny had outdone herself.

Bree's hair was all done up, and she had a veil in place.

Ginny, Temperance and Haley were there, and would be standing up with her. Ginny was still fussing a little over the dress. The other two were in dresses that were a violet color.

Johnny said, "I would like a moment alone with the bride."

"John," Ginny said, "everyone is seated. We're about to start."

"Not without the bride, you won't."

Bree smiled. She said, "I'll be right along."

Ginny gave Johnny a look that said she wasn't all that happy about this, then she, Temperance and Haley stepped out.

Bree said, "I love it when you stand up to Aunt Ginny. It reminds me of all the bickering you both did when I was growing up. It was all in fun, and we all knew it."

He nodded. "A little maddening at times, maybe, but all in fun."

He took a long look at her. "I don't tell you often enough, but you are beautiful, you know that?"

She nodded with a smile. "I know. You know how?"

"How?"

"'Cause I look a little like Ma."

Johnny nodded. "You look a lot like your Ma. You have my hair, but you have her cheeks and nose. And her smile."

He was in a tie and jacket, and his Shoshone hair was tied back, as always.

He reached into his jacket pocket and said, "I was

trying to figure what would be the perfect wedding present for a lady gunhawk. And it came to me."

He pulled a knife sheath from his pocket. From the sheath, he pulled a steel blade with a bone handle.

He said, "This is the knife that Lakota I mentioned gave me. Little Buffalo."

"Oh, Pa. It's beautiful."

She took it and held it up for a good look.

He said, "Something must have happened to the handle, and he replaced it with this one. Hand carved out of bone."

"It's incredible."

She put it back into the sheath. "Now, where to put it?"

"I can hang onto it until after the wedding."

"I wouldn't hear of it." She tucked it up her sleeve. Then she said, "Do you think Ma's watching?"

"I know she is."

Bree smiled. "Then I'm ready, Pa."

Johnny extended an elbow, and she took his arm. He said, "Let's go walk down that aisle."

Made in the USA
Monee, IL
30 June 2025

20239689R00194